LEVEN THUMPS

AND THE RUINS OF ALDER

LEVEN THUMPS

AND THE RUINS OF ALDER

✦

OBERT SKYE

SHADOW
MOUNTAIN

To Loo, Goo, Punk, Bubba, and Nay.

May your dreams fly as high as your hats.

Text © 2009 Obert Skye

Illustrations © 2009 Benjamin R. Sowards

Visit us at LevenThumps.com

Library of Congress Cataloging-in-Publication Data

Skye, Obert.
  Leven Thumps and the ruins of Alder / Obert Skye.
    p. cm.
  Summary: Leven discovers that he must travel to the island of Alder to find the answer that will save the realm of Foo from destruction.
    ISBN 978-1-60641-146-9 (hardbound : alk. paper)
    [1. Fantasy.] I. Title.
    PZ7.S62877Ler 2009
    [Fic]—dc22   2009022749

Printed in the United States of America
Bang Printing, Brainerd, MN

10   9   8   7   6   5   4   3   2   1

CONTENTS

CONTENTS

CONTENTS

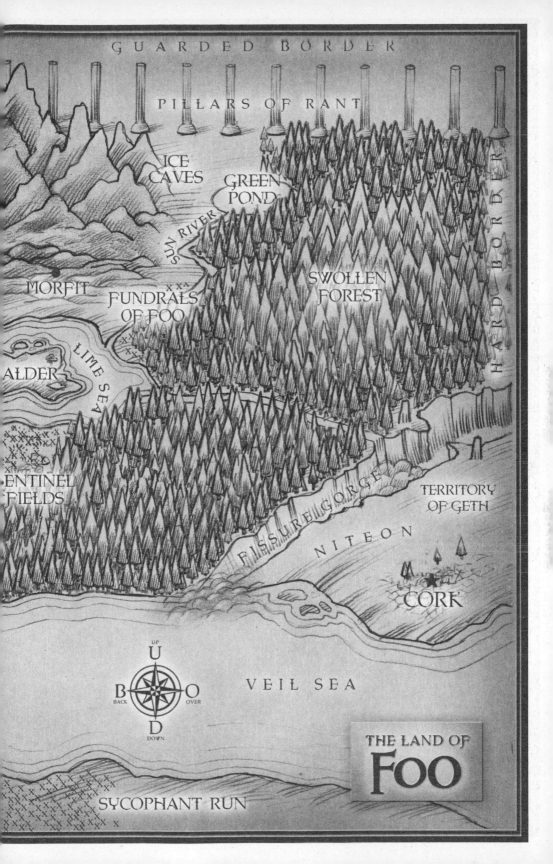

"My fellow Americans," the president began, looking straight into the camera, "and citizens of all nations. It is with complete soberness and urgency that I address you tonight. Recently our world has begun to experience some unusual events. Fields are coming alive, tornados have personalities, buildings are walking, bugs are carrying people off, and clouds are interfering with planes. We believe there are logical and sane explanations for these occurrences. We must keep a cool head and calm mind. I have been in touch with many world leaders, and this is a global concern. I want you to know that your government is doing everything in its power to keep you safe and combat this problem. We are urging everyone to . . ."

Nobody heard the rest because it was at that point that everyone's TVs, computers, and phones went temporarily dead. It was also at that point that almost everybody began to understand that the world was most definitely in a mess.

LONG NIGHT

The night was as dark as any serious sin. Only the yellow stars in the sky had any presence up above, and the ground below shook as Foo continued to transform. If you remember correctly, Leven had just cut the Dearth in half and dragged a near-dead Azure back to Geth and Winter. If you don't remember correctly, then Leven had just hosted a birthday party and Winter had come to give him a new sweater that matched his eyes.

Let's hope you remembered correctly.

Directly after Leven had returned with Azure, they had all moved their camp to some hidden tents at the edge of the Swollen Forest. The tents, built on stone, were a secret place where Azure had sometimes come to get away from the constant dark whisperings of the Dearth. Once they got safely there, they had all collapsed into a tired sleep.

Thirty minutes later, Leven jumped up, yelling. He looked around, catching his breath. The tent was unfamiliar, and the dark of night made the surroundings look like a dream.

"Are you okay?" Geth whispered.

Leven sat down on a wooden chair—nothing more, he just sat, but in sitting, the weight of the world seemed to settle. His large shoulders relaxed and he thrust his fingers back though his long black hair.

"It was a weird dream," Leven said.

"Could you keep it to yourself until morning?" Winter pleaded.

"Wait," Geth prodded. "What do you feel?"

Geth stood up to the right of Leven. His left hand was on Leven's shoulder, and his blue eyes glowed in a way they had never previously done. Geth was over six feet tall, and his dark blond hair was wild and hung in front of his right eye like a ragged curtain that was hiding something entertaining and secretive. He was muscular in his green robe and black pants and stood like a statue that nobody could easily push over or damage.

Geth smiled. "It's all changed, hasn't it?"

Leven looked up at his friend and smiled anemically. "Yes—it's all changed. I can see so many dreams."

"I don't understand," Winter said, looking around. "What's changed?"

Leven smiled a half smile. Winter was no longer a child; she was beautiful, and as strong as any nit in Foo. Her green eyes looked at Leven, the depth of them immeasurable and mesmerizing. Winter was wearing a snug white shirt with burgundy pants. She had a thin white robe hanging loosely over her left shoulder, the hood of it tossed back, exposing her lengthy blonde hair tied loosely behind her head. She blinked, and the green in her eyes seemed to rise to the surface.

"I'll take this one," Clover said, fielding Winter's question. "Leven's no longer just that boy who lived with those awful people in that . . . what was it called?"

"House," Winter answered.

"No," Clover sneered, "in that long box with wheels hidden beneath it."

"That was their house," Winter said.

"Really?" Clover shrugged. "It had wheels."

"It was still a house," Winter insisted.

"But the floor sagged and the walls were made of paper."

"It was still a house."

"Does anyone have a dictionary?" Clover asked. "I think you're—"

Leven stopped Clover by patting him on the head. He smiled at the small sycophant and stood up. Leven was taller than Geth now, and his face was well defined and framed by a strong jawbone. His eyes burned so strongly that when he closed his eyelids they still glowed lightly. Leven stretched out his right arm and Clover sprang from the ground and twisted up his arm and onto his shoulder, looking like a bulky snake.

"It was a house," Leven smiled. "But it wasn't home. And I'll tell you what's changed," he went on, looking toward Winter. "Everything."

"That's pretty vague," Winter complained. "What's coming next? Something?"

"So, how many days?" Geth asked.

Leven closed his eyes.

"How many days till what?" Winter questioned.

"He'll know," Geth said softly, nodding toward Leven. "He should be able to see the end."

"End of what?" Clover whispered excitedly.

"The end of it all," Geth answered.

"And it's in just a matter of days?" Winter asked anxiously.

"Can't you feel it?" Geth said gently. "One would have to be emotionally dead not to recognize how close we stand to the end."

Winter and Clover were quiet as Leven lifted his eyelids and let the gold shine brightly. He looked at Geth and smiled. "I should let you know that in the end you will fight yourself."

Geth rocked on his feet and grinned. "I can't wait to meet my missing piece."

"You'll have to get back to where we began," Leven added. "And you," he said, turning to Winter. "You might save us all."

"Might?" she said, blushing deeply.

"Oh, oh, do me, do me!" Clover said, jumping up and down.

Leven's expression dropped and he let his gaze fall to the ground. He raised his hands to his face and rubbed his eyes with his palms.

"What do you see?" Clover asked excitedly.

Leven was quiet, his eyes closed.

"It must be something really great," Clover whispered.

"It is," Leven said solemnly, his eyes opening slowly. "But you'll have to wait."

Clover shivered and disappeared.

Leven began to cough, and his eyes flashed. "I don't know what's wrong with me. My throat gets hot and one leg feels longer than the other and my eyes keep freaking out."

"You're changing," Geth explained. "The gifts will really start coming on now."

"Just think of it as kind of like a Foovian puberty," Winter joked.

Leven stared at her.

"So, how long do we have?" Geth asked again, looking like a soldier awaiting his orders.

"It's already begun, but once the exit opens, no more than three days," Leven answered. "That's all the time we've got."

Geth cheered.

"All of that stuff will happen in three days?" Winter asked frantically. "The end will be here in three days? Three literal days, or figurative? I mean that's only . . . seventy-two hours."

"Should be a wild three days," Leven smiled.

"Then I'm getting some sleep," Winter insisted. She stood up and gathered her blankets and furs. "I'll be in the other tent."

Winter walked out to go to the other tent, where Tim and Janet and Azure were sleeping, while Geth continued to quiz Leven.

CHAPTER ONE

WHEN PEACE IS SHATTERED

Two small sycophants stood on a tall gray rock and gazed out over the Veil Sea. The dark waters were choppy, and the largest moon was pulling and pushing huge waves up on the shores only to call them back again. The banks were covered with sycophants all poised and waiting for battle.

"They're coming," Rast whispered, his voice sounding old and tired.

"I know," Reed replied. "I'm worried that each breath might be my last."

The night felt poised to fall and shatter, as if someone had stacked it precariously on a high shelf and now the smallest motion might send the whole thing tumbling down. Orange flares shot across the sky, drawing lines from one end of Foo to the other.

"Keep your heart light," Rast pleaded. "Please."

"It's not in my nature," Reed admitted. "But I'll try."

Rast smiled at his friend. Rast was one of the most important sycophants and the brightest point in the Chamber of Stars. He had been entrusted with the well-being of Foo, and now the entire realm teetered on the brink of collapse. Rast stared at the thousands of sycophants who were all poised and waiting along the shore for battle. In the past, the only way to see the sycophants would have been to look through the special glasses he had. Now, with the secret of the sycophants floating around everywhere, and so many Lore Coils exposing the words that stole the sycophants' invisibility, there was no need for the glasses. Rast, along with anyone who had vision, could easily see every sycophant.

"Everything's changed," Reed complained. "How can we ask our children to fight when they are visible?"

"They must," Rast said. "And they still have their claws."

The claws Rast was speaking about were temporary and usually came during the few years all sycophants spent committed to guard the shores of their homeland. The claws were tremendous and razor sharp and shot out from their knuckles and could slice through just about anything. Their claws were extremely effective weapons, especially when sycophants were invisible. Now, however, they would be fighting against larger foes without the ability to disappear.

"I wish Brindle were here," Rast said. "His heart is always light."

"He'll be back," Reed said, too worried about himself to think of others. "We'll win this, right?"

Rast looked at his friend and sighed. He put his small hand on Reed's shoulder. Reed was a kind but anxious sycophant. He was one of the lower points in the Chamber of Stars.

"I can only hope," Rast answered.

"Foo can't fail," Reed argued.

"Can you hear that?" Rast asked in a hushed whisper.

Reed jumped and then steadied himself. "Hear what?"

"Look," Rast said, pointing. His voice was filled with sorrow. "The gloam now connects to our home."

Reed looked, but there was nothing but darkness and thousands of sycophants standing motionless and on guard. "I can't see anything but our troops."

"See how the black of night moves right above the gloam?"

Reed slowly shook his head.

"We should have shattered that map," Rast said.

"We tried," Reed shivered.

"Well, it's too late now," Rast said sadly. "Can you feel that in your feet?"

Reed fell to his knees and pressed his palms down against the stone. "What am I supposed to . . . the ground's shaking."

"Ready the captains," Rast ordered. "Claws out and eyes wide. Look over there now."

Reed looked toward the gloam and could faintly see thousands of twinkling bits of sliver reflecting under the moonlight. The lead rants were carrying huge silver poles, and the staffs were strung with thousands of coin-sized pieces of silver.

"Reed," Rast ordered, "I was wrong. Claws out and eyes like slits—don't look at the metal."

Reed leapt from the stone as the largest moon increased in intensity, doubling the light of the night. Rast could see the armies clearly now. The shimmering metal looked like a net of sparkling lights. All over, sycophants who should have been fighting for their home began to stare at the silver and fall into a trance. Their small bodies splashed into the water or onto the shore, lying there motionless, looking like rag dolls.

"Keep your eyes closed and fight!" Rast demanded, screaming out to those in front of him. "Remember: Without us, Foo fails."

Thousands of rants spilled onto the shores of Sycophant Run. They were swinging metal swords and wooden kilves. Rast jumped from the pointed stone and sprang up over a dozen considerably younger sycophants. He struggled up onto another flat stone and looked out over the scene.

Rast's small heart slid down into his right foot. He watched as thousands and thousands of sycophants were thrown aside or trampled over. Stunned or wounded, the valiant beings fell. Everything in him told him to turn and run, but Rast knew that this was the sycophants' last chance to stop what was happening. His eyes became wet and he could no longer see clearly.

Reed climbed up next to him. "There's too many, Rast. And the metal is putting so many of us in a trance."

"I see cogs and echoes fighting as well," Rast said sadly. "Why would they fight against us?"

"It's the whole of Foo spilling onto our shores," Reed cried. "They want out and we've failed to keep them away."

Rants circled in and around the numerous troops of sycophants. Some sycophants were slashing away with their claws out and eyes closed, but most were dropping like stones as their minds became transfixed on the shimmering metal.

"We should retreat," Reed yelled. "We should hide until these fools have gone away."

"And let them just walk out of Foo?" Rast asked.

"What choice do we have?"

Rast looked at all the thousands of sycophants. He watched as wave after wave of attackers rolled off the gloam and joined the battle. Two sycophants were hurled over their heads, flying back into the trees and crashing to the ground.

"We must retreat," Reed said.

Rast looked at Reed. "Let me at least get my hands dirty first."

"But . . ."

Rast screamed and then plunged down from the flat stone directly onto a huge rant. Reed shrugged, screamed even louder, and took on an enemy of his own.

CHAPTER TWO

I'M NOT SLEEPING ANYMORE

Leven tossed and rocked, trying desperately to find some more sleep, but the dream he had just experienced kept his mind racing. So, despite the exhaustion that had been brought on by lack of rest and even more by Leven's battle with the Dearth, sleep was not coming easily. As he lay on the floor, his mind whirled and whined like a rusty hamster wheel. He could hear Geth breathing lightly across the room.

"Are you awake?" he asked softly.

There was no answer. Geth had found sleep, and only the sound of wind pushing through the leaves above answered Leven.

"*Worry,*" the wind seemed to whisper.

Leven turned onto his side.

"*Worry.*"

Leven opened his eyes. His pupils warmed slowly, sending a ray of gold up into the roof of the tent. He could see the stitches in the fabric.

Leven lifted his right hand and held it up to his view. His fingers looked the same, but he knew that something had changed. The Dearth had been unable to kill him. He had seen the blade crash down against his own neck and nothing had happened. His mind played the image over and over in his head. Leven caught his breath and sat up.

"*Worry,*" the wind moaned. "*Worry.*"

Leven could hear the sound of splashing water in the distance. He turned his head and closed his eyes. When he opened them back up a moment later, they dimmed until they were as dark and brown as they used to be.

Leven stood up and shifted his right ear away from the wind. It was faint, but the sound of splashing water still trickled through his brain.

"Clover," Leven whispered, "is that you?"

The thought disappeared like a bubble as he looked down and saw Clover curled up in a ball, sleeping by Geth's feet. Geth mumbled something and turned over.

Again in the distance water splashed.

Leven stepped away from the tent and into the dark. He could feel stone against his feet as he climbed down the knoll. He flipped the hood of his weathered black robe up over his head and pulled it closed at the neck. The robe was tight against his back and shoulders and way too short, causing Leven to look like a wizard wearing floods.

Leven hiked deeper into the dark, pushing through long, ragged tree limbs and tall tangles of grass. He looked up and saw a couple of dozen stars rolling slowly as if the sky were being tilted and they were sliding backwards. With his eyes to the sky, Leven's feet faltered, and he fell forward onto his knees and palms. His hands scraped violently against a jagged rock.

"Perfect," Leven complained. "You'd think I'd know how to walk by this point in my life."

Leven moaned, stood back up, and dusted himself off. Had he been the normal Leven of a couple of weeks ago, his hands would have been bleeding profusely. But now there was no blood, and under the moonlight all he could see was a long, white scratch that was quickly fading away. Leven held his hand up and listened to the worrisome wind. He could still hear the faint sound of splashing water coming from beyond the trees.

"*Worry,*" the wind blew.

Leven stepped out of the thick trees and looked over the ground. The half-moons covered the landscape in shadows and shine. Up and over from where he stood was a small pond, and on the edge of the pond were dozens of smaller puddles of water.

The air smelled delicious and wet.

Leven jogged to the puddles and dropped to his knees. He thrust his hands into one of the larger puddles to rinse away the dirt from his fall. As he pulled his arms out of the water, he could hear the sound of splashing. Leven looked to his left and saw a big puddle gurgling and spitting. It looked like a boiling cauldron buried beneath the soil.

He stood up and shook his hands off, stepped over to the fizzing body of water, and looked down. The puddle shot small drops of water up into the air and onto Leven. He instinctively backed up, but the water was cool and calming, like a summer rain.

Leven watched the water in the puddle settle and then grow glassy. He marveled as an image began to take shape in the liquid. There was a small, dark room with a high window and a dirty rug on the floor.

The image began to grow clearer.

Now Leven could see every thread of the rug and the texture of the walls and floor. He could hear the sound of talking coming from outside of the window. Amazed and a bit bewildered, Leven knelt down. He held his hands out over the puddle and flexed his fingers as a coolness from the water tickled his palms. Leven looked up at the moons and marveled that it wasn't their reflection he saw in the water.

He shrugged his shoulders and stuck his fingers in the liquid.

The image of the room and small window smeared and then returned. Leven reached in deeper and fingered the edge of the small window. He could feel the wood frame. His middle finger snagged a rough splinter and Leven instinctively tried to yank his hand out.

It wouldn't budge.

The water began to swirl around his captured arms like a toilet slowly flushing. Leven growled and pulled, but the suction of the water was too strong. The puddle pulled his arms in up to his shoulders and swirled even faster.

"Geth!" Leven yelled. "Geth!"

The right half of Leven's face began to go under.

"Clo—" he gurgled.

His head went under. Leven used his left shoulder to push up on the side of the puddle, but it was no use. The pull was too strong. Leven's shoulder slipped from the edge, and in one second his complete upper body was down in the puddle. Leven twisted and shook, but the water pulled him in to the point where there was nothing but his legs sticking out. He kicked and thrashed like a maniac, but the puddle kept drawing him in—two seconds later, nothing but feet—a second after that, nothing but nothing.

The water stopped swirling, and once again there was only the sound of the wind as it pushed through the leaves of the fantrum trees.

"Worry."

Leven flew through the air in a dream. He had reached into a puddle and now he was racing swiftly toward the ground as if he were flying. He was frightened and exhilarated all at once. Flaring out his legs, he turned to the right. He wiggled his arms and lifted up and then back down a few feet. He was falling, but with some control.

Leven could see the hulking black mountain of Morfit off in the distance. The silhouette was sprinkled with thousands of small, flickering lights. Leven witnessed the darkness in the far sky as black dreams and selfish imaginations polluted it.

Leven dropped hundreds of feet. His stomach was in his mouth and his head was in his toes. He bent his legs and his body shot over the land at an alarming rate. He felt a pull, spun wildly around in the air, and then was thrown downward.

Leven could see the Lime Sea in the distance and land rushing up to him like steam. Everywhere there were large wooden buildings with pointed towers and turrets. The buildings made a large square around a giant piece of land. The ornate structures slumped and crumbled as Leven pushed through them, coming to a stop against a hardwood floor.

Leven's body sprawled out on the floor in the shape of an x. His head spun and he found it hard to open his eyes as he lay there. He breathed in deep and tried to lift his head, but a rough voice stopped him.

"Lie still," the voice said. "Keep your face to the floor."

Leven was happy to oblige, seeing how he felt as if he had just been hit by a large truck. Even with his face to the floor he could see something walking around him, the shadow of whoever it was shifting as it moved. The shape stopped above Leven's head. It moaned as if bothered and then spoke.

"He set up so many traps," the voice said. "So many traps laid out for you, and you fell for one of the tamest."

"Traps?" Leven slurred, unable to speak clearly with his mouth pushed against the floor.

"Traps—all over Foo," the voice answered. "He needed to speak with you. Devices and gadgets designed to keep you on the course. It's interesting that you fell for such a simple one. Nobody in his right mind reaches into a puddle in Foo without testing the water."

"I did," Leven reminded him.

"I wouldn't admit that," the voice mocked.

"Why?" Leven slurred.

"Lie still," the voice said again.

"No way," Leven said, pushing himself up.

"Lie still!"

Leven jumped onto his feet. He looked around, ready for a fight, but there was nobody there. "Where are you?"

"Couldn't you have just stayed down?" the voice said, sounding disappointed.

"Who are you?" Leven asked again, still looking around.

"That's not important. You've nothing to fear from me at the moment, but that could change. I speak for one who has every interest in what you're about to do. He arranged this."

"The Dearth?" Leven asked angrily.

"Certainly not the Dearth," the voice said lightly. "The Dearth moves on his own accord and for his own purpose. Even now he's pushing through the exit. What can you do but leave him be? Foo has no need of such darkness. He no longer whispers from the soil. His thoughts are on Reality."

"I can hear him still."

"Good for you."

"There must be others who still hear him here."

"Whatever," the voice said. "You nits bring nothing but selfishness and confusion."

"I'm not a nit," Leven said.

"Oh, that's right," the voice grunted. "The Want. I would bow, but I don't believe you would think I was being sincere."

"I don't want you to bow to me," Leven snapped, still searching around for the voice. "I want to know why I'm here."

"So impatient," the voice said. "You're here because someone wants to meet you."

"You?"

"No," the voice snapped. "If I had my way, you would never come near."

"So, then, who's this someone?"

"Or something," the voice answered casually. "I can't tell you. In fact, I've already said too much."

"I don't think so," Leven argued. "You haven't said enough."

"If I had my way, I would pierce your heart with a dagger and be done with it," the voice said. "No theatrics. No lessons or epiphanies."

Leven tilted his head and looked up to the ceiling. "So I guess I should be happy you're not in charge."

"What does it matter either way?"

"I think it matters."

"Why? You're fortified," the voice said. Sounding as if someone were reading out of an encyclopedia, it intoned, "Blade, poison, and accident cannot steal your life."

"Thanks for the information," Leven said.

"Unless . . ."

"Unless?" Leven asked.

"You might be safe from those who approach you, but you can still be killed by those with unfinished business."

"What?" Leven said, surprised.

"Some can still hurt you."

"I don't understand."

"You will," the voice said mockingly. "And of course you can still fail."

"What are you talking about?" Leven looked around slowly, taking in his surroundings this time. The room was small, but its ceiling was at least twenty feet high. The walls were all made of wood, and he saw a large wooden door and one tiny window near the ceiling—the same window he had viewed through the puddle.

"I mean, so what if you live, if all that you've set out to do fails?" the voice answered. "If Reality and Foo mesh, there will be no need for a Want. There will be no need for anyone."

"We won't fail," Leven said lamely, not even sounding convincing to himself.

"Unfortunately, you will, without our help," the voice said sharply. "Unfortunately, we have to step in and provide a way. You were pulled into Foo and given the power of the Want, but you know nothing about the balance of things. Nits have killed siids, nits have given up their own powers, nits have made the sky black."

"I'm not a nit," Leven said boldly.

"No," the voice said sarcastically and from a new direction. "You're their hope."

"And you're against that," Leven argued.

"It's not up to me. I'd let you dangle," the voice said. "But it's not my decision. And if you pass, you will stand before the tree, and the decision to save Foo will be all yours. I'm not happy about it."

"Pass what?"

"Nobody walks straight to the tree."

"What?" Leven argued. "I have no intention of walking to a tree. I'll find the Dearth and put an end to his plan."

"Really?" the voice questioned. "What are you going to do? Kill the Dearth? How? And if by some chance you do, then what? Plug up the exit and make everyone go back? Tell all those in Reality to ignore what they've just seen? Stupid. There's only one way for you to restore Foo, and it breaks my heart to help you."

"This is helping?"

"You will travel to Alder."

"No way," Leven said. "I'll travel to Sycophant Run. I only have three days."

The voice laughed. "You will travel to the island of Alder, believe me."

The sound of something large and creaking crackled throughout the room. The noise clicked and moaned like something pliable being bent a bit too far.

"I must go," the voice said. "I doubt you'll make it out of these walls, much less any farther. This room could be your coffin. But if you do manage to get out, follow the glass."

"What?" Leven asked, confused. "You're leaving me here?"

"Find your way out," the voice said. "Or starve, for all I care."

"What's that supposed to mean?" Leven demanded.

"Can't you do any thinking for yourself?" the voice whined. "There's a way out of this room. Find it and you're that much closer to walking the path that's waiting for you. If you can't get out, then I suppose it was fate for Foo to fall. Happy failure. And remember, if it's too much for you, in three days none of this will matter."

"You can't just leave me," Leven ordered.

"Make sure you're not followed."

"What's that supposed to mean?" Leven asked.

There was no response. The room was silent. Leven walked to the large wooden door—it was locked solid. On the back of the door was an intricate carving of a huge tree. Leven shoved his right shoulder into the door, but it didn't budge. He twisted and pulled on the wooden knob, but there wasn't an ounce of give.

"Nice coffin," he said to himself.

Leven let go of the knob and turned around. He glanced down at the ground. The wooden floor was well polished, and in the center of the room was a star-shaped rug surrounded by four chairs and a short table. On the table sat a large glass pitcher and a red clay mug. Leven walked to the pitcher and lifted it. He poured an inch of water into the mug, put it to his lips, and took a long drink.

The water was stale and flat.

Leven set the cup down and gazed up at the high window. A thick piece of rope hung from the window's latch and stretched down to where Leven could easily reach it. Leven grabbed the rope and pulled lightly. The twine broke free of the latch and fell to the ground.

Leven picked up the rope and coiled it loosely in his hands. He tossed the rope up to the window, but there was nothing for it to catch onto.

Leven closed his eyes. He could see himself lying dead on the wooden floor, his body nothing but dust and debris. He calmed his mind and pulled at the image with his thoughts. He watched the scene in reverse, seeing his decayed body reassemble itself and then stand up. He wiggled his mind and forced the image of himself to walk backwards and pick up the pitcher of water.

Leven's eyes flashed open.

With the rope from the window in his hand he stepped over the rug and stood above a bare section of wooden floor. Leven knelt down on the floor, took the length of rope, and laid it down in the shape of a large circle. He then stood up and retrieved the pitcher. Leven knelt back down and slowly poured the water into the circle of rope.

"Might as well leave the way I came," he shrugged.

The water from the pitcher splashed and ran, but as it settled it collected into the large circle of rope. When the pitcher was empty, Leven set it on one of the chairs and then looked down at the glassy circle of water.

Leven smiled—his time in Foo had made him believe in anything, and he was finally beginning to understand the power of thought and invention. In fact, he was so accustomed to the miraculous that he wasn't at all surprised to see the rocky knoll and the tents reflected in the water he had just poured out.

Again the sound of creaking could be heard outside the room through the window.

Leven quickly knelt down. He pushed both his palms into the circle of water and let the liquid pull him in. The shallow spill made the act of diving in a bit more painful. Leven could feel the floor of the room scraping against his stomach as he was dragged all the way into the spill.

Once under the water, Leven flew again. This time, however, he flew much lower and quicker across the ground. He twisted his body to dodge trees and buildings and anything over ten feet tall. Then, as if a giant fist were closing around him, he felt his lungs and body collapse. His breath was gone, and his eyes felt like they were going to jump out of their sockets. Two seconds later he was thrown to the ground ten feet away from where he had once been trying to fall asleep.

Leven caught his breath and sat up. He patted down his arms and felt his head to make sure it was still connected. Confident that he was whole, he crawled back into the tent and to his spot next to Geth. He thought about waking the others up and telling them what had happened, but he was now so tired that all he wanted was sleep. As he closed his eyes, he could hear Clover.

"Where were you?" Clover whispered.

"I'll tell you in the morning," Leven answered.

"Oh, I get it," Clover said. "Wow, that was a long bathroom trip."

"It wasn't . . ."

"I might have some leaves you can chew that will settle your stomach."

"I'm fine, really."

Clover patted Leven on the shoulder. "You've had a huge day."

"I've had a huge month," Leven added. "Hey, are there any important trees here in Foo?"

"I think all trees are important," Clover answered. "Imagine the view without them."

"I mean, is there any one single tree in Foo that stands out?"

"They talk about the oldest tree sometimes," Clover answered.

"They?"

"I mean, I was taught about it in school." Clover yawned. "I don't think very many people have ever seen it or are allowed to go near."

"Where is it?" Leven asked.

"The island of Alder," Clover replied.

Leven's stomach lurched and popped.

"You sure you don't want those leaves?" Clover asked.

"No, thanks, I'm fine, really."

Clover let it go, and Leven finally found a bit of sleep that would be disrupted well before sunrise.

CHAPTER THREE

ALLERGIC REACTION

"Careful, you knob!" Ezra barked. "Just because I have the power to turn you into a pile of green dust doesn't mean my head's not sensitive."

Dennis carefully untangled the small snag in Ezra's purple tassel and gently set the toothpick down on top of the stove.

Ezra shook his sensitive head and growled. "What kind of world is this that I have to depend on anyone besides myself?"

"It's a crazy planet," Dennis laughed.

Dennis stood up tall and stretched his back like a lanky cat. He was wearing his wrinkle-free pants and white, stain-resistant shirt. But on top of those he had on the purple robe that had once belonged to Antsel. The robe was burnt in spots and torn at the hem, but it still looked regal and otherworldly.

Dennis sat down on the small couch in the large RV that the

U.S. government had provided for Ezra and him. There were two beds at the far end, a big bathroom, and a medium-sized kitchen that was connected to a nice, spacious section just for hanging out. It was in that hang-out area that Dennis and Ezra were now relaxing.

"Nervous?" Dennis asked.

"About what?" Ezra argued.

"Things are happening," Dennis said blandly.

"What a brilliant observation," Ezra mocked. "And just to be clear, I've never been nervous in my life. I've been angry, mad, confused, and out for blood, but I'm not the nervous type."

A fly trapped in the RV began to smack up against one of the windows, trying to get out. Ezra reached out as if to help, and a tiny string of green energy shot from his hand and zapped the fly. The poor thing shook and then fell down on top of the stove.

Ezra smiled as he stood over his catch. "Do you want a wing?"

Dennis looked closely at Ezra. The thin toothpick began tearing off the wings of the dead fly. Ezra's purple tassel wriggled as he blinked his single eye. His body was covered in green nail polish and his right leg had been torn off and replaced with a paper clip. Ezra was an extraordinary toothpick, but one of his most impressive features was the fact that he now glowed slightly. Ever since he had taken a dip in a barrel of something that had been hidden in a military bunker outside of Albuquerque, he was illuminating. The dip into the goo had not only made Ezra glow, it had given him strong and fantastic powers.

Dennis rubbed his forehead with his right hand.

"Something changing?" Ezra asked.

"I'm not sure."

Ezra dropped the dead fly's wings and leapt up and off the stove.

He landed on top of Dennis's head. "Oh yeah, something's happening."

The small traces of Sabine that still remained existed only in the form of words that moved across Dennis's bald head. What was left of Sabine seemed to be able to communicate with the Dearth and spell things out for Ezra to read.

The information had been invaluable.

Ezra and Dennis had used the knowledge to impress people and convince the authorities that not only were they needed but they alone were in the know.

"What's it say?" Dennis asked.

"The exit is about to be opened."

"And?"

"And the world will never be the same again."

"That sounds ominous," Dennis said.

"I don't care about religion," Ezra said. "I just want to get my hands on Geth."

"And once you do?"

"I will make him suffer for every ounce of confusion and hurt I have ever had to experience," Ezra cackled. "And I might break a few of his bones."

"What about me?" Dennis asked. "What's my role?"

Ezra slapped his forehead. "Do I have to think of everything?"

"I'm not used to thinking," Dennis admitted honestly, his head still hurting due to the influence of Sabine. "But it seems to me that we might be in over our heads."

"Quiet," Ezra demanded.

"I mean, when thousands of people come through that entrance, what makes you think they'll listen to us?"

"Shut up," Ezra screamed.

"We don't even know who's coming."

"I know you saved my life and I promised not to hurt you, but I have my limits," Ezra yelled. "Now be quiet."

"But the Dearth might kill us all."

Ezra shook. "Do you want this to be your last day alive?"

"That's what I'm saying," Dennis said, standing up.

"No, I'm talking about *me* killing you."

"You wouldn't," Dennis said boldly, and he threw open the curtains. "You owe me, and I'm just saying that you have no guarantee that the Dearth won't just clean his teeth with you. Look at all those people out there."

Ezra hopped up on the windowsill and looked out at the thousands of soldiers and tanks all gathered around Blue Hole Lake. "What about them?"

"Most are holding weapons and anxious to use them," Dennis said. "And you might be able to kill flies, but I'm not sure even you could hold back all those soldiers."

Ezra looked at Dennis and began to tremble and shake. His single eye blinked rapidly as the tassel on his head whirled and fluttered.

Dennis stepped backwards.

Ezra leaned his pointy little head back as he shook. Then, with one amazing yelp, he sneezed. Dennis flew across the RV and into the couch as all four sides popped out and the roof shot up twenty feet. The sides fell away and the roof ended up two hundred yards to the west on top of a military mess tent. All that was left was the base of the RV, along with the stove and couch.

Soldiers came rushing over by the hundreds to see what had happened as Dennis climbed up onto the couch and then to his feet.

He looked down at Ezra.

"That was me sneezing," Ezra said. "You wanna see me belch?"

Dennis picked up the smiling toothpick and put him behind his ear as soldiers helped them down.

"To answer your question," Ezra said. "Your role is to carry me around and act like the second most important person in the room. Clear?"

Dennis nodded carefully so as to not send Ezra flying.

CHAPTER FOUR

WHEN IT COMES TO THE SUBJECT OF TIM

I t was the foggy moment between solid sleep and an approaching morning. The night, still dark, was thinning around the edges as a grey, soapy film washed over it. Those with any sense were still asleep, while those awake were either filled with worry or up to no good.

Winter was awake, and she was filled with worry.

She stormed in from the other tent and kicked the bottom of Leven's right foot as he slept. "Where's Tim?"

Leven turned over and sat up quickly. He rubbed his brown eyes, and instantly they began to glow gold. He looked at Winter and smiled as if she were a dream he couldn't fully remember.

"What are you smiling about?" Winter said, blushing. She picked up Leven's robe from the stony ground and threw it at him. "Tim and Azure and Janet—they're not in our tent anymore."

Leven stood up and quickly put the robe on. "Geth!"

Geth lifted his head up and looked around in confusion.

"Tim's gone," Leven told him, his voice filled with authority. "And so are Azure and Janet."

"Why?" Geth asked casually. "Did someone take them?"

"I don't think so," Winter answered. "I was sleeping right next to them."

Geth lit a small candle. The candle flickered to life, the tiny flames whining about being awakened.

"I know Tim wanted to get to his family," Leven said. "Maybe he thought we would stop him, so he left. How far do you think they might've gotten?" he asked Geth.

"It depends on when they left," Geth answered.

"They left about an hour ago," Clover said, materializing.

"You heard them?" Leven asked.

"Yeah, it was just after you came back."

"You went somewhere?" Winter asked Leven.

Leven shrugged. "That's not important; we should find Tim."

"I would have mentioned them leaving," Clover said. "But Tim was pretty insistent about me staying quiet. He said they were taking Azure because he promised to show them the way."

"So you saw them go?" Winter asked incredulously.

"I was writing in my dream journal," Clover said defensively.

"At two in the morning?" Leven asked. "Why didn't you tell us they had left?"

"I had an interesting dream," Clover insisted. "What does it mean when you dream about barns?"

Leven and Winter just stared at him.

"Besides," Clover went on, "Tim told me to keep it quiet."

"Since when have you done what you were told?" Winter asked.

"They didn't belong here anyhow," Clover argued. "It's always been us four . . ."

"Stop it," Leven said. "Tim can't be too far, not with Azure's condition."

"And he's going the same place we are," Geth pointed out. "There's absolutely no reason for any of us to worry about the fact that he got a jump on us."

"Tim's going to Oklahoma?" Winter asked in disbelief.

"Well, Reality," Geth answered. "Besides, there's no need to worry. Either Leven stops what's happening to all of us, or this chapter of Foo and Reality closes for good."

Winter was about to speak, but she stopped and held her finger to her lips. "Do you hear that?" she asked softly.

Clover materialized on Winter's left shoulder. His leafy ears twitched as he opened them wide.

"Hear what?" Leven whispered.

Winter kept her index finger up to her pink lips as Geth noiselessly drew his kilve up from off of the ground.

The air was silent. The ground wobbled just a bit as the bulk of Foo continued to shift and change. Leven opened his mouth to speak, but before any words came out, the sound of scraping bones against stone could be heard softly outside of the tent.

"Maybe we should just get a couple more hours of sleep," Geth pretended, moving quietly away from the side of the tent. "We have no way of catching Tim, and things will probably look better in the morning."

The faint sound of something clicking against stone could be heard. Leven looked down and saw a single black, bony toe sliding below the hem of the tent.

Leven pointed toward the toe and looked around for his kilve. Winter, however, was approaching the problem weapon free. She twisted and hurled herself into the intruder.

The tent collapsed and several skeletons showered down on top of Leven and Geth. Winter pulled herself up over the tall one she had broken apart, and with a twist disconnected his skull from his bony neck. The head of the black skeleton screamed at her as it flew through the air.

For the record, it was not screaming nice things.

Geth produced his kilve and masterfully sliced through the tent. He then tore through two black skeletons, turning them into nothing but one big pile of dark bones.

"More over there!" Geth yelled.

Leven pushed the tent away and could see five more skeletons silhouetted by the bigger moon. They were about twenty feet up above them. They pounced and clattered down on Geth and Leven, banging sticks and tossing fistfuls of dirt into their eyes. The dirt stung Leven's eyes, and as he wiped at them he could feel two skeletons brutally beating up against him with sticks. Leven looked at them, surprised to feel no wound from their blows. Then, as if it were the most natural thing he could do, he grabbed hold of both the sticks they were holding and forcefully shoved them back and into the ribs of the skeletons. Leven shook the sticks violently— bones and sinew snapped and popped as the skeletons rattled to death.

A skeleton bit Winter on the side of the neck. She wrapped her arm around it and threw it on the ground. She then stomped on it until it broke apart.

Leven just watched.

"Are you okay?" Winter asked.

Leven didn't know what to think. There was fear inside of him, but it felt like an old, outdated emotion that he should get rid of— like a shirt long out of style. Fear didn't seem to fit him any longer.

"I'm fine," he replied.

A huge black skeleton with a gigantic rib cage and massive bones jumped out in front of Leven and swung his right arm, hitting Leven in the face. Leven stumbled back and the skeleton jumped forward, throwing Leven to the ground.

"You would choose for us all," the skeleton seethed. "Who are you to decide our freedom?"

The skeleton threw his dark skull forward and cracked it up against Leven's forehead. Leven jammed his right knee up, compressing the skeleton's torso and ribs up into his neck. The skeleton screamed and rolled off of Leven, falling apart as he moved away.

"Nice," Clover said from somewhere nearby.

Leven stood up and watched Geth wipe out the remaining two skeletons. Then Leven, Winter, and Geth stood with their backs to each other searching the dark morning for any sign of more assailants.

"Those skeletons aren't much sturdier than the Eggmen," Clover said, materializing on top of Leven. "They break up pretty easily."

"So what was that about?" Leven asked, breathing hard.

"The Dearth hasn't given up on you," Geth said. "He will send who he can to destroy you before you can destroy him. And so many have been under his influence for so long that they know nothing but darkness."

"Do you think there are more?" Winter asked, her body shaking slightly from the fight.

"I don't hear anything," Geth answered.

It was completely silent.

"You know, I'm not sure I've ever seen any black skeletons alone," Geth said excitedly.

"They weren't alone," Winter reminded him.

"I mean, they almost always travel with avalands," Geth explained.

Now Leven smiled. He and Winter scurried across the stones and up over the rocky ridge from which the skeletons had just jumped down. Above the ridge, the largest moon lit the wide prairie like a giant sheet of glass. Not far from where they stood there were eight huge mounds of dirt.

Leven looked at Winter.

"It beats walking," she smiled.

"I agree," Geth added, standing by Leven's side.

"Do I have a say in this?" an invisible Clover asked.

"No," all three answered.

"Well, you still have a hand sticking to you," Clover pointed out.

Leven looked down and saw the hand of a black skeleton clinging to the side of his robe. He pried the fingers open and tossed it away.

"Creepy," Winter moaned.

Leven moved quickly, running across the prairie and directly toward the avalands. The beasts were as large as small hills and had stony, clifflike sides. Leven reached up and grabbed a small tree sticking out of the side of the biggest avaland. He pulled himself up as if doing a chin-up and then twisted his legs to the side to help push himself onto the back of the beast.

The avaland's large, stony eyes opened. It breathed in through its cavelike nostrils and then breathed out, dusting half the prairie.

"Come on," Leven said, reaching down to Winter.

She grabbed hold of the protruding tree just as the avaland stood. Winter's hands slipped, but she was able to flip one leg over the tree and shove herself up. Leven pulled her close to him and smiled.

"Remember the first time we rode one of these?"

"I think I was passed out," Winter said.

"Well, then, this ride should be better," Leven said, smiling. "Ready?"

"Of course," Winter replied, and she held onto Leven tightly.

CHAPTER FIVE

A Little Privacy, Please

There are some things in life that you just don't need to talk about. The rash in your armpit or the fungus under your toenails—clearly those things are not that desirable as subjects for conversation. It's the same thing for a book. I mean, a chapter where the villain falls into a pit and has to battle a robotic tiger is pretty necessary and cool. But a chapter where that same villain has to pull over and find a rest stop so that he can use the facilities is not only unnecessary, but hardly talked about. How often have you been reading one of your favorite stories and the main character has to hold off on wearing the sorting hat because he's in the rest room? Or what if Darth Vader, instead of admitting he was Luke's dad, had said, "Luke . . . where's the bathroom?" It's a part of everyone's life, but it's not really necessary to write about it, except for this time. You see, if Leven hadn't stopped to rest and wash up, then he would have never . . . well, read for yourself.

Leven slowed the avaland. Winter let go of Leven and climbed off the back of the beast. Leven followed her down, grasping his throat as he did. Geth pulled up next to them on a slightly smaller avaland.

"I'll just be a moment."

Leven walked quickly into the trees. The tall limbs of the fantrum trees were curling and stretching in all directions. Some branches still had a few leaves on them, but most were bare. Leven could see a thick cluster of bickerwicks lining the backside of one tree. Leven leaned over and coughed violently. The sweat on his forehead was rolling into his eyes, and his throat burned as if he had swallowed a red-hot poker.

"You okay?" Geth yelled from out in the clearing.

"Fine," Leven insisted.

"You don't look fine," Clover said, materializing in the limbs of a nearby tree. "What's up?"

"I don't know," Leven said, embarrassed. "I can't catch my breath, and when I breathe in deep, it feels like fire."

"Weird."

Leven looked at Clover and nonchalantly cleared his throat.

Clover stared at him.

"Do you mind?"

Clover caught the hint and disappeared, giving Leven some privacy. Leven moved deeper into the trees and through some short shrubbery. As he walked back, he passed a single tall tree standing next to the bushes. The weak moonlight was pushing against one side of it, creating a lanky shadow on the other side.

Leven walked through the tree's shadow to reach the bushes. But as he stepped through the shadow, his body slipped into the dark form and out of another shadow far away.

"What . . ."

Leven turned around and pushed back into the shadow. The effect didn't work in reverse. He scanned his new surroundings. He was standing in the shadow of a fat tree on the edge of a forest near the beginning of a wide dirt road. Behind him was a big beach running alongside a large body of water.

"Winter! Geth!" Leven yelled.

There was no answer.

"Clover?"

"Yep," Clover answered.

"You were supposed to leave me alone."

"I decided just to close my eyes."

"Nice," Leven whispered. "I guess I'm glad. Where do you think we are?"

"I don't know for sure," Clover said. "But look at the big moon."

Leven looked up. From where he was standing, the biggest moon was directly overhead, staring right at them.

"I've never been directly under that moon," Clover whispered. "In fact, I don't think very many people ever have."

"Why?" Leven asked, still looking up.

"Because in order to be under it you'd have to be on the island of Alder."

Leven groaned.

"The Waves are supposed to keep anyone from reaching here," Clover whispered, holding onto Leven's neck and shivering. "Nobody's allowed on Alder."

"I guess we are," Leven whispered back.

"So why are we here?" Clover asked.

"I'm not sure," Leven answered. "Last night I slipped through a puddle and was told to stay away from the exit. He said there were traps all over Foo."

"He?"

"Some person or thing," Leven said. "I couldn't see him."

"So there are shadow and puddle traps?"

"I guess."

"Well, we should get back to Geth," Clover warned. "Isn't there another shadow you can step through?"

"I don't think so."

"What about the Waves?" Clover asked.

Leven turned in the direction of the water. "Garnock! Garnock!" he yelled, calling out the name of the lead Wave.

There was no answer, only the sound of small, lifeless waves brushing up against the shore.

Leven stared at the ground. The path he was standing on sparkled under the moonlight. "Is that glass?"

Clover jumped down and touched the ground. The wide path looked like a sheet of glass that had been broken up into a million small pieces. It stretched out as far as Leven could see.

"Yep," Clover answered.

Leven turned from the water and began to walk quickly down the wide glass path.

"Are we in a hurry?" Clover asked.

"Yes," Leven answered. "We only have three days, and now we're stuck in the middle of Foo. Look for a puddle or a shadow or someone who can help us."

"We really shouldn't even be here," Clover said. "I mean, this place is sort of sacred and holy."

"I know," Leven answered. "But it's kind of cool, isn't it?"

"Extremely," Clover said, shivering.

Clover disappeared and Leven walked faster. The island of Alder was spongy and overgrown. Thick clusters of bushes grew everywhere, and rocks and hills were covered with grass and surrounded by trees. The wide path cut right through it all. Near a small hill dotted with large round rocks stood a faded red shack.

"Isn't that a house?" Leven asked, pointing down the road.

Clover snapped back and looked in the direction Leven was pointing. "Yes."

"Let's see if someone's there."

"My mother always encouraged me to go into strange houses."

"She did?"

"Well, only on certain days," Clover admitted.

Leven walked even faster, glass crunching beneath his feet.

CHAPTER SIX

So Many Misfits

The morning slowly shook the cold off to expose the warm body of day—the smell of salt and dirt and sea flowers filling the air. The mass of beings marching across the gloam added energy and excitement to the already highly charged air. Under the command of the Dearth, thousands had already reached the shores of Sycophant Run and were now moving to travel to the exit.

Lore Coils were snapping and screaming across the gloam as the passion and excitement of what was actually happening generated emotions strong enough to create them.

On the edge of the Sentinel Fields near Cusp, small battles still raged between rants and rogue nits who were not ready to give up Foo. Unfortunately, many nits from Cusp were now among those moving into the Sentinel Fields in an effort to get back to Reality.

The possibility had never been a possibility before. However, now that returning to their families and loved ones and the lives that they had been snatched from *was* possible, many were making a dash for it. It looked as if the entire population of Foo had turned into emigrants who were running for the border.

Azure leaned on Tim as they both pushed through the mountain of beings marching swiftly across the gloam. Tim stepped quickly, his thin frame and thinning hair making him look like more of a lightweight than he was. Tim had a kind face, and he was the kind of person most other people enjoyed being around. That wasn't the case for Janet, who followed right beside them in her yellow housecoat with faded red flowers. Being a whisp, she had nothing to her but a faint image, and at the moment her image was sweating.

"Where are we going?" Tim asked.

"To Sycophant Run," Azure answered, his strength slowly returning. "The exit is at the far end near the Hard Border. If we just follow this crowd, everyone will end up in Reality."

Tim smiled.

"So there really is a way out?" Janet asked.

"There must be," Azure said. "Can't you see the darkness in the soil beneath us? The Dearth's moving there as well, and soon Reality and Foo will be connected."

"I'm sacrificing my chance to be with Winter here to make things right," Janet cried. "There has to be a way out."

"There is," Azure comforted. "You'll see."

"This isn't right," Swig spoke up. Swig was Tim's sycophant. He was a kindly being who had done a fantastic job of helping Tim feel comfortable. In the short time they had been together, Tim had grown quite attached to the little guy.

"Sycophants should keep their opinions to themselves," Azure said.

Swig blushed and disappeared.

"He was just talking," Tim said. "I kind of like to hear what he thinks."

Azure looked further wounded.

"Go on," Tim said to what looked like nothing

"Foo's not meant to have an exit," Swig replied. "It is the fate of all who are here to remain here."

"That's nothing but lore," Azure insisted. "Cancerous lore. May the Dearth shrivel and die when he reaches Reality, but I believe for the rest of us it will be the beginning of a great new freedom."

"I heard you were a lithen once," Swig said, still invisible.

"I'm still a lithen," Azure snapped.

"What lithen would allow this to happen?" Swig asked innocently. "What lithen would put up with such evil?"

"The meshing of Foo and Reality is not a mistake," Azure said. "Lithens have simply been confused in the past."

"I believe him," Tim said to Swig. "It seems wrong to just steal people from their lives."

"But you've not known Foo when it was peaceful," Swig said sadly. "That is the purpose and the reason. Those who are snatched might experience temporary fear, but the wonder and the possibilities are a remarkable salve. That's what we sycophants are here for— to make you comfortable."

"Sorry," Tim tried. "I didn't mean to offend you."

Swig stayed silent as huge flocks of large birds flew overhead, screaming and shrieking at those below them. The birds dove and slid above the Veil Sea and shot over toward the direction of Sycophant Run. More and more creatures crowded the gloam, moving with purpose and speed.

Janet's large eyes swept across the landscape. She looked like a white walrus wearing a dress.

Tim saw her looking. "I don't see him either."

Janet blushed, embarrassed by Tim's having read her mind.

"But he has to be going the same direction," Tim added compassionately.

"I don't know what you're talking about," she said.

"That fiery echo," Swig spoke up. "The one you were always making eyes at."

"Osck," Tim clarified.

"An echo and a whisp?" Azure said in disgust.

"Please," Tim scolded Azure.

Azure looked at Janet and apologized. His dark blue eyes were as bruised as old fruit, and his dark hair was dirty. His long blue robe was tattered at the bottom hem, and he limped as he walked. Despite his condition, he looked more human than he ever had. The darkness that had possessed him was gone and in its place was a vulnerable, beaten man. A day ago he had been the leader of every dark soul in Foo. But after the Dearth had nearly killed him, he was a different person.

"We'll catch up to Osck," Tim promised Janet. "We're all heading in the same direction."

"What if he was hurt in the battle?" she moaned. "Or worse?"

"Echoes are a resilient breed," Azure said, trying to be helpful. "It would take a true accident to take their lives."

"And Osck seemed like one of the strongest echoes," Tim added. "The only thing he wanted more than seeing Reality was to be near you. I'm sure we haven't seen the last of him."

Janet smiled and they all walked faster.

CHAPTER SEVEN

WHEN THE WHISPERING FADES

L even stood in the middle of an abandoned shack. It was the largest of three shacks clustered together, partially hidden behind a run of fantrum trees, on the side of a wide dirt road somewhere near the bottom of the island of Alder. The shack's red fabric curtains and gold roping made Leven feel as if he were a prop standing in the middle of some poorly funded Arabian movie. The shack was built over a large square of stone ground. Inside, the floor was covered with thick, dusty rugs and plush roven hides. Thanks to Leven, there was now a small fire burning in a round pit to the side, the smoke from the fire dancing up and out into the dark sky as the flames sang softly.

Leven's on Alder, now we shall see
If while on Alder he'll reach the tree.

Leven stared at the fire, and it began singing about something else.

There was nobody else inside any of the shacks. But once inside, it would have been hard not to feel comfortable. It seemed as if the whole of Foo had washed away and there was nothing but the safety and warmth of the shack.

In the center of the largest shack, hanging on a thick wooden beam above a small sink, was a square mirror. Leven gazed into that square and marveled at what he saw. He reached out and touched his own reflection, his pointer finger tracing the flat image of his gold right eye.

"I'm old," Leven whispered. He shivered and pulled his robe up tighter around his wide shoulders.

Of course, to the boy who had been fourteen not too many weeks ago, anything over seventeen was old. Everything Leven had experienced since swimming into Foo had caused him to grow at a tremendous rate. His body was now hovering somewhere between ages eighteen and twenty.

Leven studied his reflection. His face was fuller and his chin more defined. The ears that had seemed too big on him were considerably more fitting; they were also hidden behind the long, dark strands of his hair, which curled slightly. The few freckles Leven had once sported had long since dissolved like raw sugar in milk, leaving his skin clear and unspotted.

"I look like a man," Leven said.

Leven stared into his own eyes and marveled at all the things he had seen with them in the last few weeks. He had seen his life in Reality disappear and the realm of Foo grow up around him. He had seen a host of unimaginable creatures and beings flood into his life.

He had seen his grandmother taken away from him by the gunt. He had seen Geth change from a toothpick to a man. He had seen his grandfather selfishly pass on to him the mantle of the Want before dying in his arms. Leven's eyes had seen the dreams of his own father, a father he had long thought dead. Leven had also seen Winter change from a girl to a woman.

Leven's thoughts warmed.

Winter was far different from the unsure child who had first found him at his school not too many weeks ago. Leven caught his breath. He could feel his emotions and soul catching up to the rapid growth of his body.

Leven pushed his hair back behind his ears and sighed. The sigh was as heavy and significant as any air he had ever released before.

Through the walls of the shack, Leven could still hear the Dearth whispering from patches of distant soil. Ever since Leven had returned from fighting the Dearth, his head had been filled with the incessant hissing and beckoning of his enemy. The hissing sounded wounded and forlorn, as if Leven had hurt the Dearth and the Dearth now mourned his absence. Leven put his palms up over his ears and growled to himself. He dropped his hands and breathed in deeply.

"I'm not sure I can do this," he whispered, telling himself the secret. His reflection just stared back, looking sad.

Leven shook his head and turned the wooden spigot above the sink. He pushed his hands into the cold flowing water and washed them in the small basin beneath the mirror. He dried his hands, pulled back his hair, and tried to listen better to the wailing of the Dearth. Leven's one long white streak of hair slipped from his hold and hung loosely in front of his right ear. He sighed and watched it happen in the mirror.

"You're quite handsome," Clover said casually.

Leven jumped slightly. "I thought you were checking out the other shacks," he said.

Clover materialized on Leven's left shoulder. He wore his small purple robe, the hood of it folded back. He was crouched and smiling innocently. His large, leaf-shaped ears fluttered and his small, hairless face scrunched as he sniffed and then blinked. The hair on the rest of his body was long and clean and he vaguely smelled of corn chips.

"I was in the far shack," Clover admitted. "But it's not as warm as this. Why are you staring at yourself?"

"Nothing, really," Leven answered. "I guess I just can't believe how old I am."

"Everybody ages," Clover waved. "Maybe you should try some cream or something."

"Not that kind of old," Leven laughed, shallow dimples appearing like grey smudges on his cheeks. "I was fourteen, and now? Well, I don't exactly look fourteen any longer, do I?"

"I'm not good with ages."

"It's like I skipped five years of my life," Leven explained.

"What you've been through this last little bit was not skipping," Clover said defensively. "You just got a whole lot of living crammed into a short bit."

"I know," Leven agreed. "And now look at me—I look old."

"You look like Leven," Clover pointed out. "Besides, how can you see anything? It's so dark in here."

"Not to me," Leven whispered reverently. "I can see the dreams everywhere."

"Really?"

"Everywhere," Leven insisted. He reached out his arms and brushed through the darkness. "I can feel the hopes and sadness of thousands of dreams. They feel like tiny pins. Look." Leven clenched his right fist and grasped a spongy string of light. The dream glowed softly in his grasp like a limp glow stick. Leven pulled on the light with his left hand and stretched it like taffy. The elongated image of a small wooden boat blushed like a radiant tattoo.

Clover pointed at the bugs covering the boat. "Sarus," he said. "They're carpeting the whole thing."

"Dreams are being destroyed already," Leven whispered. "All of them are tainted with bits and pieces of the Dearth."

"How?" Clover asked. "Has the Dearth already gotten through? I mean, the sarus are already there?"

Leven stared at the image in the dream, brushed away the bugs, and cleared the image. He left Clover's question hanging and went to work on a strong dream filled with tall, dark humans throwing sticks and stars. Had Clover thought about it, however, he might have remembered the day he carelessly let a single sarus slip from his void while he was still in Reality. He might have also felt some pride and deep dread over the fact that his mistake was now helping to wreak havoc on hundreds of thousands of people and dreams. The single sarus Clover had set free had now multiplied into millions of bugs and was speeding up the destruction of dreams.

A wounded hissing floated lightly through the air.

"Can you tell if anyone is dreaming about me?" Clover asked in hushed tones.

Leven let go of the dreams he was holding and smiled. "Anyone in particular?" he asked.

"I'm not sure what you're getting at," Clover said, his blue eyes glowing softly. "I'm just wondering if one of the many things I have met in my life is now dreaming about me."

"Things?"

"You know," Clover said, closing his eyes and fading. "Things . . . people, stuff."

"Stuff like Lilly?"

Leven couldn't see Clover, but he could feel him shiver as he hung onto Leven's right arm. A weak whispering floated through the air.

"I need to speak to someone," Leven said suddenly.

"Who?" Clover asked, confused. "Jeffery?"

"Who's Jeffery?" Leven smiled.

"That guy with the limp and the really tight pants?" Clover said snidely. "I mean, come on, move up a size."

"Not Jeffery."

Leven stepped from the large shack, pushing the splintery door open and letting the deep gray of an oncoming morning swirl around him. Alder felt different from the rest of Foo. It seemed like there was more oxygen, and the air was more moist.

The ground was rumbling slightly, the whole of Foo unstable and unsteady. Besides oxygen and moisture, the air was filled with emotional Lore Coils of different strengths and volumes. Leven could hear the words *Alderam Degarus* faintly drifting all around him, and he knew each one he heard represented the frightened and passionate concern of some poor sycophant somewhere.

Clover materialized.

"I should have kept my thoughts to myself," Leven whispered, thinking back to the night the Dearth had pulled the secret from his mind.

"That was a pretty big mistake," Clover admitted.

"Thanks."

Leven walked a hundred feet over and stopped and stared down at the dirt on the edge of the island. The ground shivered like an old refrigerator with a tired motor. Leven could see spots of deep, dark swirls in the dirt where dreams were blocked by the presence of the Dearth.

Leven stared at the ground. Then, as if it were only natural, the weight of early morning seemed to push him down onto his knees. Leven knelt on the ground, fighting the urge to lean forward. His body felt like a heavy eyelid that insisted on closing. Leven bent forward and his face pushed down into the soil. He opened his eyes, expecting dirt to fill his view—instead the soil seemed to lighten. Like on an old TV slowly warming up, he began to see fuzzy images and warped definition beneath the ground.

"Wow," Leven whispered. His eyes swept the sand, taking in roots and rocks and long-buried objects. He could see an underground river flowing miles away and a colony of three-armed tharms digging a long tunnel off in the direction of the Swollen Forest. He could also see beneath the Lime Sea, and then, like a flip of a light switch, Leven's view beneath the soil was as focused and clear as staring at a mountain landscape on a cloudless day.

"I can see everything," Leven mumbled.

Leven's life was tumbling and shaping at such a rapid pace he could barely keep up with the changes. Ever since last night, when he had wrestled with and sliced the Dearth in half, he could feel new gifts working their way into his being. He knew that as the Want he could possess multiple gifts, but he was surprised by how quickly they were now coming on. He felt like he was a giant magnet and the abilities were being drawn to him.

As Leven stared into the dirt, he saw a sea of darkness a few feet beneath the surface. The blackness stretched out as far as he could see, and it was wriggling like a serpent away from the spot where he now knelt.

Leven thrust his hand deep into a square of dark dirt. He moaned and clenched the bits of black with his hand. He yanked upward hard, pulling a thick strand of the Dearth out of the dirt. The ooze stretched out and melted in his palm. It pushed through his fingers and dripped down his arm. Leven pulled the blackness up and stood. He stared at the tarlike substance in his hand and on his wrist.

"That's real nice," Clover said, disgusted.

"I can hear you," Leven said to the muck, the gold from his eyes lighting up the strand of Dearth. "I know your head's miles away, but I can hear you whispering."

The black ooze hissed.

"I'm not the same person anymore," Leven explained to the goop on his hand.

The dirt sizzled.

"If you push through to Reality, I'll have to stop you," Leven growled.

The black gunk in Leven's right fist bubbled, and dozens of small, dark faces swelled like boils. The multiple faces whined and screamed in anger and agony.

Leven squeezed the muck and it popped from his hand and

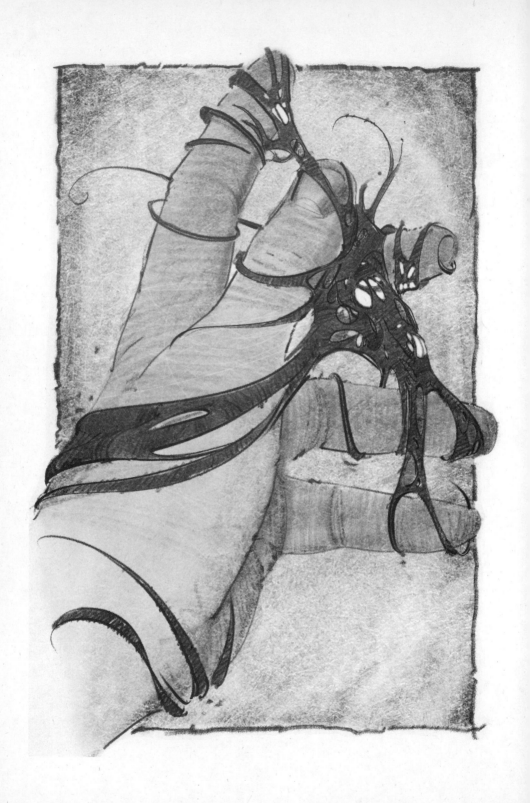

wriggled back into the dirt and away. Leven reached down and pulled out more. It too slithered and pulled, trying to escape his grasp.

"He's trying to get away," Leven said. "Pulling out of Foo."

The ooze burped.

"Ugly and no manners," Clover observed. "He doesn't have a whole lot going for him."

The tar dripping down Leven's arm hissed and whistled. Dozens of tiny, agonized faces swelled like zits in the muck. Collectively the faces began to hiss. They screamed, popped, and then withered. Leven stared at the black mess of Dearth he held. The glare of his gold eyes lit the ooze up from the inside out.

Leven pulled at the blackness and twisted it up like a stubborn root. With his left hand he yanked up more of the Dearth from the ground and tore at it. The strings of sticky evil pulled between his fingers as if he were a child playing with mud.

Leven could feel how long and stretched out the Dearth was. He knew he reached beneath the soil in all directions, slithering to an escape. The tiny faces in the black ooze began to laugh and snort.

Leven's throat constricted. He coughed twice and could feel his lungs expanding.

"Are you okay?" Clover asked, patting him on the back.

Leven stood tall and then, as if he knew exactly what he was doing, he breathed out. Thin flames leapt from Leven's mouth and wrapped around the ooze of the Dearth. The tiny faces melted and screamed as the fire turned them to ash. Leven watched the fire race down the black strings and extinguish itself against the ground. He closed his mouth and placed his hand over his lips.

"Wow," Leven whispered, a weak wisp of smoke escaping from behind his hand. "I can breathe fire."

Clover materialized on Leven's left shoulder. "That's one way to wash up—pretty cool."

"Yeah," Leven agreed.

"You look dazed," Clover said.

Leven shook his head, "I'm fine. But the gifts seem to be growing. I woke up last night and couldn't see the bottom half of me. A few minutes later the rest of me materialized."

"Nice," Clover said.

"Plus I can see under the soil," Leven continued. "And just now I breathed fire."

"You shouldn't brag," Clover said jealously.

"I'm not bragging. In fact, I can't decide whether I'm confused or amazed. All I know is that the Dearth's moving out and we're stuck here on this island."

"We could eat something," Clover suggested.

"The world's ending and you want to eat?"

"Maybe just dessert."

Leven's shoulders flexed as he stood up taller and smiled. The white T-shirt he wore stretched across his chest tightly.

"What?" Clover said defensively. "It could be like a portable dessert. Like an ice-cream cone or a splotch-sicle."

"Maybe we should hike to the center of this island and find that tree," Leven suggested.

"I guess," Clover said reluctantly.

Leven reached out his arm, and Clover twisted around it and onto his head.

"Then," Leven said, "maybe we can find some dessert."

Clover disappeared and shivered contentedly for the next ten minutes.

CHAPTER EIGHT

A Very Important Piece of Land

Something was up, or perhaps it's more fitting to say that something was going down in the small town of Burnt Culvert, Oklahoma. Up or down, over or under, either way there was a palpable unease in the air, an unease that seemed to prophesy that something big was coming. Yes, at the moment you couldn't see it, but, like staring down a vacant railroad track and feeling the empty rails beginning to shiver, you could tell something thunderous and large was barreling toward you.

A fine mist of rain began to drop like glitter and then the wind blew, causing the entire town of Burnt Culvert to chatter and chirp like a large, rusty wind chime. Doors slammed closed, trees whistled, and clouds shivered as leaves and litter raced over the landscape. The sky above grew dim, making the scene feel like an outdated den with grassy carpet and dark walls.

It was Wednesday morning just after ten, or at least that was what the TV inside the manager's office had just announced. The day would be cool and windy, and there was a slight chance of twisters touching down. The man watching the TV was Dooley Hornbackle. He was as old as any respectable grandfather, and his weathered face appeared friendly despite the drooping skin and large nose—he was like an honest version of the Dearth's fake self. Mr. Dooley Hornbackle had owned and managed the Rolling Greens Deluxe Mobile Home Park for many, many years. He was a widowed Irishman with a soft heart and brittle knees. Currently his mobile home park was filled almost to capacity. The only vacancies were 1845 Flatline Circle, where someone had just moved out and the new home had not been brought in yet, and of course 1712 Andorra Court was still available. But other than that the park was full up. The manager's small office sat just inside the entrance of the mobile home park. It was a tiny portable shed that he had rigged with electricity so as to be able to watch TV or run a fan on one of the hot summer Oklahoma days. There was also a short counter with a black phone on it. On the wall there was a calendar with pictures of World War II planes.

The black phone rang. Dooley Hornbackle picked it up and said, "Yes?"

The voice on the opposite end of the phone squawked and gnashed at Dooley's saggy right ear. Dooley held the phone three inches away and listened.

"I know the sky looks bad . . . yes, I'll keep an eye on it . . . I'll unlock the shelter now if it will make you feel better."

Dooley hung up the phone and grabbed his keys from a small copper hook screwed into the bare wall. He stood up, took in air, and let his bones settle just a bit, his knees popping like hot corn.

Then, with the agility of a wooden statue, he shuffled over to the door. He pulled the door open, and wind raced in like heavy curtains. Dooley stepped back and then pushed himself out the door and into the open.

The voice on the TV had been spot on about it being windy.

Dooley fought against the wind, walking down the first lane in the mobile home park and toward the center. He walked through the small playground he had built years ago and over to the storm shelter he had put in when the park was first opened. The shelter was used a dozen or so times each year, but so far no tornadoes had actually worked through or damaged Rolling Greens Deluxe Mobile Home Park.

That was about to change.

Dooley reached the storm shelter. There were already seven residents standing near it waiting to get in.

"Hurry, Mr. Hornbackle," one of the oldest residents ordered. "Hurry."

Dooley unlocked the heavy steel door and turned on the light. The residents began to shuffle as quickly as they could into the storm shelter.

"You should sound the alarm, Dooley," an aged woman said as she stepped in.

"I didn't think it would get this bad," Dooley replied. "And so quickly. I'll—"

The warning sirens began to scream all over town.

"Saint Peter," Dooley said to himself.

He looked over at the swing set he had installed twenty years back. The beat-up, rusty swings squealed and hollered at one another as the tough air pushed them around. Small trees peppered throughout the park shook their bare arms. The sounds of honking cars and gusting wind snapped and whirred all over like invisible pinwheels.

"Get in!" Dooley yelled as more residents worked their way to the shelter.

The air stiffened, and anyone trying to breathe had the sensation of trying to choke down a cup full of warm, glassy cubes of oxygen. Standing still, a person might feel pelted or stoned by Mother Nature herself simply because of the wind.

The sign above the entrance of the Rolling Greens Deluxe Mobile Home Park broke off at the top right corner and swung down, crashing into the line of beat-up old mailboxes and sending them flying. The old cars lining the road inside the park rumbled like tethered dogs wanting to break free.

Two new warning sirens began to scream and holler while three odd-looking funnel clouds touched down.

In the far corner of the Rolling Greens Deluxe Mobile Home Park, past all the homes and on the edge of a dry riverbed, sat the piece of land that Leven had once lived on—1712 Andorra Court. There were still bits and pieces of the home Geth had lifted up, Winter had frozen, and then Leven had helped shatter all over. They were tiny pieces, most of them completely unrecognizable and covered in dirt and weeds.

Nobody had ever moved in after Leven's house had been destroyed. The lot was spooky and ugly and covered with thick, wicked weeds and prairie-dog holes. On the back side of the lot was the stump that had once been the bottom part of Geth.

A thick black funnel cloud touched down just over a mile away. The sound of it settling was like that of a tall building reluctantly imploding.

It was beginning to feel as if the town of Burnt Culvert was going to be sucked up.

Then, as if daylight were frightened, all light scurried off. The scene became as black as the darkest alley.

A twenty-year-old boy with long hair yelled for his mother and ran down the sidewalk toward the shelter. A man who had been painting the side of his mobile home ducked for cover as his open paint cans blew high-gloss paint all over him and his yard. Speckled and scared, he ran for the shelter.

Birds in the air no longer had any control of their flight patterns. They were flung sideways and backwards, riding the thick streams of wind. Two birds smacked into each other and fell to the ground inches away from where the bottom of Geth was.

The tree stump didn't notice. In fact the stump was long dead. It had been many weeks since Geth had been cut down, and the wood had officially given up and was now hardening at a quick pace.

Boom!

The entire globe seemed to rock on its axis as a twister flicked its tail down into the ground.

Boom!

A second twister touched down in the park. It picked up the tiny office and threw it three miles south.

Another funnel cloud touched down. It caught the tip of one mobile home on the far side of the park and flipped the entire thing up and over. The home crashed onto the ground upside down. The wheels that had been hidden beneath its skirt now spun like roller skates that had been struck against the ground.

Two more residents ran into the shelter and Dooley struggled to close the door. He looked around, knowing full well who should be there. Any kids were off at school, and most of the residents were away at work. So, unless someone had stayed home sick, the shelter now held everyone it needed to.

"Everyone's here," an old woman yelled.

The sky drew in its breath and then, like an overzealous child blowing out candles on a birthday cake, blew it out. Dozens of tall, skinny funnel clouds shot down like strands of black licorice. The whirlwinds pummeled and ripped apart the mobile homes, roofs and windows shattering into confetti. As one funnel cloud would pick up a trailer, another would strip the tires from beneath it and send them flying like discuses into the dark sky.

One after another, every mobile home was picked up and slammed to the ground. The air was filled with swirling particle-board, linoleum, and carpet.

The atmosphere burped and belched, filling the air with the smell of sulfur and dirt. Then, as if the sky were suddenly winded, it gasped and died, leaving the air completely still. Tiny bits and pieces of what were once dozens of people's homes fell to the earth like clumsy rain.

Dooley looked at all the anxious faces huddled in the shelter. He was surprised the shelter had held up, the way the concrete walls had shook and wobbled.

But now it was silent.

"Is it over?" an old woman in a housecoat asked.

"I figure it is," Dooley answered.

"Maybe it's the eye of the storm," an even older gentleman said. "It's just a short calm."

"I don't believe it was one proper tornado," Dooley said. "It was a mess of tiny twisters, and the storm's blown through."

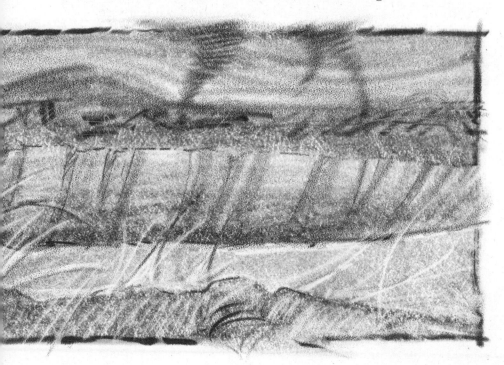

Dooley stepped up the concrete steps and pulled the latch over. He pushed against the door; it moved outward about six inches and stopped. Dooley looked out and up at the sky. He pushed the door harder and it opened another two feet, pushing debris away.

Dooley swore, and rightfully so. He stepped out, and for only the second time in his life, he began to cry. There was nothing left of the Rolling Greens Deluxe Mobile Home Park. Unless, of course, you consider piles and piles of shredded-up homes and trees "something."

Dooley stepped out farther. He looked around, putting his hand to his chest. Not a single home remained. The other residents pushed out behind him, crying and swearing—one woman fainted.

"Saint Peter's mercy," Dooley whistled.

It would take more than mercy to make up for the mess that stood before them all. Sadly, for the second time in less than twenty years this particular piece of the world had been completely worked over.

Everything in the mobile home park was lost.

Of course, it would take hours for anyone to realize that the far corner lot, 1712 Andorra Court, the spot where Geth had once stood and Leven had once lived, was now just a giant crater—no debris, no topsoil, just a big hole with a huge tree stump sticking out of it. The crater was the size of the lot and perfectly round. All the residents of the mobile home park would have marveled and wondered over it if it weren't for the fact that they were temporarily blinded by their entire lives being in shambles.

Despite their lack of attention, however, it was pretty significant that the very spot where Antsel had planted Geth and Leven had grown up had changed shape again.

In the history of time, 1712 Andorra Court was one very important address.

CHAPTER NINE

DIVIDED WE RIDE

Geth stepped out of the bushes and looked at Winter. "Nobody's there. I looked everywhere, but he's gone."

"Clover!" Winter called, the early morning air cooling her words.

Geth put his hand on Winter's shoulder. "They're not there. Something happened."

"They have to be there," Winter insisted. She pushed back into the bushes, calling Leven's name. "Leven! Lev?" Winter whipped her head around and looked at Geth. "Where could they have gone?"

"He's disappeared," Geth answered. "I was right by him and I didn't hear a thing."

"Did he fall in a hole?"

"There are no holes," Geth said.

"Maybe he just needed privacy," Winter suggested. "Lev!"

There was no reply.

"Listen, Winter," Geth said calmly, "he's okay."

"How can you possibly know that?" Winter asked, her green eyes as wide as apples. "We've been together since the start, and I'm not going to just walk off without him. Why would you have some sort of radar as to whether he's okay? I'm the one who . . ."

Geth waited patiently for her to figure out what she wanted to say.

"Well, how would you know?" she finally said, exasperated.

"I just know I'd feel different right now if he were harmed," Geth answered. "Leven is walking where fate wishes."

"You lithens are . . . I don't know a kind word that would represent the word I really want to call you."

"We've been separated from Leven before," Geth said. "He's very strong."

"That's true," Winter said, exhaling.

"Fate's in control," Geth said kindly.

"I hate that."

Geth smiled. "Look what it's done for you so far."

"Should I list all the times I was almost killed?" Winter asked.

"If you include the fact that you're still alive after each listing," Geth said. "And Leven has Clover."

Winter's shoulders dropped. "So they're okay?"

"I think so," Geth soothed. "I'd be more worried about us."

"You're so comforting."

"We'll get to Oklahoma," Geth insisted. "That's what Leven said, so that's what we'll do."

"So we just leave them?" Winter asked. "We hop back on the avalands and act like this is how it's supposed to be?"

Geth nodded.

"You're so infuriating," Winter smiled. She turned around and headed out of the trees and back to the avalands.

"You want to ride on mine?" Geth asked.

"No way," Winter answered. "I've always wanted to control one of these things myself."

Winter awkwardly climbed back up onto the avaland that she and Leven had been riding. She grabbed onto the long grass growing from the forehead of the beast and yelled. The avaland took off, and for a very brief moment she was rather happy that Leven had gone missing and she was in control.

CHAPTER TEN

ALWAYS SOMETHING THERE TO REMIND ME

The largest sun was now up, its orange body causing the biggest moon to take its leave. The morning was quiet, and only the sound of bit bugs buzzing in the foliage could be heard. The island of Alder smelled like soap—clean and good for you. Of course, it didn't *look* clean—it looked like a place that had once thrived but was now abandoned and grown over.

Leven moved carefully across a thin rope bridge. The bridge stretched out across a narrow but deep crevasse that had water running down in the bottom of it. Leven and Clover had been following the wide glass road and it had come to an end at the head of the bridge.

"Don't look down," Clover said.

"Great," Leven replied while looking down. "You know it's impossible to not look down when someone says that?"

"*Impossible* is not a word," Clover mimicked Geth.

"Your impression has gotten much better," Leven congratulated him. "I—" Leven's grip slipped on the rope and he grabbed to get ahold of it again. As his right hand grasped the rope, his left leg slipped and he had to balance himself on the bridge until it stopped swinging and he could stand tall again.

"Are you okay?" Clover asked. "You look uneven."

"I'm fine," Leven lied. "My balance is sort of freaking out."

Leven looked at his left hand and watched it shrink back to normal size. He quickly put it behind his back.

"What's up with that?" Clover asked.

"Nothing," Leven's voice cracked.

"Geth said you were changing," Clover reminded him. "Is this what he meant?"

"I don't know what Geth meant," Leven said defensively. "As if I haven't changed enough. I'm already a completely different person."

"Maybe Winter was right about that Foovian puberty thing."

Leven wanted to argue that fact, but he was afraid his voice would crack again. They stepped off the bridge and onto a mossy knoll with white flowers and orange bushes growing all over it. Leven turned around.

"Do you hear that?" he asked.

Clover shook his head.

"I think someone's following us," Leven whispered.

Clover looked back at the empty bridge. "Well, there's nobody there now."

"Good," Leven said, beginning to walk down the glass path as it snaked away from the bridge.

"How do you know you're going the right way?" Clover asked.

"I don't," Leven answered. "I just know I'm supposed to follow this glass."

"What if we should be going the opposite direction on that path?"

"Then we'll probably turn around at some point."

"We should get back to Geth," Clover complained.

"Why?"

"Because he's so old and wise and has a really good sense of direction."

Leven stopped. "Can you hear that?"

"What?" Clover said nervously.

"The sound of you making fun of my sense of direction."

"Oh," Clover waved. "I thought you heard somebody again. Anyway, I wasn't saying you were bad with directions, I was saying Geth was good."

Leven smiled. "I would love to be with Winter and Geth, but it seems that fate has placed us here for the moment. Show me a way to them and I'll take it." He started walking again.

After some time Clover spoke up. "I never mentioned Winter."

"What?" Leven asked.

"You said 'I would love to be with Winter and Geth,' but I had never mentioned Winter."

"Well, they're together," Leven pointed out. "Wherever they are."

"Still, you said *Winter* first."

"Can I take it back?"

"No," Clover insisted.

"Well, then, read into it what you want," Leven said, frustrated.

"I think it means you were thinking about her."

"I'll tell you what," Leven said. "I'll talk about her if you talk about Lilly."

Clover disappeared.

Twelve minutes later, still invisible, Clover said, "Winter's changed."

"What's that supposed to mean?" Leven asked, pushing through long droopy branches and tall purple grass.

"Well," Clover said, "you've changed . . . and Winter's changed."

"You mean we grew up fast."

"And her hair's nicer," Clover said. "When I first saw her it was a mess."

"I've never seen Lilly," Leven admitted. "What's she like?"

Clover shivered on Leven's shoulder. "She's all white, with green eyes, and she's real picky about who she talks to."

"Really?"

"Yeah," Clover said sadly. "I think she's refined."

"Are you sure she's not just stuck—" Leven smacked into a large stone wall. It had been completely hidden by the tall trees, and its mossy covering had disguised it perfectly. "Ouch."

Leven stepped back and ran his hands along the wall. From where he stood, he could see that it stretched on for quite a while in both directions. It was also about three feet taller than him.

"What's this?" Leven asked needlessly.

The stone wall was covered with mossy carvings. There was a picture of a boat and a carving of what looked like a siid. Leven looked over at the nearest tree. He grabbed onto a low branch and pulled himself up into the tree. Wriggling through the branches, he crawled out onto the top of the wall. The ground behind the wall wasn't as far down. Leven pulled out his kilve, pitched it forward, and then jumped down after it.

The ground behind the wall was spongier and covered in small brown stones. Leven picked up his kilve, accidentally striking a rock with it. The rock screamed and then flew at him, smacking him behind the right knee.

"Careful," Clover warned. "Those are woe stones. If you can catch one, I would love to keep it."

Leven stepped back and kicked another one. The stone screamed and flew up, hitting Leven under the chin.

"What the—"

Clover reached down and picked up a small woe stone. The tiny rock whined and jumped from his tight grip, then slammed Clover on the right side. Clover hollered and disappeared.

Leven looked around. The entire ground was covered with the rocks. He looked back up at the wall.

"What do we do?" Leven said out of the side of his mouth. "Any direction I go, I'm going to step on one."

"I don't know," Clover whispered back. "You could throw me back over the wall."

"To be honest, I'm not that worried about you."

"Oh," Clover said, sounding hurt. "Maybe if *you* walked really slow."

Leven pushed his right foot forward, steering clear of as many rocks as possible. His toe gently brushed a fist-sized stone. The rock barked and flung itself into Leven's stomach. Leven held his gut.

"You've got to be kidding."

"They don't go on forever," Clover said from the top of Leven's head. "I can see more glass about three hundred yards from here."

"Where?"

Clover pointed.

"And the path leads somewhere?"

"Most paths do."

Leven slid his left foot past his right and wove it around six rocks before he nicked another. The woe stone flew between his legs and smacked him in the back of the head. Leven stepped with his right, brushing a stone. As it launched itself toward him, he swung down with his kilve and knocked it like a baseball hundreds of feet away. The woe stone squealed as it flew through the air. Had they been in a ballpark, it would have been an easy home run.

"Wow," Clover whispered. "You should do that again."

Leven smiled until the sound of something screaming began to increase in volume.

"It's coming back!" Clover yelled.

Leven looked in the direction he had hit the stone and could see a small brown spot racing toward him. He shifted his stance, and right before the rock reached him he gripped his kilve and bunted the stone down into the ground. The rock hit several other stones, and those stones dog-piled the offending stone, beating and burying it.

"Lucky," Clover said reverently.

"If that thing had hit me going that fast I would have been dead," Leven said in awe.

"Those stones can't kill you."

"Well, it would have hurt," Leven complained. "We don't have time for this—hold on."

Leven leapt forward, landing on two stones. They twisted up his legs, scraping his left knee. He kept running, the rocks screaming and popping up around him like bubbling stone. Leven swung his kilve, hitting as many away as possible, but there were just too many to dodge or hit. One whacked him on the back of the left shoulder while another whacked him on the front. A flat stone with rough edges popped him in the ear as dozens yelled and whipped up against his legs.

"Run faster!" Clover screamed. "Can you see the path?"

Leven looked to his left and saw the wide, stone-free path. He kicked through a thin patch of woe stones and dove for the glass path. Once on it, he crumpled into a ball and covered his head with his arms. Tiny bits of glass dug up into his forearms as the few remaining stones finished screaming and pelting him.

Leven breathed heavily. As the onslaught ended, he uncovered his head and knelt up. "That's insane."

"Yeah," Clover agreed. "Some stones don't know their place. There must be something of value nearby."

"Why?"

"Woe stones don't just happen," Clover said. "They're pretty rare, and they're usually surrounding something of value. I've only seen a few in my life, and they were protecting a bunch of birds that had just been born."

"So what is this place?" Leven asked, standing up all the way. "I don't see any birds."

Leven looked around. In the distance he could see another stone wall, and near that was a two-story stone structure. It looked like a small castle with rock chimneys and a miniature drawbridge. Leven glanced down at the glass path and let his eyes trace out the direction it wound. It appeared to lead straight to the small castle.

"See that?" Leven pointed.

Leven could feel Clover nodding on the top of his head.

"What is it?" Leven asked.

"Some sort of home," Clover answered. "It looks deserted."

"Let's hope it has some answers."

Leven pushed his shoulders back and slipped his kilve over his shoulder. He walked with purpose down the path.

"Are you sure about this?" Clover asked.

"No."

"Maybe we should sneak up on the place."

Leven reached up and scratched Clover's head. "Where's the fun in that? Besides, what do we do, go back to the rocks?"

"I'm just saying that if something was out to get you, that would be the perfect place for that something to wait."

"Let's hope something could care less about me."

Clover looked at his knuckles. "I wish I had claws."

"You never got yours?" Leven asked kindly.

"It's a sore spot," Clover said. "They should have grown in when I was taking my turn guarding our shores, but they didn't."

"Your teeth are pretty sharp," Leven tried.

Clover flared his gums and showed his teeth as they moved closer.

The stone structure was small and decaying in several places. The rock chimneys on top of it tilted, and a couple of them had crumbled down altogether. The wooden roof was splintered and parts of it had been torn apart or blown away completely by the wind. Moss and weeds had captured almost the entire bottom half of the building, whereas decay and rot had been working steadily on the top half.

"Lovely," Clover observed.

With each step closer, the place looked more ugly and dilapidated.

"There's no lights on," Clover complained.

"It's daytime," Leven pointed out. "And it's not like they have electricity."

"I miss electricity," Clover lamented.

They stepped closer to the castle. A large, dry moat circled the entire structure, but a thin drawbridge was down, creating a way for them to cross the moat. Leven glanced downward into the empty trench as they moved over it. Ghostlike creatures were swimming through the air in the empty moat.

"Are those fish?" Leven asked.

"No," Clover said. "They're spunk. They're like fish, except they live in empty bodies of water and they'll suck wormlike pieces of your soul out if they bite you."

"Really?"

"You'll end up more confused than when that one pretty lady flew over you."

Leven moved to the middle of the drawbridge.

"Their meat is supposed to be really stringy and hard to chew. And . . ."

"And?" Leven prompted.

"And they'll give you really awkward gas."

"Just what I need," Leven complained. "Maybe I should know more about Alder," he whispered. "This place seems a little bit different from the rest of Foo. The ground is spongy, the fish swim in non-water, and it feels like I'm on a boat with the ground never staying completely still. Are we rocking?"

Clover looked around. "I thought it was just you and your lack of balance."

Leven stepped off the drawbridge and walked under a large stone arch and into a rock courtyard. On the other side of the courtyard there were two double doors that were wide open.

Clover disappeared as if instructed.

"Hello," Leven called out as he walked through the doors. "Anyone here?"

Inside the building, the ceilings were ripped up and there were pieces of beat-up furniture all over the place. The wallpaper on the wall was torn and moldy, and the smell of animal urine and rotting wood was so strong that Leven had to plug his nose.

"Who decayed in here?" Clover whispered.

Leven waved his right hand in front of his nose. In the far corner of the filthy room was a small round table with a couple of empty glasses tipped over on it. There were also some crusted plates of petrified food.

"Hello," Leven hollered out again. "Anyone?"

"No need to yell," a sickly voice sounded from the far corner.

"Who's there?" Leven asked, holding his hand above his eyes.

On the far side of the table, hiding in the shadows, Leven could see a blurry definition of a dark, ragged being. The body shifted and gasped.

"Hello," Leven greeted. "I was . . ."

The shadowy figure began to cough violently. It hacked something up and out of its throat and then moaned pathetically. Whatever had come out of its throat was now on the floor. A swarm of bit bugs scurried over to it and began to feast.

"That's disgusting," Clover whispered.

"Shhhh," Leven insisted.

More coughing, but no throat glob.

"Is this your home?" Leven asked.

"Yessss," the figure hissed, sounding as if it didn't have the energy to finish the word.

"I don't know where I am," Leven said.

"I do," the voice rasped. "You're making your way to the tree, Leven."

Leven stepped closer. "How do you know me?"

"I was one who failed to stop you," the voice said sadly.

Leven moved in even closer. He could see the being much more clearly now. It was missing bits and pieces of itself and looked like a smeared version of the person Leven remembered. But the image still caused the hair on the back of Leven's neck to stand up.

"Sabine?"

Sabine nodded and coughed violently.

CHAPTER ELEVEN

ON THE ROCKS

Like everyone else, including you, I occasionally make assumptions based on too little information. If, for example, you were to tell me that you grew up in a small town, I would instantly assume that you spent your afternoons swinging from tire swings or skipping rocks in a small stream. Or maybe you used to sit out on the front porch while your apron-wearing mother brought you tall, chilled glasses of homemade lemonade. I would also blindly assume that the small town you had grown up in had no more than a few quaint buildings, and that in the center of town there was an old courthouse with a town clock that didn't quite keep correct time. Life was slower, people were kinder, and the cost of living was well below that in the Big Apple or Madrid.

Well, if someone were to say they were from the small town of Santa Rosa, New Mexico, I would assume all the above, but maybe instead of a courthouse with a clock I would envision a battlement covered in stucco. And maybe, in the past, my assumption would not have been too far off. But right now? Today?

Well, things were considerably different from the way my assumptions would have painted them. The small town of Santa Rosa, New Mexico, was exploding. Never had their borders experienced so many people flooding their streets and taking up their space. Every motel was full, and many of the residents had rented out parts of their homes to news crews and people who had money and were interested in what was happening.

What was happening was that the small sinkhole known as Blue Hole Lake was now the most talked-about body of water in the world. Dennis, the one-time janitor, with the help of Antsel's robe that Terry had found, was now challenging the world to gather around the hole in anticipation of its opening. He challenged them to be ready for those who would soon be storming into Reality from Foo.

Of course, anyone who was anyone knew that the real power and drive were coming from Ezra, one very powerful and ticked-off toothpick. Ezra was not the same toothpick he had been just days ago. After being captured by the military and placed in a jar, he had accidentally caught on fire. And the only way Dennis could put him out was to kick him into a barrel of orange glowing liquid that had been sitting there since three wars ago. Ezra now glowed, his hue changing with his mood. His green-nail-polished body shone like a glow stick, and his paper-clip right leg was shiny and sharpened. And whereas he had been a bothersome and insulting little pest before, now he was completely evil and seemed to possess powers that were growing and changing daily, thanks to the orange goo bath he had soaked in.

At the moment Ezra and Dennis were being flown in a helicopter to Clovis, New Mexico. Apparently the president of the United States was there and wanted to talk to them. Dennis was shaking, his wrists wet with perspiration. Ezra, on the other hand, was salivating and fighting himself to keep from laughing.

Elton Thumps was in the front seat of the helicopter with the pilot. Elton was wearing a light brown suit and had his dark hair slicked back. He had on scholarly, large-rimmed glasses that fit his elitist personality and strong chin. Elton was tan and tall and had more arrogance than his thin frame seemed capable of holding. Yes, he was Leven's father, but he had been brainwashed for years and now, much like some of those in Foo who had let selfishness dictate their fate, he was confused and very much touched by the prospect of power.

Dennis had large earphones on to muffle the noise of the helicopter. There was a microphone attached to the right earphone. The microphone bent down and in front of Dennis's mouth. Ezra pushed the left earphone up and wiggled beneath it.

"You ready for this?" he screamed in an effort to be heard over the whirl of the helicopter.

Dennis put his hand over the microphone and pushed it up so as to not be heard. "I think so," he replied, scrunching his large, bland facial features into a tight wad.

"What have I told you about thinking?"

"Right," Dennis said.

"I'll tell you what to say," Ezra hollered. "But you've gotta make it sound important and powerful. You've gotten better."

"Thanks," Dennis yelled.

"Stop being so polite," Ezra ordered, his body pulsating with green light. "I told you I'd lay off the insults, seeing how you saved my life, but I'm only wooden—don't make it so easy."

Dennis growled.

"That's better," Ezra said happily.

The helicopter veered hard to the right, tilting like a toy in a child's hand. It picked up speed and raced forward.

"The president of the United States," Dennis blurted out. "I can't believe that I'm going to meet the president of the United States."

"I suppose if I were you I'd find it hard to believe as well," Ezra said nicely.

"Not too many weeks ago I was a janitor—a janitor being yelled at for not filling the copy machine with enough paper," Dennis reminisced loudly. "Or being picked on because a trash can was put back a couple of inches in the wrong spot, or a computer screen had smudges on it." Dennis opened and closed his fists. He held them tight until they were white and then slowly relaxed them.

Ezra hissed. He looked at Dennis and smiled as if Dennis were a stew he had been brewing for years, and he could tell it was now done and ready to be served to mankind.

"Now?" Ezra asked maliciously, his voice a loud static cackle. "How do you feel now?"

"I feel invincible," Dennis said softly.

"And?" Ezra egged him on. "Invincible and . . ."

"Invincible and better than the same people who once made it perfectly clear that they were better than me," Dennis barked.

"Which, if you remember correctly, was everyone," Ezra screamed.

"Everyone!" Dennis chanted.

"Nice," Ezra glowed. He himself was shaking from a small, self-induced frenzy. His purple hair was twisting madly and his single eye stared directly at Dennis. "Go on! You're invincible and better than everyone. And . . ."

Dennis considered for a moment. "I think that's it."

Ezra smacked his forehead with his right palm. "That's it?" he yelled. "That's it? Don't you feel evil?"

Dennis shrugged and patted his arms. "Not really."

"Ahhhhh," Ezra screamed, jabbing his metal leg into Dennis's shoulder. "I need you to feel—"

The helicopter dropped a few feet and sped in a diagonal line to the east. Dennis's headphones came to life.

"The military base is a few miles away," Elton Thumps said. "We have word the president is already there and waiting."

Dennis just nodded.

"The president will want to know everything you know—and quickly," Elton said.

"We weren't planning to reminisce," Ezra balked. "But we'll tell him what we want or he can go jump in a cake."

Dennis snorted. "Don't you mean 'jump in a lake'?"

"What's so bad about jumping in a lake?" Ezra screamed.

"What's so bad about jumping in a cake?" Dennis argued.

"All that frosting and sugar and sticky stuff," Ezra pointed out. "It would take hours to wash it off. Plus, a cake is small, and you'd jam your head on the plate. A lake, you jump in, jump out, dry yourself off, and you're fine."

"It doesn't make sense," Dennis yelled.

"Then tell them that we will say what we want and if they don't like it we will tie them to a pole in the coldest region of the world, strip them of everything but their stupidity, and use their frozen fingers and toes as ice cubes to cool our drinks." There was no bounce or lilt in Ezra's voice.

Dennis just sat without replying.

"You can paraphrase if you want," Ezra growled.

"I'm not saying that to anyone," Dennis insisted.

"Fine," Ezra growled. "I'll do the talking."

The helicopter dropped rapidly and then leveled out a few feet above the ground. It twisted a full circle, swung over, and settled on a cement landing pad without so much as a bump.

Elton Thumps took off his headphones and jumped out of the front door. He opened the back door and waved Dennis and Ezra out. The dying blades of the helicopter blew back the hood on Dennis's purple robe. Dennis's head was clear, with no trace of Sabine on it, and he walked as tall as a person with extraordinarily high self-esteem might walk.

The path from the helicopter was lined with soldiers all standing at attention, weapons in hand. Ezra jumped up on top of Dennis's head and crouched down, facing forward. He looked up at the rising sun and blinked his single eye. He eyed the line of soldiers and laughed.

"Do they think this will scare us?" Ezra yelled.

Dennis didn't answer.

Ezra opened his arms, and the soldiers lining both sides of the path flew back and onto their rears. Their guns scraped against the ground, and one gun down the line accidentally went off, firing into the air. The soldiers scrambled to get back up and stand at attention as Ezra laughed.

"Having fun?" Dennis asked.

"I've had funner," Ezra replied.

A round man in a general's uniform came storming toward Dennis, his right fist raised and shaking. The man had a large, blocky head, short arms, and legs as thick as garbage cans. The steam coming from his ears was a pretty good indicator that he wasn't in a pleasant mood. He stopped six inches in front of the two of them and shoved his large red face up into Dennis's grill. His wide brown eyes looked up at Ezra, who was lying casually on Dennis's forehead.

"General Lank," he informed them.

"Dennis," Dennis replied.

Ezra yawned.

"Listen up," General Lank said, pointing toward the shaken soldiers. "Did you do this?"

Ezra raised his hand. "Guilty."

"I don't know what kind of trick this is," General Lank said. "A mobile toothpick. But the president feels you're worth talking to. If you were my assignment, I would treat you differently."

"There's some green stuff in your right ear," Ezra said.

General Lank stuck his right pinkie into his ear and twisted while his big, blocky face reddened. "You caused one of them to fire a weapon into the air. Bullets come down, you know."

Ezra stood up on Dennis's head, stretched, and reached his right hand up. Two seconds later a thin whistle could be heard. One second later Ezra extended his wooden arm farther and caught the bullet as it fell to the earth. "Was this the bullet you were talking about?"

General Lank's mouth dropped open, exposing how poorly the military had taken care of his teeth. "How?"

"Don't question us," Ezra swore. "Take us to the president, and if we are in the right mood, we just might enlighten him."

"But—"

"Don't call yourself names," Ezra growled.

"You have—"

Ezra bit off the tip of the bullet and spat it at General Lank's forehead. The bit of bullet bounced off and fell to the ground.

"Now," Ezra said sweetly, "are you ready to take us?"

General Lank gritted his teeth, turned on his meaty heels, and reluctantly led the way.

The landscape around the military base was dusty, hot, and barren, with an oppressive feeling of isolation. But once they were inside in a secured room, things didn't look too bad for Ezra and Dennis. The room was filled with soft chairs and four couches. There were plush rugs on the floor, and the walls were covered with real artwork. The room was rectangular, and on the far end there was a giant wooden desk with a small American flag on the corner of it.

Dennis and Ezra were alone in the room.

Dennis was sitting with his legs crossed in a green wingback chair, wearing the purple robe. Ezra had thrown a fit about there being no chair his size, so a couple of soldiers had fashioned a small seat out of an empty Coke can and some fabric. Ezra was so happy about his throne that he had been sitting in it humming for the last few minutes.

"This isn't too bad," Ezra stopped humming to say. "Just think what it will be like when we rule the world."

"And how are we going about that again?" Dennis asked.

"You ask the worst questions," Ezra answered, sitting up in his throne. "Why are they making us wait?"

Dennis just shrugged.

"Have you ever impressed anyone positively?"

"I don't care if I have," Dennis said honestly.

"What?" Ezra asked. "That almost sounded gutsy."

"My mind's clear."

"You mean empty?" Ezra asked. "Now, what does this president of yours look like?"

Dennis pointed to a huge oil painting behind the desk. At the bottom of the painting was a gold plaque that read, "President Myron H. Topple."

"That's him," Dennis said.

"Really?" Ezra smiled. "He looks weak—I know I can take him."

Dennis shook his head. "I'm all for stopping this Dearth, and I can see how I might enjoy being one of the leaders of this movement and all that will come with Foo. But I'm worried about you and the power you now have."

"Worried about me?" Ezra laughed.

"You're not real stable," Dennis pointed out.

Ezra jumped out of his chair and pumped his fist. "I can't believe what I'm hearing."

The far door opened, and four armed guards came into the room. They were followed by a dozen other important-looking people. Finally a man matching the portrait hanging behind the desk walked in. He smiled like he did in the portrait and walked directly over to Dennis.

Dennis stood up and awkwardly bowed-curtsied-nodded.

President Topple stuck out his hand, still smiling. Dennis wiped his right hand on his robe and then reached out to shake the president's hand.

"President Topple," the president said. "And you must be Dennis."

Dennis nodded.

"Sit down," President Topple said. "Please."

Dennis sat down as President Topple took a seat on the edge of the large desk. "I've been excited to meet you, but I must admit I am most interested in your friend."

"That's using the term *friend* a little liberally," Ezra said. "Now, what do you want?"

President Topple looked at Ezra in awe. "You know, if I hadn't seen some of the things I've seen in the last few weeks, I'm not sure I would have believed this."

"You haven't seen anything like me," Ezra said, bothered. "If you're comparing me to a bunch of wind or bugs or dirt monsters in the field, then you're a larger dolt than that painting makes you out to be."

President Topple's smile faded. He tugged on the cuffs of his shirtsleeves and sniffed. "I apologize. I certainly didn't mean to offend you."

"Ezra's offended by everything," Dennis said casually. "Don't let it get to you."

President Topple smiled weakly.

"And Dennis is baffled by everything," Ezra retorted.

"Listen," President Topple said, "I'm sorry if I don't know the proper etiquette for talking with a toothpick, but there are very important things we need to discuss. If what you have told my staff is true, some very big things are about to happen, and I need to know what we should do to prepare for them."

"You're asking me?" Dennis said happily.

"We want not only to be ready for whoever or whatever is coming but to be prepared to occupy the land they have come from." President Topple was not smiling now.

"Occupy?" Ezra asked. "I'll decide who occupies."

President Topple stood up. "We have tremendous resources lined up and in use," he said. "We have built large, fenced-off stations to hold those who might come through, and we have organized thousands of troops to march into this Foo, when the time is right, and make sure our interests are taken seriously. And I'm prepared to extend you every courtesy, but I will not have a toothpick calling the shots. I am the president of the—"

President Topple stopped talking because he was caught off guard by the sensation of floating. He drifted up with his arms and legs failing. Ezra stood on the edge of the desk raising his arms and laughing. The guards that had come in with President Topple pulled out their guns and pointed them at Dennis.

"Whoa," Dennis said, standing. "Don't point those at me."

"Who's doing that?" the tallest guard asked.

"It's not me," Dennis insisted.

"Hold it," the president yelled as he floated in midair. "Put your guns away and step back."

The guards reluctantly returned their weapons to their holsters and backed up.

"What do you want?" President Topple asked Ezra.

"To be taken seriously," Ezra seethed. "Even I don't know the full extent of my powers, but I'm pretty excited to find out. And I have no problem testing them on you and the 'resources' you've lined up. If you want me to just turn a blind eye at all those who will be coming through, then go for it. You deal with them. Either way, in the end I'm going to take the credit and finish off those beings in Foo who have created me with so much anger and confusion. In the end I am going to stand over Geth's dead body triumphantly. Then and only then will I begin to reason and barter." Ezra was breathing hard.

"Who's Geth?" the president asked, still floating in the air.

"That's not important to you," Ezra said. "We will return to the exit and call the shots. Then, if I complete what I must, I will make sure you get yours."

"Could you put me down?" President Topple asked.

Ezra waved and the president fell to the floor. Dennis

and two guards helped him back onto his feet. He leaned against the desk again and rubbed his head.

"I can't let you just have the run of our country," President Topple said. "I need to know what's happening."

"Come with us," Ezra said. "I don't care."

"We've already decided that wouldn't be wise, so I'm sending General Lank. He has a clear understanding of our military and my mind."

"Wow," Ezra said sarcastically. "Are you complimenting or insulting him?"

"Do we have a deal?" the president asked, ignoring Ezra's last jab. "I can't just let you fly around untethered."

"So the guy with the square red face has to tag along?" Ezra asked.

President Topple nodded his head.

Ezra looked at Dennis. "What do you think?"

Dennis flipped the hood of his purple robe up over his bald head. "I think we should get going."

"Of course," President Topple said. "We'll get you back to the site as fast as possible."

"Can I fly the helicopter?" Ezra asked.

Dennis looked at the president and frantically shook his head.

"I believe our pilots can get you there even faster," President Topple said.

"Whatever," Ezra complained. He hopped off the desk and crawled beneath the hood of Dennis's robe. His head popped back out. "Have someone bring that throne."

President Topple picked up the can and fabric and handed it to one of the guards. "Good luck," he said. He then smiled like his portrait again and walked out of the room.

CHAPTER TWELVE

TAG, YOU'RE WRONG

Brindle was tired. His small body and old knees were pleading with him to please take a break. He climbed slowly up over a lip of stone and across a thin wooden bridge that connected a bit of the Sentinel Fields with the beautiful shore of the Veil Sea. From the shore Brindle could see the thousands and thousands of beings marching across the gloam toward Sycophant Run.

The sound of their feet rumbled like low, endless thunder.

Brindle swore. He lifted Lilly up from around his neck and set her gently on the ground. The small white sycophant was still blissfully asleep, thanks to the bite Brindle had given her a few days before.

Brindle stretched and rolled his neck. His fur bristled and his eyes blinked softly. He was a kindhearted sycophant who had no desire to be doing what he was now doing. He had been sent by Rast to retrieve Rast's daughter Lilly. Rast felt that Lilly might know more about the key that was missing and had been used to unlock the Dearth. Brindle had found Lilly in the Invisible Village and pleaded with her to come. When she had refused, Brindle had bitten her and heaved her up over his shoulders. He had been working his way back to Sycophant Run ever since.

Brindle picked up Lilly and carried her over to a large rock. Laying her down on the rock, he took a seat next to her, then pulled a small piece of fruit from his leather satchel and smelled the skin. The green twizberry was ripe and spongy. Brindle bit into it, and purple juice ran down his furry chin.

The thundering of the marching armies continued.

Brindle's small heart could barely take it. He knew that everything was different now. With the secret of the sycophants' immortality out there, everything had changed. Bringing Lilly back would do little good, now that every soul in Foo knew how to dispose of the sycophants or at least to make them visible.

"It will never be the same," Brindle whispered to himself as he watched the marching hordes. "So much destruction and devastation, in a place where beauty and peace have always prevailed."

Brindle turned and looked at Lilly. She was smiling, and her small left foot twitched. Brindle bent down and whispered into Lilly's ear.

"Arise and dream of Foo."

Slowly Lilly's green eyes blinked open. She looked at Brindle and smiled.

The bite of a sycophant is a marvelous thing. Sycophants long to serve, but every once in a while they need a big dose of me time. By biting those they serve, they are able to spend a few days doing the things they want to do. People who are bitten simply sleep peacefully, their brains showing images of sycophants and how wonderful they are. When they wake up from the bite, they are not only calm and happy but filled with kind thoughts about how spectacular and needed sycophants really are.

Lilly smiled even wider.

"Hello," Brindle said.

"Hello," Lilly blushed. "Where am I?"

"I'm taking you to your father," Brindle answered. "He needs you."

Lilly's eyes scrunched closed and she shook her head softly. "I'm tired."

"You'll be fine."

"What's that noise?" Lilly asked.

"Those in the distance," Brindle pointed. "They are moving toward Sycophant Run."

Lilly gasped. "Why?"

"Come with me," Brindle said. He swung Lilly back over his shoulders. She braided her fingers together under his chin and held on.

Brindle moved swiftly. The short rest was all he had needed. He ran over a web of stone and down onto the shore of the Veil Sea. Ten minutes later he had caught up with the armies of rants. Brindle dashed beneath their feet and bodies, racing out onto the gloam.

The gloam was about thirty feet wide and divided a section of the Veil Sea down below Sycophant Run. The water on both sides of the gloam was churning wildly and spraying everyone. Rants and nits marched with speed down the gloam. Brindle could see groups of echoes and cogs and troops of black skeletons marching between the rants.

"Why are they going to Sycophant Run?"

"There's an exit there," Brindle said. "They're moving to escape Foo."

"The sycophants will stop them," Lilly said, her head still in a daze.

Brindle didn't have the heart to say anything else. He ran as fast as he could down the gloam, weaving through the throngs of beings. Some rants were chanting, and tall black skeletons on onicks were herding the masses and yelling to keep the armies moving. The sky above was filled with hovering birds curious over what was happening.

"The sycophants will stop them," Lilly said again.

"Not this time," Brindle answered. He ran through the legs of an onick and farther down the gloam.

"Wait a second," Lilly yelled. "Did I want to come with you?"

"I can't remember," Brindle yelled back.

"Where was I?"

"Lost." Brindle jumped up over a cluster of slow-moving rants. He came back down against the gloam and shot like a rocket right down the middle.

"I was in the Invisible Village," Lilly declared.

Brindle didn't answer.

"You bit me?"

"Don't think too much about it," Brindle said loudly, his breath labored from the run. "Foo is gasping for air and there's little time to worry over things like that."

"It looks to me like Foo's dying," Lilly said sadly. "I didn't want to come with you, did I?"

"No."

"I won't speak to my father," Lilly insisted, her head clearing as she clung to Brindle.

Lore Coils were still drifting all over Foo, and most of them were whispering the words of the sycophant secret. Brindle watched two sycophants appear out of nowhere as the words *Alderam Degarus* rolled over them.

"How can they know the secret?" Lilly asked.

"The Dearth got it," Brindle said. "He stole it from Leven's mind."

"Who?"

"Leven Thumps."

"Just like a nit to ruin everything."

"He's no nit," Brindle said, still running. "He's the Want and he's our one chance."

"Our one chance?" Lilly seethed, the hate in her rising. "Then why was my burn needed?"

"Winter brought him back."

"Don't say her name," Lilly ordered. "Don't say her name ever."

Brindle and Lilly ran in relative silence, with her holding on to his neck and him running as fast as he could. The troops of rants were organized and vast, and they marched toward Sycophant Run with a great sense of purpose and speed. A harsh scraping and the sound of screaming began to rise from the distance. It grew louder and louder.

"What's that?" Lilly asked.

"It's the sound of war," Brindle answered. He weaved along the edge of the gloam and directly toward the point where the gloam now connected with Sycophant Run. Brindle could see hundreds and hundreds of sycophants valiantly fighting the throngs of rants that were spilling onto the shore. The armies of rants held large poles with fluttering leaves of metal that twinkled like bright lights under the morning sunlight. All over rants were hollering the words that stole the sycophants' invisibility.

"*Alderam Degarus!*"

Some sycophants were trying to fight, but the shimmering metal put them into a trance, and their visibility made it simple for the armies invading their shores to kick and swat them away. Some sycophants had their claws out and were trying to make a last-ditch effort to protect their home. But, sadly, for the most part the beaches were littered with wet, dazed sycophants. Many were simply in a trance, thanks to the metal, but some lay suffering from wounds.

Brindle stopped. Lilly slid down from off of his back, and they both stood there staring in awe. Lilly's eyes became wet as Brindle breathed slowly.

As they stood there, hundreds of beings continued to rush past them, racing onto Sycophant Run and toward the direction of the exit. Some refugees kicked the sycophants out of the way; others just stomped over them.

"I don't believe it," Lilly said, her voice cracking. "It's so horrible."

Brindle was quiet.

"Couldn't someone stop this?" Lilly asked angrily.

"Winter tried," Brindle said softly.

Lilly's small knees buckled. She put her tiny hand to her heart and gasped for air. A couple of careless rants pushed Brindle aside and almost trampled Lilly. Brindle reached out his hand and Lilly took it.

"She never wanted to leave you," Brindle said. "But at the time it was the only way. She argued to bring you with her, but it was not right. Antsel and Geth both thought it too much for you."

"I could have helped," Lilly said, her pink eyes still taking in the horrific scene.

"It wasn't how it happened."

"So I was wrong?"

Brindle was quiet. He was wise enough to know the power of silence.

"Now look how they trample us," Lilly said. "We have served since the first day of Foo, and now they use us as a road to walk upon. How could they?"

"It's hard to find any good in this," Brindle said.

"There is no good," Lilly cried. "How could there be?"

"All is not lost," Brindle argued.

"How can you say that?"

"Leven still fights."

"And . . . Winter?" The name did not come easily to her.

"She fights just as hard," Brindle said. "Many Lore Coils whisper her name and her intentions. She's very strong—it took everything she had to leave you."

Lilly let her eyes run. The sound of the marching armies and the sight of so many of her kind being pushed around bobbing in the waves made her stomach sick. She had known the world was full of bad things, but she had never imagined the kind of evil that could have ruined and stripped the innocent land of Sycophant Run.

"What do we do?" Lilly asked, sobbing.

"We find your father," Brindle answered.

Lilly began to run, and Brindle followed closely after.

CHAPTER THIRTEEN

WHEN WORLDS COLLIDE

The cavern burned bright—hundreds of torches being held by hundreds of beings lit the wide space like a tunnel of Goth love. Rants and nits and cogs and all other beings stood shoulder to shoulder quietly holding up the lights. The scene smelt like a campfire where someone had thrown something plastic into the flames. An acrid, burning scent drifted back up the tunnel looking for more oxygen.

At the head of the line stood the map of glass, lit beautifully from the fire. The swirling colors shifting over it were mesmerizing. The map cast shadows and waves of light up against the cavern walls. It also showed quite clearly the current course one could take to walk through the water and get out of Foo.

The three overly protective thorns buzzed around the map, making sure nobody touched it.

"Read, if you want," the black thorn buzzed, warning the crowd. "But if you touch her . . ."

"She's not just yours," the green thorn argued.

"She's more mine than yours," the black one said.

"You're both thick in the heart," a brown thorn said. "Look how she gazes at me."

All three thorns looked at the map.

Next to the map, trying to ignore the thorns, wearing a soft yellow wool sweater and a corduroy cap, hunched the Dearth. He had on felt pants with patches at the knees, and his bare feet were woven into the soil he needed contact with to live. He had a bushy mustache and kind old eyes. In fact, Leven's having chopped him in half in his true form had unwittingly made the disguised Dearth that much more endearing. Now the old man walked hunched over and holding his back, looking like the spokesman for some very mild English tea. The Dearth lifted his right hand, and everyone aside from the thorns grew quiet.

"This is it," the Dearth commended them. "You've done well."

Loud cheers echoed off the walls of the cavern as the excitement rolled like a wave down the line of all those who wished to get out of Foo.

"For years I have whispered from the soil," he said. "And now, in a few moments, all that we have fought for, all that we have dreamed of, will be ours. We will walk through and possess the soil of Reality. Move quickly—the waterways will stay clear for only three days and it is the desire of all to touch the dirt of Reality. And you will—"

"Die!" a voice screamed as a nit broke from the ranks and

shoved a small knife toward the heart of the Dearth. "Long live Foo."

Before the man could reach the Dearth, hundreds of thin black strands shot out from the dirt and wrapped around the man's arms and legs. The nit tried to scream, but the strings of ooze quickly wrapped him up like a spider encasing a fly. The black wad was dropped to the ground in front of the map, where it sank into the soil.

"Some people are so shortsighted," the Dearth tisked. "Anyone else wish to complain?"

Even the thorns were quiet.

"Good," the Dearth clapped. "Now, let's put that out of our minds and begin our final march."

The crowds cheered. The map shifted just a bit, and the thorns praised it. The Dearth observed the change and marked a paper he had in his hand.

"We should be there shortly," the Dearth said, turning and heading into the darkest part of the cavern. "I will mark the trail for those who follow." Those in the cavern were all too happy to do just that.

After a couple of hundred feet the cavern narrowed just a bit, and a large torch hanging on the wall was singing a song about curiosity.

Next to the torch was a gigantic wooden door. The door was over fifteen feet tall and as wide as the cavern. There was a large carving of the land of Foo on the wood and the illustration was current, showing the gloam reaching all the way to Sycophant Run. Beneath the wooden doorknob was a large keyhole. The Dearth reached out and twisted the knob.

It was locked.

There was a small murmuring from behind him, but the Dearth quickly pulled out a key that was hanging from a cord around his neck. The key was gold, with two circular swirls at the end and two large metal teeth. It was a copy of the key that had belonged to the sycophants.

The Dearth fingered the key and slid it into the lock. A crisp clicking sound like that of a gun loading sounded throughout the cavern. The Dearth turned the key, and the lock turned and tumbled in a series of clacks and snaps. The Dearth reached out, and this time the knob twisted easily and the door popped open with a gust of wet wind bellowing in.

The crowd cheered as the Dearth and two cogs pulled the door all the way open. The Dearth then stood with his right hand raised and his eyes on the long line of refugees.

"This is it," he said. "I am not a sentimental being, but this is a step that so few thought would ever be taken."

The cheer was much louder.

"Come," the Dearth waved. He walked through the large door. In the distance, a shimmering square of weak light seemed to mark the way.

The Dearth walked quickly, consulting the map in his hands whenever tunnels branched off. There was not much talking, but the sound of feet scraping the trail and shoes clomping down gave the air an urgent and bustling feel.

"The light," the Dearth said. "It's water."

The trail became an invisible cavern running right through water. The liquid flowed in waves above and beside them. The path glowed where the Dearth moved.

"Don't touch the sides, and follow carefully," the Dearth said.

The Dearth shuffled speedily through the tunnel of water, following the path that the map of glass had pointed out. If he had possessed a heart, it might have jumped right out of his chest. But he had no heart. And if he'd had a brain he might have been too giddy to think straight. But he had no brain. In fact, all he really had under his facade was an unending, wicked desire to see everything but the soil obliterated. He couldn't wait. He was growing sick of pretending that he cared, and he longed with all his non-heart for the day when not a single nit, cog, human, rant, or any other being existed.

He was a simple man, with a simple wish that was about to come true.

CHAPTER FOURTEEN

DRAINED

Sometimes people are so clueless. Yes, sadly, many spend their days oblivious to half the things going on around them. For example, there are those who don't notice when someone gets a new shirt or a new pair of trousers. And there are those who pay no attention to the fact that someone might have gotten braces put on his or her teeth, or switched from glasses to contacts. Some people are clueless that others have gotten a haircut or are now parting their hair on the other side.

What does it take? I wonder.

I mean, how hard is it to simply say, "Nice haircut," or "Your new shoes are smashing"? I met a man once with a large facial tattoo who was still bothered that his mother had never said anything about it. I guess we get so caught up in our own lives that we fail to notice some of the amazing things going on right around us.

Well, in an effort to be less clueless, I suggest we give a young private with freckles and big ears a nice congratulations for noticing that the small body of water he was standing near was now beginning to drain.

"The water's lowering!" the private hollered.

Every eye and camera focused intently on Blue Hole and its water level. The small spring running from it had stopped flowing and was now beginning to recede.

The military had taken over the white stucco scuba shop at the edge of the lake. It was now filled with a select group of important people—generals, majors, presidents, congressmen, Dennis, and Ezra. Circling the scuba shop were hundreds and hundreds of military troops, all organized and waiting for something exciting to happen. Mixed in with the chaos were people from the media, and behind all of that were large sections of civilians in RVs and cars hoping to get a peek at what was going on. There were also massive numbers of protesters protesting the arrival of any being from any other place other than Reality.

"The water's lowering," Elton Thumps said.

"Finally," Ezra yelled. "Move me closer."

Dennis pushed past two large soldiers and right up to the short wall surrounding the small lake. The water vibrated and the uncomfortable sound of something big being shoved through something small could be heard gurgling in the water.

"Brilliant," Ezra laughed.

"So, what exactly is happening?" Elton asked.

"The entrance is opening," Ezra said. "And if Dennis's head was right, in a short while thousands of beings will come flowing through the bottom of there and climbing up and out into your world."

"And we shouldn't shoot them?" General Lank asked.

"Not at first."

"They're allies?" General Lank asked.

"Maybe—of course, it has been a while since I've read Dennis's head," Ezra growled. "But the last time I read, they were allies. So, now if you could shut your gaping mouth and try using your brain for something other than an ear-and-nose spacer, that would be appreciated."

General Lank's eyes bulged and his ears turned the color of cherries. It was one thing to have a civilian telling a high-ranking military leader what to do, but it was a whole other thing when that civilian was a toothpick.

"Watch yourself," Lank said, steaming.

"Slap him, Dennis," Ezra ordered.

Dennis ignored Ezra, shaking his head slightly.

"Fine." Ezra stood up tall on Dennis's right ear. He extended his hands and shot visible waves of electricity directly at the general. The electricity created two tiny black craters on General Lank's face and filled the air with the smell of burning flesh. General Lank jumped back screaming and swearing and holding his cheeks with his hands.

"Does anybody else wanna tell me to watch myself?" Ezra asked. "I have told your president that it is best to let those who are coming just flow through. Then we will have them on our soil, and if their intentions have changed we will be able to easily take them."

"But what about—" a young private started to ask.

Ezra didn't allow the poor kid to even finish the question. He put his small arms forward and the unlucky private began to fold into himself. His head flopped down into his neck and his arms and legs retracted like telescopes. In a couple of seconds he was just an odd-looking torso with fingers at the shoulders and toes at the corners. His frightened eyes peered out of the folds of his neck where his head had been shoved. Ezra counted to three and the young private sprang back into his normal form.

"I will not be talked to by just anyone," Ezra declared. He turned to look at Elton. "Is the preparation complete?"

"Of course," Elton said, signaling to a couple of huge tractors that were still moving fences.

"Good," Ezra sniffed. "Tell me when the water's only a few feet deep."

"Yes," Elton said coolly. He smoothed back his dark hair and tightened the cloth belt on his trench coat. He too did not enjoy taking orders from a toothpick, but he was smart enough to act as if it were no big deal.

"Take me to my new trailer," Ezra ordered Dennis.

Dennis didn't move.

"What, did you not hear me?" Ezra raged. "I'm standing on your deaf ear?"

Dennis just stood there calmly.

Ezra slapped his own forehead with his right hand and sighed—civility didn't come easy. And here Dennis was standing his ground and demanding he be treated right.

"Please," Ezra said, defeated.

Dennis turned away from Elton and walked confidently toward the new RV the U.S. government had brought in for Ezra.

"Some people and their inflated egos," Ezra sniffed.

Dennis just smiled.

ii

There has been much debate and discussion concerning just how long the tunnels under Blue Hole Lake really are. Some people say the tunnels run as far as the Atlantic Ocean, or to the Gulf of Mexico. A popular story is told of a diver who swam into the tunnels and never came back out. Weeks later, however, his body was discovered in Lake Erie. Other divers and explorers have tried to map the tunnels out many times in the past. But the few maps that were made were crude and incomplete. Then, in the early seventies, a couple of divers got lost down in the tunnels and one of them died. After that the government locked up the tunnels and forbade anyone to explore them further.

Of course, that didn't keep people from speculating and wondering just where the tunnels went. I think it's a pretty safe guess, however, that nobody ever thought about the tunnels actually connecting to another realm. Well, that's not completely true, seeing how a kid named Todd once did a school project on how the tunnels were a gateway that connected to one of the worlds of *Star Trek*. But Todd also claimed that cooties were an actual virus, so his theories were largely ignored. No, I believe for all the speculating and imagination that has gone into wondering just where the tunnels led, nobody could have ever guessed the truth.

Foo.

And nobody could have ever predicted that someday those same tunnels would provide a way for thousands of beings to invade our world. Of course, the list of things nobody could have ever predicted is longer than the tunnels themselves.

The Dearth moved easily through the watery passage. The map

of glass had worked perfectly, exposing a complex dry and safe way through the caves. The Dearth dragged his feet along the wet soil beneath him, marking the route with a dark streak for those to follow.

The torches everyone carried lit the water in a surreal and ethereal way. Light swirled off of the water and drifted around like colorful nymphs. If the Dearth hadn't been so evil and his purpose so selfish, the scene would have almost felt reverent. But the Dearth was completely evil and cared for nobody but himself, so the scene felt confusing.

The cavern turned and the water overhead changed from purple to blue.

"There!" a rant yelled. "Up ahead."

A pinpoint of light shone through the tunnel like a third eye. It blinked and then shone even brighter. The Dearth moved quickly toward it, and as he got closer the water overhead tapered off and he could feel air filling the space around him. Ten steps later he was standing at the bottom of Blue Hole looking up eighty feet at the ring of faces and weapons pointed down at him. He turned to those behind him and announced, "I believe we've made it."

A great cheer rose from the ranks and snaked back deep into the watery caverns. In fact, it continued all the way until it burst out of the opening in Sycophant Run.

Come what may, Foo and Reality were finally joined.

CHAPTER FIFTEEN

SOMEWHERE THERE'S A PLACE WHERE WE BELONG

Have you ever gotten rid of something bothersome only to have it pop back up at some other point in your life? Don't answer that—it's probably not wise to talk to strangers. If you know me personally, however, go ahead and shout it out. Have you ever? Have you ever thrown out an ugly, itchy sweater some cruel relative knitted for you, only to have your mom pull it from the trash and present it to you to wear on school picture day? Or have you ever hidden a pile of mushy, rubbery brussels sprouts in your napkin, only to have your mother find them as she was cleaning up, and she made you eat them even though they were now mushy, rubbery, cold, and dirty? Some things are just better left lost or gone. Certain things should never resurface.

Things like Sabine.

Leven gasped and pulled his kilve out. Clover fell from the top of Leven's head and couldn't catch himself until he was down by Leven's left knee. It had been many weeks since Leven had last seen Sabine whole. Now here he was again, looking at Leven from across the decaying room. There were bits and pieces of him missing, but from a distance he looked almost complete.

Sabine coughed, and chunks of him splattered down to the floor.

"That's really, really unbecoming," Clover whispered, now back on Leven's right shoulder.

Sabine's thin weasel eyes glared at Clover.

"I don't understand," Leven said. He moved closer to take a better look. "You're dead."

"I suppose it does me no good to lie now," Sabine said. "I'm as surprised as you are to find myself here. This is the island of Alder?"

"I think so," Leven answered, his kilve still drawn.

"You must be nearing the last of it," Sabine wheezed. "I am just a marker on your path to the end."

"End of what?"

"Or the beginning," Sabine coughed.

"Of what?" Leven asked impatiently.

"I would have walked the path you are now upon," Sabine swore. "I would have been the one to tie the two realms together."

"I'm not sorry I stopped you," Leven said boldly, stepping closer.

"Now this is where I'll spend my days," Sabine moaned. "Unless . . ."

"Unless?" Leven questioned.

"Unless I take your life." Sabine stood up and reached forward.

Leven looked down at himself. His right hand and a chunk of his left shoulder were frozen. "What are you doing?" he asked.

Sabine closed his eyes, and a tiny bit of Leven's left elbow froze. Leven shrugged his shoulders and straightened out his arm. Flakes of ice drifted off, giving him full range of motion.

"Are you doing that?" Leven asked.

Sabine dropped back down in his chair and coughed until it became uncomfortable for all of them.

"Come on," Clover begged. "Could you at least cover your mouth?"

Sabine wiped his mouth with the back of his hand and moaned.

"Were you trying to freeze me?" Leven asked.

"I'm too weak."

"And I can't be killed," Leven said. "A few things have changed since we last met. You are an incomplete mess, and I am the Want."

Sabine reached into his tattered robe and pulled out a short knife. He lunged pathetically at Leven. The knife nicked Leven's right forearm and fell to the ground.

Leven looked down at a small trickle of blood on his arm. "I'm bleeding," he said in disbelief. "I thought . . ."

A strange noise filled the room. Leven looked around, confused until he realized the sound was Sabine's laughter.

"What's so funny?" Leven asked.

"You thought you were invincible," Sabine wheezed. "Any unfinished business can still kill you. It's only fair that you finish or be finished by what you started. Alder will do you in."

Leven looked at the small knife on the ground and kicked it away.

"I can't believe how pathetic you are," Leven said softly.

"Don't pity me," Sabine snapped. "I want no pity."

"Don't worry," Leven said. "I have no pity for you."

"I was once the stronger one," Sabine cried. "The Dearth needed me."

"Not anymore," Leven said.

Sabine looked at Leven and froze his right ear.

"Pathetic," Leven repeated.

"You don't understand," Sabine wheezed. "I've been brought here to finish what we had between us. This castle is my coffin, unless I finish you."

"I don't see that happening," Clover said.

"You're walking a crooked trail to the oldest tree," Sabine spat.

"That makes no sense."

"You can't reason with the tree unless the things you've touched in Foo are resolved," Sabine whined. "He won't even talk to you."

"I'm not looking to reason with any tree."

"You have no choice." Sabine hacked, and dark chunks flew from his mouth and slapped down on the stone floor. "What you desire requires a conversation with the tree, and that conversation cannot happen if you have unresolved business." Sabine's shoulders raised a couple of inches—he growled like a wounded kitten, and the tips of Leven's right thumb and pinkie froze.

Leven looked at his hand. "Are you still trying to freeze me?"

Sabine's torn body slouched against the floor. His head hung back and his open mouth breathed deeply.

"So, if you were strong enough, would you really be able to kill me?" Leven asked.

Sabine's head flopped to one side.

"Just because I'm unfinished business?"

More head flopping.

"So what do we do?" Clover said. "Do you have to kill him?"

"I'm not going to kill him," Leven complained. "Look at him."

Sabine moaned, looking like a pile of worn-out dirty rags.

"Maybe if you just pushed him or something," Clover suggested. "He looks pretty weak."

"Push him?"

"Actually," Clover said, "he looks so weak that if you called him a few names he might keel over. Hey, dirty-towel boy!"

Sabine turned his head and snarled weakly at Clover. The tip of Clover's nose froze. Clover looked cross-eyed at his nose and frowned.

"This isn't a very dramatic final battle," Clover complained.

Leven stepped up to Sabine and gently grabbed his shoulders. He pulled Sabine up and held him in front of him, staring directly into his beady, dark eyes. There was no soul there, no life, and, in the right eye, no pupil. Sabine was nothing but the few leftover pieces that had once possessed Tim, fought with Ezra, and spelled out things on Dennis's head. He was an incomplete being who had been brought to this point to finally perish.

"You wanted this," Leven said. "You listened to the Dearth and chose evil."

Sabine breathed out, sounding like a raspy accordion.

"So much of what has happened is because of you," Leven whispered.

The quiet words were more damaging than names. The truth swiped at Sabine like a saber, cutting the last few bits of his life from his rotting being.

"I'm . . ." Sabine started to say, but his thoughts never made it to fruition. The tiny remaining bits of his body slipped out of his tattered rags and splashed down against the floor.

Leven watched the dark bits puddle together. Then the puddle hissed, dried up, and disappeared.

"Eeew," Clover said, disgusted. "He's not a comfortable person to be around."

Leven let go of the dirty bits of robe in his hands, and they fluttered to the floor like wounded bats.

"Do you think it's because I called him 'dirty-towel boy'?" Clover asked guiltily.

Leven reached up and patted Clover on the head. "I don't think so," he said.

"And we're sure he's gone?" Clover asked, jumping down and messing with the empty rags.

"I think this was his last stop."

"I wonder what it would be like to have lived such a dark life," Clover said casually. "It would drive me crazy."

"Yeah," Leven smiled. "We're lucky you're on the good side. Now, we need to keep moving."

"I think we should get something to eat first," Clover suggested.

"Really?" Leven said. "You could eat after that?"

Clover looked at the mound of robe. "Maybe just something light."

"Eat something out of your void," Leven instructed, kicking the pile of Sabine's clothes with his toe. "I know you have stuff in there."

A strong wind snaked through the stone castle and rattled bits of decaying wood and uneven stones.

"Come on," Leven said. "We've gotta go."

Clover jumped up and grabbed onto Leven's left arm. He then crawled around Leven's back and settled on Leven's right shoulder.

"What other unfinished business do you have?" Clover asked.

"I don't know," Leven answered honestly. "But I hope it's as easy to settle as that."

"I hope it's in a nicer place."

Leven and Clover walked the two floors of the castle searching for anything or anyone else. Finding nothing, they set out through a back breezeway and kept walking toward the center of Alder.

CHAPTER SIXTEEN

PULCHRITUDE APLENTY

The day was coming into its own. The weather was cool, but a warm string of air was hovering waist high, reminding every being in Foo that, as pleasant as it was, it could be even better. The mountains of Morfit in the far distance were reflecting the green sunshine off their highest peaks and sending the light back out as shimmering waves.

Winter reached the edge of the Sentinel Fields and pulled her avaland to a graceful and impressive stop. The beast settled just feet from the fields near a low stone wall and a line of thick purple trees. Through the growth, Winter could see thousands and thousands of beings in the distance still moving across the fields toward Sycophant Run.

Winter looked over and saw Geth racing toward her. Geth was bouncing around on his avaland and trying desperately to bring it to a halt. It finally stopped, but only because it ran directly into Winter's beast. Winter flew off her avaland, landing on her side and scraping her left shoulder. Her kilve tumbled over the dirt with her.

She came to a stop on the stone ledge that ringed the edge of the Sentinel Fields right by the shore. Geth jumped off his avaland and ran to her side. Blood was running down her left shoulder, and she was trying to rip her sleeve to look at it. Her blonde hair was hanging in her face, making it hard for her to see.

"I'm so sorry," Geth said, kneeling down right next to her. "Those avalands are impossible to stop."

"I stopped mine," Winter pointed out, her voice giving away the fact that she was hurt.

"Do you mind?" Geth asked, motioning to Winter's arm.

Winter shook her head, and Geth ripped her sleeve up to the shoulder. He stopped to stare at her arm.

"What?" Winter asked. "It's not that bad, is it?"

"No," Geth said softly, beginning to wipe off her arm. "It's not that at all. It's just that when I tried to help pull you up out of the gunt, back when I was a toothpick, your arm was that of a child. Now you're a . . . well . . ."

Winter blushed. "*You* at a loss for words?" she finally asked.

"I forget how much we've been through," Geth smiled.

Geth took a leather bladder of water and poured some onto the swatch of Winter's shirt he had ripped off. He cleaned up her scratch, dried it, and then covered it with the remaining material.

"Thanks," Winter said self-consciously. She pulled herself up and looked out over the Sentinel Fields at the marching armies of refugees and escapees. The large trees above them brought their branches down just a few feet to make the scene even cozier. "Look at all those people—it's like a river."

"Impressive," Geth whispered, sitting next to Winter.

"You're impressed?" Winter asked. "What, you want to help them?"

"I want to stop them," Geth answered. "But there's no harm in marveling over what we have to conquer—it keeps me humble."

Winter pulled her blonde hair back with her right hand and looked directly at Geth with her deep green eyes. "Do they train you lithens how to speak?"

"Nope," Geth said. "It comes naturally."

Winter smiled. "You look taller. Are you, or is it just your state of fluctuation?"

"I think you're just finally beginning to look up to me," Geth grinned.

Winter couldn't stop herself from blushing again, and the branches on the trees closed in even more.

"You know, Winter," Geth said calmly, "you really do . . ." Geth's words went unfinished due to the arrival of a new voice.

"How pretty," the melodious voice said. "I've been searching all over Foo for you, Geth, and here you are on a stone wall beneath the purple boughs of a fantrum tree with one very lovely nit."

Both blushing, Geth and Winter turned to look at Phoebe smiling at them. She had come out of nowhere and appeared to be at least seven times prettier than when they had last seen her. Her wide blue eyes and soft features were hypnotizing, and the short green wrap she wore made her look like a very womanly fairy. She was hovering two inches above the ground, her thin wings humming so quickly that you couldn't tell she even had them.

"Phoebe," Geth said happily.

"I hope I'm not interrupting anything," Phoebe said playfully.

"No," Winter replied, the red in her cheeks barely subsiding. "We just got here ourselves."

Geth stood up slowly, as if any quick movement might scare Phoebe away. "Where have you been?"

"All over," she smiled. "It seems that Foo was in dire need of some passion. But now I'm here and alone."

Winter cleared her throat.

"Yes, *you're* here," Phoebe amended. "But there are no longings left. What a sad thing for Foo."

"I'm so sorry," Geth said compassionately.

"Is there someone to blame?" Phoebe asked honestly.

"There are plenty to blame," Geth answered. "But it's way too late to punish any of them. Can't you see Foo is falling?"

"The balance is off," she agreed. "There are only four siids. And you're the last of the lithens."

Winter stood up to remind the two of them that she was still there.

"So, do you mind if I travel with you?" Phoebe asked.

"No."

"Yes."

Geth and Winter answered simultaneously.

"I mean, yes, we'd like that," Winter corrected. "But don't you have other people you need to push into love?"

Phoebe smiled—it was a nice smile, with no hint of guile. "I'm not Cupid. My effect will mellow now that I'm free. I've moved over Foo and done my part to bring a balance back to desire. But I don't follow up with arrows or lessons in love."

"Oh," Winter said, clearly disappointed.

"I don't mean to make things harder," Phoebe said.

"Well, you've definitely made things more interesting," Geth smiled.

Phoebe blinked slowly, and Winter cleared her throat again.

"So what are you doing?" Phoebe asked.

"We're going to move into that horde of beings," Geth pointed. "Then we'll march down the gloam and onto Sycophant Run. We'll slip though the exit and work our way to a place called Oklahoma."

"How exciting," Phoebe smiled.

"Many of the beings who are moving through now won't live long in Reality," Geth reminded them. "Echoes will eventually fade; rants will harden. We have less than three days. Of course . . ."

"Of course?" Winter asked.

"Well, eventually even the nits will die. If the exit has been opened, that means all dreams have ended. With the Dearth slipping out, not a single new dream will survive. Nits will forget their purpose and possibilities, and many will simply fall to the earth, never to get up again."

"So it really is too late?" Winter asked.

"Not if Leven can pull off what he's supposed to do."

"We don't even know where he is," Winter said, frustrated.

"Fate will make things clear," Geth said softly.

Winter put her head in her hands. "You're so confusing."

Phoebe patted Winter on the back.

"I might not know everything," Geth said honestly, "but I believe in Leven. Besides, there's a bit of me missing, and I know that piece is in Reality. I wouldn't mind being my whole self again."

"Don't say that," Phoebe cooed. "You're perfect."

Winter rolled her eyes. "Yeah, perfect."

"We've never really been introduced," Phoebe said to Winter.

"I'm sorry," Geth said animatedly. "This is Winter. She's a nit who came to Foo, then slipped through the gateway to bring Leven back."

"Important *and* pretty," Phoebe said.

"Thanks," Winter said suspiciously. "So, we should get going."

"First of all, Phoebe will need to cover up her wings," Geth said.

Phoebe smiled, and her thin wings folded into her bare back and disappeared. Geth stared at her.

"You're still going to be noticed," he said. "We need robes to cover you two up. Wait here and I'll be right back."

"Where are—" Winter couldn't get her question out fast enough. Geth had already jumped over the short stone wall and was running sideways through the trees and into the bushes.

Winter sat there on the wall and cleared her throat. The tree limbs above her lifted two feet. Phoebe just stared at her. Winter drummed her long fingers on the stone wall.

"Do I make you nervous?" Phoebe asked innocently.

"No," Winter replied, her cheeks red. "Why would you say that?"

"That's odd," Phoebe said. "I didn't take you for someone who doesn't tell the truth."

"What?" Winter asked defensively.

"I can tell that I make you nervous," Phoebe said, confused. "But you said I didn't." Phoebe's voice was so soothing and unaggressive that Winter couldn't help but calm down.

"All right," Winter admitted. "Maybe you make me just a little nervous."

"I wonder why?" Phoebe asked, without sounding like she actually wanted an answer.

Winter bit the corner of her lip and tugged on the bandage Geth had put on her arm. "Really? Have you looked at yourself?"

"Many times," Phoebe answered. "I'm quite pretty."

"There's an understatement," Winter grumped.

"But you're beautiful as well," Phoebe said.

"It's different," Winter waved.

"So, do you love Geth?" Phoebe asked, sitting down next to Winter.

"Geth?" Winter laughed. "Why would you say that? He's like my grandfather, or my father, or my brother."

"But, being a lithen, he looks and acts as young as you," Phoebe pointed out.

"I said, 'or my brother,'" Winter pointed out. "Besides, can't you tell when people are in love?"

Phoebe shook her head. "No more than you can. Of course, I'm aware of the effect that we longings have on others. So I usually assume that everyone I meet is either in love or wishing they were."

"You must be popular at funerals."

Phoebe just blinked.

"What about you?" Winter asked. "Do you love Geth?"

Phoebe nodded innocently.

"You do?" Winter questioned. "Really? You mean, like you love your brother?"

"The one brother I did have, I couldn't stand," Phoebe said. "I love Geth in a far different way."

Winter just stared at her.

"Are you okay?" Phoebe asked.

"Are you always so honest?"

"I hope so," Phoebe answered.

"So you love Geth?"

"Why do you think I came back?"

"I don't know," Winter answered, amazed. "Didn't you just meet him a few days ago?"

Phoebe nodded.

"And you've said maybe ten words to him since then?" Winter questioned.

"We haven't spoken much," Phoebe admitted.

"But you love him?"

"Should I not?"

Winter laughed. "What if he has some weird habits?"

"Does he?" Phoebe asked innocently.

"He's incredibly positive."

"I hope that doesn't change."

"He has a tiny bit of him missing."

"We all seem to have something we're deficient in," Phoebe said. "My right wing is torn at the bottom."

Winter rubbed her forehead.

"So," Phoebe asked, "if you don't love Geth, then who do you love?"

"Do I have to love someone?" Winter argued.

"No," Phoebe said, "but I can see a name on your lips."

"Really?" Winter asked incredulously, putting her hand over her mouth. "A name on my lips?"

"It looks like the *L* sound," Phoebe smiled. "Oh, of course, Leven."

Winter's mouth dropped open.

"I can see I was right," Phoebe said, staring at Winter's open mouth.

Winter closed her mouth.

"I've met him," Phoebe said needlessly. "In fact, I believe he rescued me. And you love him? That's wonderful."

"I'm not . . . I can't . . . really, you . . ."

"You don't have to find the words to say to me," Phoebe said nicely. "Silence is an acceptable answer."

"No, it's not," Winter stormed. "You're assuming a lot of things."

"You don't love him?"

Winter closed her green eyes and breathed in deeply. Behind her eyelids she could see some of the things that she and Leven had been through. She could see the boy who had mistakenly touched her and caused the shadows to find them, and she could see the man who had last pulled her up on the avaland only hours before.

"This time I can't tell from the silence," Phoebe said honestly. "Do you love him or not?"

"This isn't the place," Winter insisted.

"Where would you rather admit it?"

"I just . . ."

"You love him?"

"I guess I do," Winter said, defeated.

"The word *guess* makes your answer confusing." Phoebe bit her lip.

"Well, I know I miss him," Winter said softly. "Is that good enough?"

Phoebe smiled. "Sometimes missing is stronger than love. So have you—"

Phoebe's question was cut short. Geth burst through the bushes holding two robes and smiling as if he had just cured the world of all rashes.

Winter had never been so glad to see him. She jumped up and grabbed one of the robes. It was big, but not as huge as the one she had been forced to wear the day before. It was also red, and Winter was happy to be wearing a bit of color.

"Sorry to take so long," Geth said as Phoebe slipped on her robe.

"No problem. It gave us a chance to talk," Phoebe replied.

"What'd you talk about?" Geth questioned casually.

Winter looked at Phoebe and shook her head lightly.

"Nothing," Phoebe answered smoothly.

"How informative," Geth said. "Well, we might want to get going. The two rants I borrowed those robes from should gain consciousness soon."

"Nice," Winter smiled.

Winter then headed in the direction of the soldiers, followed by Phoebe and Geth but thinking about Leven.

CHAPTER SEVENTEEN

SIZING UP THE COMPETITION

Anticipation is a fascinating thing. There's nothing like the anticipation you experience the morning before Christmas or your birthday. Of course, there can be great disappointment following that anticipation, like when on that same birthday you get a flamethrower that doesn't even work right.

Sad.

People anticipate all sorts of things—elections, movies, romance, sports—but never, in the history of mankind, has there been the kind of anticipation the entire world felt as Blue Hole Lake drained and word spread that something was now climbing up out of it.

It was a very pregnant pause. You might not remember it, but even you put down what you were doing and stared in anticipation at the TV, wondering what was coming next.

I chewed off most of my fingernails.

The scene in New Mexico was awe inspiring. It looked as if the whole of humanity was spread out across the desert staring at a tiny empty lake. For a place filled with so many thousands of people, it was relatively calm. There were a few helicopters in the sky, but there were no birds singing or cars rolling down the interstate. The whole world had come to a halt, anxiously anticipating what was coming.

Everyone held their breath as the soft sound of scraping and shuffling rose from the bottom of the lake bed. At the cement steps on the lake's edge, General Lank stood with ten of his best men. Leading out from the lake was a wide path lined with soldiers and tanks all pointed in the direction of the hole.

General Lank held his right hand up, signaling that something was coming.

A small head covered in a dark brown felt hat rose up.

"Hello," the Dearth yelled cheerfully, using his British accent. "You there, soldier, how about a hand down here?"

A dozen soldiers began sliding down into the empty lake. Climbing the sides of the lake wasn't too difficult, due to a natural slope. The Dearth was helped by two strong soldiers who kept calling him sir and asking if he was comfortable.

Don't get me wrong, I'm all for people being comfortable. And if they happen to be elderly, then all the better. But I don't think that in the history of mankind there was a time when we were more gentle or accommodating while ushering evil into our midst. Never had we so willingly put forth our hand and pulled vile into our lives.

"Thank you, young man," the Dearth said as he was helped up.

"No problem, sir." The soldiers boosted him onto the lake's edge near the waiting general.

The Dearth stood as tall as he could, took off his felt cap, and smiled for the cameras. General Lank looked at the Dearth's feet where they were connected to the dirt. He then extended his right hand, and the Dearth shook it.

"Are you in charge?" Lank asked.

"I believe so," the Dearth said softly.

The Dearth stepped away from the edge as hundreds of beings began to spill up over the lip of the empty lake behind him. Rants by the dozens crawled up and over each other, anxious to get a look at Reality.

Groups of U.S. soldiers moved in and began as politely as possible to usher the visitors into the large, fenced-in areas that had previously been set up. The river of rants and nits and cogs moved down the wide, guarded road and into their designated areas. There were tables all over the place filled with bottles of water and some sort of military fruit bars for the visitors to eat.

A tall rant stopped and looked up at the single sun. He pulled back the hood of his robe, and his body began to solidify into one complete being. Other rants followed suit, looking at their now-whole bodies while cheering and crying triumphantly.

General Lank took the Dearth by the elbow. The Dearth shuffled slowly, his bare feet attached to the earth. Soldiers lined the dirt road, holding their weapons and standing at attention. The Dearth, escorted by three huge soldiers, was taken into the old scuba shop, where Ezra and Dennis were waiting. The scuba shop was so old that part of the floor had rotted away, allowing the Dearth to stay connected to the soil.

Dennis was wearing the purple robe that Antsel had once worn. He was rubbing his head, amazed at how clear his thoughts suddenly were. Ezra was perched on Dennis's right ear, staring at the Dearth with his single eye.

"He looks weak," Ezra complained. "And that mustache? Come on."

Next to Dennis and Ezra was Elton Thumps, who was busily looking at something on a clipboard while talking on his cell phone. He snapped his phone shut.

The Dearth stopped in front of Dennis and bowed slightly. Dennis was trying hard not to throw up. It hadn't been too many weeks ago that he was an ignored and underachieving janitor. Now the whole world was watching him and expecting him to say something important. He cleared his throat and shifted on his feet.

"Hello," Dennis finally said.

Ezra slapped his toothpick forehead.

"Hello," the Dearth answered, his British accent in full form. "I am the Dearth."

"The Dearth," Elton asked. "Is that your first or last name?"

"My only name," the Dearth said with charm. "And your names?"

"I am Dennis, and this is General—"

"I'm Ezra," Ezra said as if that was the only introduction that needed to be made.

"Pleasure to meet you all," the Dearth said. "I'm not one for crowds. But here today, so many people—certainly this large welcome isn't for us."

General Lank spoke. "The entire world is interested in you."

The Dearth smiled, and everyone in the room seemed to relax.

"Come on!" Ezra screamed. "You're really the Dearth? I don't believe it. You're a walking pile of dust. Shouldn't you be home napping or planning an early high-fiber dinner?"

"Ah, youth," the Dearth said, still smiling.

Ezra's eye widened to the size of a pea. "Listen, you senile old bump, I find it hard to believe that you can command *anything*, much less the thousands of beings now flowing in from Foo."

"I don't command them," the Dearth said sappily. "They're here of their own free will."

"Still, Ezra raises a good question. What are your intentions in coming here?" the general asked. "What exactly do you want?"

"We seek a new place to live," the Dearth said defensively. "We seek to coddle our curiosity and know more about Reality. And, in return, you will be given access to Foo. Not everyone is coming to Reality. There are those who are happy in Foo. But there are many thousands who have family here and wish only to return to them . . . or to know more about you."

"What about Leven Thumps?" Elton spoke up.

The Dearth's right eye twitched just a bit, and Ezra took notice.

"Leven Thumps?" the Dearth asked. "What is your connection with him?"

"We have questions for him," Elton said. "And I especially am interested in his well-being."

"Yeah, yeah," Ezra complained. "This gutless twig is Leven's father. It's a real touching story. If you're ever in the mood to puke and cry, just let him tell it. What we need—"

"You're Leven's father?" the Dearth interrupted.

Elton nodded. "He was raised by others."

The general's radio crackled and buzzed. He spoke into it, then turned to the Dearth. "Just how many of you are there?"

"Quite a few," the Dearth said, taking out a handkerchief and wiping his forehead. "I hope we're not causing you trouble."

"Oh, no," the general grumbled. "We do this for everyone."

"A bit of sarcasm," the Dearth said. "I suppose it's merited."

"Listen," General Lank said. "This is the United States of America, and we take security very seriously. Now we have thousands and thousands of unidentified beings marching out of a hole in the earth, and the only guarantee we have that you aren't our enemy is the word of a toothpick."

Ezra was sitting on top of Dennis's head, yawning.

"That fellow there?" the Dearth asked. "What a surprise."

Ezra stretched and stood up.

"The surprise is that you're *their* leader?" Ezra asked casually, hopping down onto Dennis's left shoulder.

"I suppose it is," the Dearth smiled. "But I'm really just a volunteer helping my fellowman."

Ezra looked disgusted. "You're an impulse guided by darkness."

"Now, now. They needed someone to walk them out, and I had the key." The Dearth pulled a gold key out of his sweater pocket. The key was tied to a leather strap. He handed it to the general as a gesture of trust.

"There's a door down there?" the general asked.

"A large one," the Dearth smiled.

The general looked at Elton and then at Ezra. He gritted his teeth.

"Listen," Ezra said, his tiny body buzzing. "I'm not sure who this old man is, but the things I've read on Dennis's dumb head don't match up with him."

"What do you mean?" General Lank growled.

"This doddering old coot can't possibly be the Dearth I read about on Dennis's head."

Three soldiers raised their guns and pointed them at the Dearth.

"Now, now," the Dearth said again, holding his hands up nervously. "I'm not sure what this splinter's been telling you, but we're not here to hurt you. There are those from Foo who are here to become whole, and others who wish to reunite with loved ones, but there are not any here who wish to do you harm. Let our people come, and you'll be free to walk in and experience Foo."

"I think I'll hold onto this key," General Lank said, "just in case."

"Suit yourself," the Dearth said pleasantly.

"It's a copy anyway," Ezra grunted.

"How do you know that?" the Dearth said, looking genuinely surprised for the first time.

"See this noggin?" Ezra asked, pointing to Dennis's large bald head.

The Dearth nodded.

"Up until a few hours ago, it used to tell me things," Ezra informed him. "All kinds of things. Now it's just a large skin ball."

"Thanks," Dennis said.

"You're welcome," Ezra replied. "I've gotten soft. But I'm not mental, and I know that there's something up with you, Dearth. What's the deal with your feet?"

"Beg pardon?" the Dearth said, not sounding quite as cute as he had just a few moments ago.

"Your feet," Ezra pointed. "Am I the only one here who can see that he's like a potted plant, rooted to the ground?"

"People are different," Elton said.

"I'll say," Ezra growled. "Just look at your hair. But I'm not talking about choices in wardrobe or dry skin, I'm talking about the fact that this elderly chump's feet are intertwined and growing into the ground."

The Dearth blinked his eyes and then spoke slowly. "I am connected to the soil. I'm sorry if that is unsettling to you, but my type need to stay connected to the dirt. You'll soon see things stranger than I."

"What would happen if we were to lift you off of the dirt?" Ezra asked.

It wasn't very obvious, but a person looking closely enough could have seen a slight flush of red rising from the Dearth's collar and crawling up his neck.

"I thought we were walking into a civilized nation," the Dearth said coolly.

"Civilized but suspicious," General Lank said.

"I'm attached to the dirt." The Dearth shrugged. "I can step off of the dirt, but it is more comfortable and wise for me to stand upon soil. Is this a problem?"

"I suppose not," the general conceded.

The noise outside the scuba shop grew louder and louder as more and more beings spilled up out of Blue Hole Lake and into Reality. The large strips of land where those who were coming were being corralled into were filling up fast. And there were some screams and some additional photos taken as a large bunch of black skeletons leapt from the hole and marched proudly in a line toward the fenced areas. The rhythm of their feet shook the ground and their bones clicked and clacked.

"Keep the troops on high alert," General Lank said. "No one is to use force of any kind unless they hear my voice say so." He turned to the Dearth. "We have others we'd like you to meet."

"It would be my pleasure."

General Lank escorted the Dearth to the other side of the scuba shop, with Elton tagging along. Ezra jumped up onto Dennis's left ear.

"Something's wrong," Ezra said.

"I don't understand," Dennis replied.

"That should be your motto," Ezra snapped. "I just don't see how that fossil could lead anyone anywhere. Once all those who are flowing into Reality arrive, he's going to be easier to slap around than you."

Dennis cleared his throat.

"Right, you saved my life," Ezra conceded. "I'm just saying that taking care of him and ruling the world might be even easier than I had anticipated."

Dennis flipped up the hood on his robe, hiding his bald head and the small toothpick on his ear. He stepped out of the tent and watched in wonder as wave after wave of fantastic-looking beings marched into Reality and past him.

"Nervous?" Ezra said from beneath the hood.

Dennis nodded his head.

"I can tell by the sweat," Ezra commented. "You know, you might want to invest in some sort of head deodorant."

"Thanks," Dennis laughed, still watching the river of beings flowing in.

"You're lucky I've got your back."

Dennis felt the rumble of those marching roll up through his feet and shake his entire body. He felt anxious, he felt worried, he felt scared, he felt inadequate, he felt alone, and he felt like he was going to hyperventilate.

Dennis felt a lot of things, but not one of them was lucky.

CHAPTER EIGHTEEN

NEVER IN HIS WILDEST DREAMS

The island of Alder grew greener and greener and steeper and steeper with each step. The trees were so thick it was hard to pick out one trunk from another. Birds with long feathery wings jumped from treetop to treetop, spreading their wings like umbrellas and drifting down to lower branches. The ground was covered with dark, rich soil and rocky outcrops forming intricate patterns. The path of glass was still visible, but it was almost completely overgrown in spots.

"Okay," Clover said, "so what about in fourth grade?"

"I don't want to do this," Leven protested weakly.

"You should be prepared," Clover pointed out. "Fourth grade?"

"I can't remember fourth grade," Leven insisted. "And I don't think the unfinished business that Sabine was talking about has to do with what happened in fourth grade."

"Okay," Clover said. "What about fifth grade?"

"Honestly?" Leven asked.

"All right," Clover conceded. "What about here?"

"I don't know," Leven said. "To be honest, I thought Sabine *was* finished."

"What about that rant he hung out with?"

"Jamoon?" Leven asked.

"Sounds like a made-up name," Clover said. "But yeah, him."

"He fell hundreds of feet and was buried by a mountain of stone."

"People can be resilient when stressed."

"He wasn't stressed," Leven pointed out. "He was dead."

"Okay," Clover said. "Then what about your grandfather?"

"We finished that."

Clover was silent as Leven hiked between two mammoth boulders and through a meadow filled with braided orange grass. Leven turned around. "I really think someone's following us," he whispered.

"It makes me nervous," Clover admitted.

"That somebody's following us?"

"No," Clover said. "It makes me nervous not knowing what's coming."

"Well, then, pretend you're Geth," Leven smiled.

Clover cleared his throat. "Oh, I can't wait to be killed by whatever comes my way," he said in his best Geth imitation. "I hope it happens soon."

Leven laughed and walked quicker. Once past the meadow he stepped carefully across a stream filled with thick red water and through a large, tree-covered patch of ivy. The incline of the path was getting steeper, and all around were moss-infested piles of stone and dilapidated walls and structures. It was obvious that at one point long ago this section of Alder had been fairly well populated.

"Hello, Leven," a voice sang out.

Leven stopped and looked around quickly. He could see nothing but trees and ruins.

"Did you hear something?" Leven whispered.

"Maybe," Clover whispered back. "Did it sound like a rooster coughing?"

"What?"

"Never mind," Clover said, disappearing.

Leven took another step, moving around a leaning pillar of stone.

"Hello, Leven," the voice repeated.

Leven looked to the trees. Something was moving beneath the shadows of a wooden structure. Leven's heart began to thump like a foreboding drum.

"Who's there?" he called out.

The sound of ivy being stepped on rubbed against Leven's ear. He slowly and quietly pulled his kilve out from behind his back.

"See anyone?" Leven whispered to Clover.

"Not a thing."

Someone was moving behind the trees; then, as if she had been pushed out, a woman sprang from the woods. The woman stumbled a bit and then gained her balance. She stood up straight about ten feet from Leven. It wasn't the most graceful entrance ever, but the visitor was beautiful. She wore a white dress with a blue robe over it. Her long, brown hair was pulled back behind her head with a white, twisty ribbon. She smiled with her eyes, and Leven was struck by how familiar she appeared. The wisdom behind her dark eyes made her look a bit older than Leven.

"Hello, Leven," she said again, taking one step closer to him.

"Hello," Leven said cautiously, slipping his kilve back behind him. "I'm sorry, but do I know you?"

"Sort of," she laughed.

Leven's heart began to beat even faster. "We've met?"

"The circumstances were not pleasant," she laughed. "And I was a bit different in appearance, but I'm your grandmother."

Clover materialized on top of Leven's head and gasped loudly enough for all of them.

"My grandmother?" Leven said, staring.

She nodded.

"Amelia?" he said bewildered. "That's . . . you were . . . I don't . . . how?"

"Gunt's an amazing substance," Amelia smiled. "If I remember correctly, it was gunt that Winter used to revert back to a baby. You didn't leave me to die, Leven, you left me to grow younger."

"But you're so much younger," Leven said, walking slowly around her looking for strings or mirrors or some sort of explanation for what he now saw. He stopped in front of her, pushed back his long, dark hair, and smiled. "Amazing."

"You've changed as well," she said. "You're not exactly the child I pulled through the gateway."

Leven stepped closer. "I don't understand. How come you're here?"

"This is Alder?" she said, looking around.

Leven nodded and Clover disappeared.

"And you're moving through the ruins and toward the center?" she asked.

"To be honest, I'm not sure where I'm going," Leven said, sounding a bit more like an actual grandkid. "Clover and I slipped through some thick shadow and started walking. I've already run into what was left of Sabine."

"What a useless soul," Amelia cursed. "Well, I suppose I'm more unfinished business. Fate snatched me from the gunt and placed me here."

"Unfinished business?" Leven asked. "You?"

Clover showed himself again, this time clinging to the front of Leven's robe. "He doesn't have to kill you, does he?"

Amelia smiled. "No, I've come simply to see you and wish you well."

"Really?" Leven said with relief in his voice. His body relaxed and he rubbed the back of his neck. "So the unfinished business can be good?"

"Of course," she answered. "In the past, most unfinished business was good. Foo was a remarkable place."

"I wish I'd known it then," Leven said.

"Hopefully you'll see it that way yet again," she said. "But for the moment let's just be happy to be here."

Amelia opened her arms and Leven ran forward. She grabbed him and hugged him as if he were indestructible. Leven leaned his head onto her shoulder and picked her up two inches off the ground. He set her down and stepped back two feet.

"I can't believe it," he said happily.

"You must have been through a lot," she praised him, patting his left arm. "You're so tall. And you look like your grandfather."

Leven looked down. "I met him," he said solemnly. "He was the Want."

"That wasn't your grandfather," Amelia said. "That was a selfish old man who had been ill for so long his soul was nothing but a sick sludge."

"But he's dead," Leven said.

"He died long ago," she said softly. "I'm so sorry for what you've been through."

"I'm not," Leven said honestly. "Sometimes I think about none of this having ever happened and I get so anxious I can't breathe. It's been hard, but it's been what it should be."

"So you're the Want?" she said with respect in her voice.

"I am," Leven tried to say confidently.

Amelia let go of Leven's hand. "I have great blank spots in my memory, but I can remember there were good times long ago. I can feel the soft afternoons and long days of Foo when the darkness was but a whisper in the halls of Morfit."

"I'm so glad you're alive," Leven sighed.

Amelia just smiled.

"You'll travel with Clover and me?"

Amelia looked up and put her right ear to the wind. "I'm afraid not. I'm going a different direction."

"What?" Leven asked, shocked.

"I love you, Leven," Amelia said. "Remember that. It's important you know."

"Why can't you stay?"

"I am so proud of you."

"But you can't just leave!" Clover wailed.

Amelia looked up and laughed at Clover. "It's obvious Leven's in good hands. If fate is kind, we will see each other again."

Amelia smiled one last time and then slipped into the trees and back behind some ruins. Clover waved good-bye and then blew his nose. Leven reached up and patted the sad sycophant. "It's okay," Leven said, trying to comfort him.

"I really do like this pretty version of her better," Clover said honestly.

Leven smiled, happy to have real family once again wandering Foo.

CHAPTER NINETEEN

The Disadvantages of Following the Crowd

Sadly, Sycophant Run was no longer the tranquil, beautiful haven it had always been. Gone were the sounds of laughter and soft winds. Buried in the stench of war were the smells of food and fresh tavel growing in the fields. Even beauty had fled. The huge flowers that had covered the land had closed their faces and were now deep in hiding. The legions of sycophants who had once guarded the shores were now either wounded or had retreated into the hills, hiding for their lives. A few still fought, but being visible they lost all advantage and were too easily picked off.

A large rope bridge with wide wooden slats had been constructed over the gorge on Sycophant Run. The structure was remarkably strong despite how haphazardly and quickly it had been thrown together. At the moment, crowds of beings were hiking across the bridge, heading for the exit.

Tim and Azure clomped across the bridge with Janet in tow. Swig was under Tim's robe, hiding from danger and avoiding the sight of his damaged and destroyed homeland.

The air was filled with excitement and anticipation as people continued to hike through the tunnels and push out into Reality. Azure's face was hidden beneath a green robe; thanks to the amazement of the moment, nobody gave him a second glance.

Tim stepped off the bridge and headed toward the marsh. "Are we close?"

"I have no idea," Swig answered from beneath the robe. "I've never even been to this part of Sycophant Run."

"We must be getting there," Janet answered. "I can see people up ahead moving underground."

"Can we sit for a second?" Azure asked. "I'm still pretty weak."

Tim would have loved to just leave Azure and Janet and run until he was back in Reality with his family, but Tim was not that kind of person. He had come here in the first place because he cared about Winter, and he would stay with Azure because he believed it was the right thing to do.

"All right," Tim said. "We'll rest for a moment. But we've got to hurry."

Tim led Azure to an overturned wooden cart that someone had abandoned. They sat down on the bottom side of the cart and watched the crowd of beings push past them.

"I don't believe it," Azure said, emotion tainting his voice.

"You don't believe what?" Tim asked.

"I'm a lithen," he said sheepishly. "I grew up believing there was no way out of Foo. Now I see that the very things we taught others were false. I'm not a sentimental being, but the moment I step into Reality, I believe my heart might burst."

"It's a remarkable place," Tim said. "I suppose it might seem a bit pale in comparison to here, but the heart of Reality is no smaller than that of Foo."

"What do you do there?" Azure asked Tim.

"I gather people's trash," Tim answered proudly.

"I don't understand," Azure said.

"I take control of what others throw out."

"Do you like that?" Azure asked.

"It gives me a lot of time to think."

"And that's a desirable commodity in Reality?" Azure asked.

"I believe time to think is a desirable commodity in any realm," Tim said, smiling.

Azure smiled wide and his blue eyes lightened.

"When I get out I can't wait to give myself what-for," Janet butted in. "I only hope that I will listen to myself."

"How can a whisp exist in Reality?" Swig asked from beneath Tim's robe. "I don't understand."

"Can't you tell him to keep to himself?" Janet asked.

"It is a travesty to all that is sane when the voice of a sycophant is the only voice of reason," Swig argued.

"Perhaps you should leave us," Azure said. "Certainly, as the voice of reason, you can see the wisdom in you staying here."

"No," Tim insisted. "Swig comes with me."

"I'm afraid Azure's right," Swig contradicted. "This is my leaping-off point."

"What?" Tim asked. "I need you. I want my sons to see you."

"I'm sorry," Swig said. "But it's not the role of a sycophant to abandon Foo. If you wish to leave, then my duty is over."

Tim looked wounded from the neck up.

"There's no need for me to help you adjust to what you are already comfortable with," Swig pointed out. "You're messing with the balance of everything."

"Please, Swig," Tim said.

"It wouldn't be right."

"Well, then, we'll come back and visit when everything settles."

Swig crawled out from Tim's robe and stared at him. "It is interesting to me what you nits can tell yourselves to make yourselves feel better. Does it make things easier?"

"I don't like you," Janet said.

"I'm not sure it's important that you do," Swig pointed out honestly.

"We should go," Tim said, changing the subject abruptly. He stood and helped Azure up. "Are you doing okay?"

Azure nodded. "I feel stronger. I should be well when we reach Reality."

The four of them were sucked right back into the thick string of refugees who were tromping across the marsh. Mud seeped up around Tim's feet and dragged at the hems of his and Azure's robes.

Janet commented on how fortunate she was that mud couldn't cling to her, but she was ignored by everyone.

They followed the masses, walking on a wide, spiral dirt path into the tunnel. Quickly the outside world disappeared and there was nothing but darkness and torchlight. The cavern walls were lined with lit torches that cheered and giggled as everyone walked past them.

The tunnel was around fifteen feet wide and seven feet tall. The walls were all dark stone, and the floor was covered with black, dry dirt. The sounds of footsteps and excited voices bounced off the rock walls and filled everyone's heads with constant noise.

The cavern wound down farther. A number of beings became too impatient to walk at the speed they were going and quickly ran past Tim and his group in a race to get out.

"Swig, are you here?" Tim asked.

There was no answer.

"Are you gone?"

Again nothing.

"Don't worry about him," Janet said. "You'll see your kids."

Tim looked back down the cavern.

"He's just a sycophant," Azure said hotly.

"We've all given up something we will miss," Janet reminded him. "Azure used to lead all of these people, and I had . . ."

"Osck," Tim said, pointing.

"Yes," Janet admitted sadly. "I just—"

"No," Tim said with excitement. "There's Osck."

Janet looked to where Tim was pointing. Down the tunnel, standing near a wall of colored glass, was Osck. He was standing still, watching everyone who walked by.

"Osck!" Tim yelled.

Osck turned and spotted Tim. He then saw Janet right behind him and smiled. Janet glided through everyone and right up next to him. She tried to touch Osck, but her hands and body kept slipping though him.

"You're here," she said.

"Of course," Osck replied. "I felt certain you would eventually come this way."

"And you waited," Janet said happily.

"I figured there was little harm in waiting a short while longer to enter Reality," Osck said without emotion. "I have waited my whole life; why not wait a bit longer and enter with you, whom I love?"

There almost wasn't room enough in the tunnel for Janet's smile.

"Love," Janet finally said.

"We're not much," Osck said. "You are but a whisp and I a simple echo, but we are meant to stand together."

Tim greeted Osck and quietly introduced him to Azure. Osck was too busy staring at Janet to really acknowledge him.

"We should keep going," Tim finally prompted.

All four of them walked into the darkness toward the large wooden door. Tim was the first to step through. Janet and Osck were laughing as they moved into the wet part of the tunnel that the map of glass had mapped out. The watery walls were dark and rippling and the floor was marked clearly with a luminous smudge that the Dearth had left.

"That's water above us?" Janet asked.

"It is," Tim said.

"How does it not crash in around us?" Osck asked nervously. It wasn't the greatest feeling for a fiery echo to be surrounded by water.

"The map of glass," Azure answered. "The course is made clear on the map. But it is not a set course; it will shift in three days. That's why it is so important to move quickly."

Osck picked up his pace, pushing into a group of rants in front of them. The tunnel of water turned and then slanted up five feet. It grew wider and then twisted around almost into the reverse direction. Osck stuck to the middle of the tunnel with Janet by his side.

At one point the tunnel twisted in such a way that it almost felt like they were walking upside down.

Just as Tim was beginning to doubt his ability to distinguish up from down and over from under, he saw a round circle of light ahead. Soon the light grew bigger and the deafening sound of cheering could be heard. Everyone in the tunnel surged forward, trying to contain their excitement.

Osck reached the exit first. He looked up from the bottom of Blue Hole Lake and marveled at the light. He began to scale the walls of the tiny, empty lake. Janet was scrambling right next to him.

Osck looked at her. "Is this real?"

Janet was too happy to speak.

Tim helped Azure climb the walls of Blue Hole Lake. Azure's robe kept getting caught underfoot, making it hard for him to move.

"Throw it off," Tim said, peeling off his own robe.

"But . . ." Azure tried to say.

"But nothing," Tim smiled. "Robes aren't really a Reality thing."

Azure and Tim dropped their robes behind them and climbed the walls quicker. Five minutes later, on the heels of Janet and Osck, they all busted up over the edge of Blue Hole and climbed up the concrete steps. All four of them blinked and marveled, finding it hard not to just stop and take it all in. But there was a wide stream of beings behind them pushing them forward. The air was filled with the sound of cheering and helicopters hovering overhead.

Tim stared at the rows and rows of soldiers and military vehicles as he was herded past the crowds and into the large fenced-off areas.

"We made it," Tim said to Azure.

Azure bent over and grabbed his stomach.

"You okay?" Tim asked.

"I'm fine," Azure lied.

All four of them shuffled down the path toward their designated waiting area.

CHAPTER TWENTY

THE WORST SHALL BE THIRD

There are billions and billions of different dreams. There are the boring ones that simply put you in normal situations doing normal things, like grocery shopping, or picking out school clothes, or doing the dishes. There are the messed-up ones, where you can see you're somewhere, but your brain is telling you you're somewhere else, like you see yourself on a ski slope but your brain tells you you're back in your old elementary school serving detention. There are the painful ones, where you spend the whole time looking for a bathroom only to wake up and realize you'd really better find one fast. And there are those amazing, not-to-be-missed dreams where you're flying and you wish you would never, ever, ever, ever wake up—not even to use the bathroom.

And then, of course, there are those dreams that you feel you never really wake up from, and you stumble about the next day just trying to clear your head.

It was that kind of dream Leven was now hoping to shake.

He walked quickly over the broken glass. His feet bounced with each step, making his knees hurt more than usual. He looked ahead and saw nothing but trees and fog and green and mist and stone. That, mixed with the thoughts of Amelia in his head, made his mind a wet and confusing place.

"She was real, right?" Leven asked Clover.

Clover materialized, hanging from Leven's left elbow. "She looked real to me," Clover answered. "But remember that time in Reality when I thought I saw that barn in the distance but it was just a mirage."

"It was just a *garage,*" Leven clarified. "A garage—no barn."

"Yeah," Clover said. "That's what I mean. Maybe Amelia was just a trick of the mind. But she seemed real to me."

"Me too," Leven said softly. "Look at that."

Leven pointed to a tall, dark wall that ran across the path in both directions. It was made of black stone and was at least twice Leven's height. At the point where it crossed the glass path, there was a crumbling archway. Only a few precarious-looking rocks were still holding together at the top of the arch.

"Come on," Leven waved.

When they reached the wall, Clover hopped off Leven's arm, climbed up, and jumped over. Leven glanced beyond the piles of crumbly rock and looked through the archway.

Clover jumped back over the wall and landed on Leven's left shoulder. "Looks safe enough. I saw a sharp stick and a couple of rocks you might want to avoid."

Leven climbed over the pile of rock and through the archway. Once through, he noticed two people kneeling on the ground with their heads down. They were a long way down the glass path and looked harmless, but Leven pulled his kilve out just in case. Before he got all the way to them, he recognized them from the clothes they were wearing.

"Aunt Addy?" Leven questioned. "Terry."

They both lifted their heads. Their eyes were ringed with red, and tears were slipping down their cheeks. Leven felt no compulsion to run to them. In fact, if he felt anything at all, it was an urgency to run away.

"What are you doing here?" Leven asked, dumbfounded.

"Leven," Addy sobbed.

"I don't understand," Leven admitted. "You're here."

"We're dead," Terry cried. "As dead as Elvis. We got hit by a truck, and just as we was settling into an eternity of misery, we was zoomed here."

"You're dead?"

"Completely," Terry wailed.

Addy cried harder. "We were awful to you."

"That's true," Leven said.

"I should have treated you like a son," Terry yelped.

"You should have treated me like a human," Leven threw out.

"Even just before we died, we was thinking of exploiting you," Addy said. "Can you ever forgive us?"

"Of course," Leven said without pause, his voice in perfect control. "I forgave you a long time ago."

"Why?" Terry asked, looking up at Leven.

"You two are who you are," Leven pointed out. "I couldn't let your cruelty make me something I couldn't stand to be."

"Cruelty," Addy wailed.

"You had a chance to make my life better and you chose not to," Leven said calmly. "You made it very easy for me to walk away."

The two of them were still kneeling and their shoulders shook as they sobbed. Addy finally looked up. "So you're okay?"

Leven smiled. "I think so."

"We're so sorry," Addy blubbered.

"We really are," Terry added. "My stomach feels like a loaf of lead when I think of how we treated you."

"Well, then, stop thinking about it," Leven insisted kindly. He stepped up to them and patted them on their heads. They wrapped their arms around his legs and cried like the world had just run out of fried food. Leven patted them in such a way as to say, "It's okay that you treated me like dirt; these things happen."

Addy glanced up. "You look important."

"I'm just the same person I always was."

Terry wailed.

"I was a horrible aunt," Addy hollered.

"Well, actually, you were my mother's half sister."

Addy cried even harder.

"Sorry," Leven said.

"Wow," Clover whispered from the top of Leven's head. "You've got some emotionally unfinished baggage."

As Leven continued to pat their heads, their bodies began to break up into myriads of little pieces and drift away. Addy smiled before her fat face was gone, and Terry looked relieved. Eventually there was just a small pile of dusty residue at Leven's feet.

"I still don't like them," Clover insisted.

"Well, don't waste your time on it," Leven smiled. "They're gone." Leven looked down at the thin skiff of white dust. He thought of all the times he had been yelled at and ignored. All the abuse and anger they had brought into his life. He thought of the times when he would have given anything to have them simply be kind to him. Now they were gone, and everything in the past had the ability to either drag him down or propel him forward. He was sad—not at the loss so much as at what could have been.

"So, all this is supposed to prepare you?" Clover asked.

"I'm not sure."

Leven jumped over the residue of his once-guardians and continued on the glass road.

"What time do you think it is?" Leven asked.

Clover pulled out a deck of cards from his void. "Does this tell time?"

Leven shook his head.

"This?" Clover asked, pulling out the bottom half of a Barbie.

"Really?" Leven asked in amazement. "How would *that* tell time?"

"Don't clocks have legs?"

"If somehow we really do save the world, I'm going to be amazed," Leven laughed.

"That's so weird," Clover said honestly. "I was thinking the same thing."

CHAPTER TWENTY ONE

FINDING WHAT YOU DIDN'T KNOW WAS MISSING

Winter, Geth, and Phoebe had joined the ranks of refugees working their way to Reality. Winter and Phoebe were wearing the red robes that Geth had borrowed for them, and so far not a single being had given them a second glance. The masses of refugees were made up of rants and nits and cogs and echoes and every other being that had ever been curious enough to wonder what Reality had to offer. Foo was a place of wonder, but it was also a place of service, of making the dreams of those in Reality become huge. So many now wanted to get out and have the chance for *their* dreams to come to life.

The three of them were in line directly behind two fat nits and in front of a dozen black skeletons. Winter looked back over her shoulder at the endless stream of beings.

"I hate this," Winter said. "I feel like we're abandoning Leven."

"That's sweet," Phoebe said kindly.

Winter wanted to reach out and throttle Phoebe. It wasn't that Phoebe was mean to her; it was just that she was way too perfect. Whatever Winter said, Phoebe would always react in an interested, happy manner.

It just wasn't right.

Plus, Winter couldn't count on her own feelings. She knew Phoebe's effect was mellowing, but she didn't know how much. So she couldn't tell if she was feeling like she did because of Phoebe's ability to make people nuts, or because she really felt that way.

"There's nothing sweet about leaving Leven," Winter argued.

"Look at you," Phoebe said kindly. "Your cheeks are as red as our robes."

"Geth," Winter seethed. "Are you going to do something about her?"

Geth smiled at Phoebe and back at Winter. "Let's just keep moving. I know you're tired, but the sooner we get through, the sooner we can start looking for Leven."

"Looking for Leven?" Winter asked, disgusted. "We're leaving him behind."

"We're going where he said we should," Geth pointed out.

"Geth's right," Phoebe added.

Winter held her own head in her hands and shook. "Is that you?" she asked Phoebe.

"Excuse me?" Phoebe asked nicely.

"Is that you making my mind so nuts?" Winter questioned. "I feel like my brain is on fire and my cheeks are going to burst into flame. My stomach is hungry and yet repulsed by the idea of eating. I can't see straight, I keep thinking about Leven, and my feet hurt."

Phoebe smiled. "I can't help your feelings for Leven. If they've intensified, it's because of things moving in the direction they should. And I'm sorry about your feet."

"She's not to blame," Geth said.

"What do you know, Geth? You're useless," Winter moaned. "You're too smitten to be objective."

"That's probably true," Geth agreed. "But even with Phoebe around I am not distracted by what fate has us doing."

"And just what is that?" Winter asked, frustrated.

"Helping Leven," Geth answered. "Come on."

Geth's line of reasoning made no sense to Winter, but she walked quickly and with determination, looking as if she truly believed in what she was doing. The three of them reached Sycophant Run, and Winter was struck dumb by the sight of so many sycophants floating in the water along the shoreline.

"Are they dead?" Phoebe asked.

"No," Geth said. "They're wounded or stunned, but not dead. It would take the bones of their own to completely steal their lives. Of course, they probably wish they were dead. Look what all this has done to their home."

Winter looked around. Sycophant Run, once beautiful, was now trashed. The beaches were trampled and covered with unwelcome visitors and debris. And a thick river of beings ran from off of the gloam into Sycophant Run.

"This is so horrible," Winter whispered. "I can't look at it."

"It's one of the reasons you felt so passionately about helping us," Geth said. "You wanted to prevent this from happening."

"It looks like I failed big time."

"You've done your part," Geth said kindly. "This is the result of selfishness. It has come about due to hundreds of wrong decisions."

"So do we follow the crowd?" Winter asked.

"Of course not," Geth smiled. "Follow me."

The three of them broke from the string of beings and hiked toward a distant, mushroom-shaped hill in the opposite direction. Nobody seemed to notice or care that they were marching to their own beat, and in a short while they were off the beach and surrounded by beautiful trees and large, empty sycophant farms.

"It's so quiet in this part," Winter pointed out. "Where are we going?"

"I have friends here," Geth said. "I need to see if they're all right."

"Really?" Winter asked. "Isn't that kind of silly? I mean, is anyone all right?"

"I need to check," Geth said.

"You're so thoughtful," Phoebe said sincerely.

Winter rolled her dark green eyes again.

Away from the shores, Sycophant Run was quiet and still. There was no sign of a single sycophant anywhere.

"Where are all the 'phants?" Phoebe asked. "When I flew over this area a couple of days ago, there were so many out and about."

"Most are probably hiding," Geth answered her. "They've never known this kind of fear and chaos. There." Geth pointed to a tiny dirt trail that twisted up and onto a thin knoll where a large, bare tree stood. "Come on."

Geth walked quickly, sliding down a grassy slope and jumping onto the trail. Phoebe followed him and Winter took up the rear, still bothered by what she had seen on the shores and wishing her complete memory would come back. She could still recall only the things she had last been through in Reality. She couldn't remember her first stint in Reality, before she had ever been snatched into Foo. She couldn't remember her first time in Foo, and the things she had done to fight against Sabine and to put into motion the plan to bring Leven in.

Winter jammed her right foot against a hard root and tumbled to the ground. She sat there in the dirt wondering who she really was and wishing Leven were here.

Geth ran back and helped her to her feet. "You okay?"

"No," Winter said. "I feel like rot. Was this the plan?"

"Yes," Geth said happily.

"Seriously?" Winter argued. "Our plan was to come to Sycophant Run and see all the hurt sycophants and then wander off without Leven and end up in the dirt? That was the plan?"

"You—" Geth started to say.

"Don't talk about fate," Winter growled. "If you say one more thing about fate, I think I'm going to puke. Of course, it does seem sort of fateful that you're here making eyes at Phoebe, but for the rest of the world things are falling apart."

"Making eyes?" Geth smiled.

"It's like you're a child," Winter complained.

Phoebe raised her hand as if she needed permission to ask a question. "Are you sure you don't have feelings for Geth?"

"What?" Winter guffawed.

"Feelings for Geth," Phoebe said again. "You seem to have more than a usual amount of intensity over all this."

"I . . ." Winter scoffed. "You're insane. Just because I have a strong opinion doesn't mean I'm hot for Geth."

Geth just stood there staring at Phoebe.

"Besides," Winter argued, "when you're around, he has no clue I'm even alive."

"That's not true," Geth said, looking at Winter. "Phoebe's not insane."

Winter threw up her arms. "I give up. Where are we going?"

"Excellent," Geth said as if he had not noticed she was being sarcastic. "We're almost there."

The three of them stepped quickly up the small, jagged trail. On top of the hill stood a bare tree with dark bark and thousands of thin, naked branches. The branches swayed in the light wind. The tree itself was only about three times the height of Geth, with an exceptionally fat trunk. Geth reached out and touched the tree.

"This is what you were looking for?" Winter asked.

"It's a sacred place for the sycophants," Geth answered her. He gently tapped the bottom of the tree with his right foot. Five seconds later a small section of bark in the upper part of the tree slid back to reveal two tiny eyes looking out. The black eyes widened, and then the bark snapped quickly back into place. A large piece of the trunk at the bottom of the tree hinged open like a door, and an older sycophant with light fur and wide, wet eyes emerged.

"Geth?" the sycophant said happily, clapping his small hands.

"Rast," Geth bowed. It seemed as if the two of them were going to hug each other, but they held back and respectfully just nodded toward one another.

"You're alive," Rast said. "Nothing could please me more."

"And you, as always, are too kind."

"There must always be room for kindness," Rast said happily.

"It would be a mess even uglier than the scene before us if all kindness were gone."

"Oh, great," Winter whispered to Phoebe. "He talks like Geth."

"You're right," Phoebe said. "How fortunate."

"Yeah, we're pretty lucky." Winter dropped her kilve and pulled off her robe, then sat down in the long, soft grass. She folded her robe up, placed it behind her head, and lay down on it. Phoebe sat down next to her with her legs crossed and her eyes barely open.

Geth and Rast continued to talk.

"This is the second great surprise I've had today," Rast told Geth. "How I wish the feelings in the air weren't so heavy. We would be celebrating, and the whole of Sycophant Run would be filled with laughter. Instead . . ."

Rast let his last word hang like a wet towel on a sagging clothesline—heavy and damp.

"Instead we hide and hope that others can fix our mistake," Rast finally concluded. "It is a sad day."

"Your mistake?"

"It was our responsibility to keep the exit hidden," Rast reminded Geth. "We let the key get away and failed to shatter the map. Now hundreds of thousands flow freely through the exit."

"It's the failures of many that have brought us here," Geth said. "Not you and your people. The darkness had been building in the sky for years. However, there's still much to take place."

"But is there hope?" Rast asked desperately.

"Oceans full," Geth smiled. "Keep your people safe, Rast, and in the near future we will celebrate in a way much more fitting."

"You always were my favorite lithen," Rast smiled. "Now tell me, who are the beautiful beings you travel with?"

Geth looked at Phoebe and introduced her.

"Of course," Winter mumbled from her spot on the ground. "Her first."

"And this is Winter . . ."

Rast's smile faded and his fur seemed to fade to a lighter shade.

"She's been . . ." Geth started to say.

Rast held up his small right hand. The sign of the star was visible on his palm. "I'm sorry to interrupt you, but could you hold for just a moment?" Rast moved back into the tree trunk and shut the door.

"Did you offend him?" Phoebe asked.

"Yeah," Winter said, her eyes closed as she rested. "Was he mad that you were trying to out-philosophize him? Or that you said *fate* two times more than he did? Or that you were spending precious time introducing me when there was more to say about Phoebe?"

Geth sat down next to Winter just as the trunk of the tree opened once more. Rast stepped out, followed by another sycophant.

"Lilly," Geth said happily.

Lilly's eyes were red from all the tears she had cried in the last few hours. The sight of Sycophant Run and the horror over what others were doing was too great for her. More than that, however, had been the realization that Winter had left her to save her people and that she, Lilly, had behaved like a spoiled child. She had also been the one to retrieve the key to the sycophant secret. All the misery and pain her people were now going through was due to her. Winter had only wished to help. Lilly's white fur was dusty, and her tall ears were folded forward. Geth looked from Lilly to Winter.

"Winter," Geth said urgently. "Sit up."

"What is it?" Winter asked.

"It's Lilly," Geth said, smiling.

Winter sat up and looked at Lilly. "Lilly?"

"Your sycophant," Geth said.

Winter's mind raced like a toy car that had been overwound and quickly released. She looked at Lilly, searching her brain for any hint of recognition. Lilly, on the other hand, needed no reminder. She bound up from where she stood and sprang toward Winter. She wrapped her small white arms around Winter's neck and chattered excitedly.

"You're back," Lilly cried.

Winter began to cry—she wasn't exactly sure why, but the moment just seemed to call for it.

CHAPTER TWENTY-TWO

PEEL AWAY THE SKIN AND
WE'RE ALL QUITE SIMILAR

T he New Mexico sun beat down like a high-voltage heat lamp,
warming up all the thousands of beings locked behind the tall
chain-link fences. At first those from Foo were pretty patient, waiting calmly behind the fences for someone to tell them when they
would be free. But as the scene became more and more crowded and
the day got hotter and hotter, nits, cogs, and other beings began to
lose it. There was hollering and shoving, and over the past few minutes the chain-link fences seemed in danger of being pulled down.

Still, despite all the anxiety and unknowing, the stream of
refugees continued to flow up and out of Blue Hole Lake.

The Dearth was currently tucked away in the scuba shop waiting
for the president of the United States to make a visit. Ezra, Dennis,
General Lank, six guards, two other generals, the ambassador from

France, a Mexican liaison, and a doctor who was currently examining the Dearth were waiting with him.

Dr. Nook listened to the Dearth's chest with his stethoscope. He moved the stethoscope around and then looked into the Dearth's ear with a small light. Dr. Nook then took a pen from his pocket and jabbed it into his own leg.

"What the heck?" General Lank said.

Dr. Nook moaned, "Oww."

"What are you doing?" Ezra hollered.

"I thought I might be dreaming," Dr. Nook said. "I mean, a toothpick that's alive, and now this person with the feet growing into the ground who has no heartbeat or pulse . . . or blood, for that matter."

"He's from Foo," Elton explained.

"Amazing," Dr. Nook said. "He will need to be further studied."

"Now?" the Dearth asked mildly. "I have been most patient with all this, but I think it is about time you let me and those who have come go free. We were told that America was the land of the free."

"That might be," General Lank said. "But we just can't let a couple hundred thousand aliens start wandering around the desert."

"Aliens?" the Dearth said, bothered.

"You know," General Lank said. "The Reality-challenged."

"Stop being so nice to him," Ezra barked. "I know we're waiting for that bulb-headed president of yours to come here and tell us nothing we don't already know, but you don't have to treat this dirt clod so gently."

The Dearth laughed as if Ezra were joking.

"I think what Ezra's trying to say is that our feelings have changed," Dennis informed them all.

"What?" Elton asked.

"Ezra and I have talked," Dennis said. "We're being fooled."

"Fooled?" General Lank said.

"This old man sits here saying nice things and winking, and we're falling for it," Dennis said. "While he winks, all those he has brought with him are getting restless. They're planning something."

"Excuse me," the Dearth said, half smiling. "I don't understand."

"Stop it," Ezra yelled. "You come here with your accent and sweater and mustache and figure that all these dolts are going to just gobble you up. Well, they might, but I'm not."

Ezra leapt across the room and landed on the Dearth's nose. He pulled and pulled, as if the Dearth's face were a mask and he was about to expose it.

"Ah-ha!" Ezra screamed while pulling.

The Dearth patted Ezra away, and the tiny toothpick flew across the room and landed in front of Dennis's right foot. Ezra stood up on the ground and turned back to look at the Dearth.

"That was a dumb move, older man," Ezra seethed.

The small, angry toothpick stood still. He closed his single eye and raised his hands as if marshalling his power. Then he waved his arms and opened his eye. A tiny wave of light radiated from it, expanding rapidly as it moved up and across the room. The wriggling glow reached the Dearth's head and washed over him.

The Dearth began to cough and sputter. He bent over, grasping at his own stomach in pain. As he looked back up, his once-friendly face began to melt away. His eyes dripped down onto his cheeks, his nose melted to his chin, and his ears slid down the side of his neck.

"What the . . ." General Lank said, backing up.

A black ooze ran down his forehead, but when the Dearth reached up to try to make things right, all he managed to do was to get his chin stuck to his hand. He pulled his chin away.

Five seconds later there was no sign of the kind elderly gentleman. There was nothing but a huge pile of black that was writhing and stretching. The Dearth opened his large, sticky mouth and screamed.

"Shoot it!" General Lank said.

The six guards pulled their pistols and immediately began to unload into the Dearth. The bullets shot into the dark tar but did no damage. The Dearth just laughed.

"Smother him!" Ezra yelled.

Two of the guards jumped onto the Dearth. One tried to choke him at the neck while the other wrapped his arms around the back of the Dearth and squeezed.

The Dearth shook, and hundreds of thin strings of sticky black shot out from him and wrapped around the two unlucky guards. The Dearth then began to sink down into the soil beneath him.

"Stop him," General Lank yelled. "Stop him!"

"How?" one of the guards screamed back.

The Dearth sank even lower into the dirt floor, dragging the two soldiers with him. Ezra shot off from the floor and pierced the Dearth's torso. He flew out the back of the Dearth and slammed up against the far wall.

Dennis stood up, watching helplessly with the others as the Dearth disappeared beneath the soil with the two soldiers. Everyone just stood there dumbfounded. Suddenly, a thick root of rubbery blackness shot up like a snake. It flew across the room and jabbed itself into Elton's stomach. The blackness took a bite into Elton's belly, shook, and then retracted into the soil. Elton clutched his stomach and fell to the ground moaning.

General Lank grabbed a phone as two soldiers ran to Elton's side.

"I told you so," Ezra seethed.

"Yes, sir," General Lank said to someone on the phone. "No, we have a real problem. Really?"

Ezra jumped back to Dennis and took a few moments to berate him for doing nothing.

"There was nothing to do," Dennis argued.

"What a nub you are," Ezra yelled.

General Lank hung up the phone.

"What now?" Dennis asked.

"The president will be here shortly," Lank said. "And the Eiffel Tower just got up and walked away."

"It's going to get worse," Ezra yelled, "now that the Dearth's in the soil."

"What do you suggest?" General Lank asked.

"I suggest you lock up Elton there, and then shoot everybody you currently have captured behind those fences."

General Lank laughed uncomfortably.

"What are you laughing about?" Ezra asked.

"You're serious?" the general said.

"As a decapitation," Ezra screamed. "The Dearth took a bite out of Elton and is now in the soil. Even as you stand here, he's wriggling about and spreading out. In fact, right now he's probably whispering to every soul that will listen behind those fences, commanding them to start taking their own freedom a little more seriously."

"Ha," General Lank laughed. "My troops built those fences themselves."

"You're a fool," Ezra laughed back. "It would take only a couple dozen of those from Foo to push those fences down. And once they see it's possible, they'll all follow—"

"Shut up," General Lank interrupted.

"Excuse me," Dennis and Ezra said together.

"I can't think," General Lank said.

"That's obvious," Ezra growled.

"We keep this a secret," General Lank insisted. "Until the president arrives, we make no mention of losing the Dearth."

"You seem to believe the president has some control over all of this," Dennis said calmly. "I believe it's time you start thinking a totally different way."

Ezra almost looked proud.

"This Dearth," a soldier asked, "how far can he go?"

"According to what I read on Dennis's head two days ago," Ezra answered, "he can move just about anywhere there is soil or sand. He can even move under oceans if there is dirt. You can go ahead and keep it a secret, but I guarantee that it won't be a secret to those who he will first start messing with."

General Lank's red face looked like it was going to explode. He swore, making it clear that he would rather be anyplace other than where he was at the moment.

Unfortunately for him, it was about to get much worse.

CHAPTER TWENTY-THREE

FUZZY

Everyone's forgotten something at some point in their lives. Many have forgotten their keys; some have forgotten where they parked their cars; and a man with a really crooked back and a greasy forehead forgot to meet with me last Tuesday to give me the rest of the notes I needed about Foo. In the eternal scheme of things, his mistake is far more bothersome than simply forgetting where you placed your keys. We had to meet later, in a dark cave where it was hard to see clearly and it strained my eyes to look over the papers he was delivering. Of course, it was so dark that he didn't notice that I paid him considerably less than agreed upon.

Win-win.

But the worst thing a person can forget is another person or friend. There's nothing more uncomfortable than meeting people who claim to know you, but you can't remember a thing about them. Such was the case, and then some, with Winter and Lilly. Lilly had been Winter's sycophant many years before, and she had been set free when Winter went to Reality. Since then, Winter had lost all memory of her earlier life in Foo and of Lilly, and had no knowledge of how Lilly had become remarkably bitter and destructive.

Now, as Lilly began to see the light, Winter still had no recollection of the small friend she had loved for many years.

Winter held the white sycophant out in front of her and looked her over.

"You look different," Lilly said. "But the same."

Winter smiled as if she had been instructed to.

"You don't remember me at all, do you?" Lilly said softly.

"I don't," Winter said sadly. "I'm so sorry."

Winter was leaning against the trunk of the bare tree on the grassy knoll. Geth, Phoebe, Rast, and Brindle had walked off to give Winter and Lilly some much-needed catching-up time. From where they were now all sitting, it was hard to imagine the rest of Foo falling apart. The weather was cool, and a breeze filled with the scent of tavel wound though the air like a ribbon of caramel. A strong Lore Coil rippled across the scene, announcing the birth of a sycophant named Sunrise.

"I wish I could remember," Winter said. "It's maddening sometimes."

"Don't worry," Lilly said submissively. "I remember you."

"I know I had to set you aside," Winter said. "Geth told me that. I'm sure I must have been sad about that."

"I was angry," Lilly admitted. "And I still don't understand everything, but I've seen now what you were trying to stop. I should have understood how important it was—seeing all those sycophants floating in the water and watching everyone tear apart our land. My anger was misplaced."

Three huge rovens flew overhead. One was carrying a large trunk in its talons and the other two were screaming at each other.

"So you're my sycophant?"

Lilly bowed. "You'll get used to me again. Having a sycophant can be an adjustment, but we're made to make things better."

"You know, it's weird," Winter smiled. "I've kind of always felt like I had a sycophant because of Clover."

"Clover?" Lilly asked, the hair on the back of her neck sticking up.

"Leven's sycophant."

"Leven's sycophant is named Clover?"

Winter nodded.

"You could leave me," Lilly said. "I realize now how wrong I was. I have thought of nobody but myself, while you did just the opposite."

"You know, there have been moments . . ." Winter smiled.

"Moments?" Lilly asked.

"Where I thought it would have been nice to have my own sycophant," Winter admitted. "And a girl one at that."

Lilly's pink eyes widened to the size of pool balls.

"I mean, I love Clover," Winter said. "But his taste in . . . well, just about everything is pretty much the opposite of mine."

"You mean it?" Lilly asked.

"I guess I do," Winter replied. "But—you know I'm going to Reality. It's not your responsibility to go with me."

"I'd love to make up some time," Lilly begged. "It scares me, though."

"Really?" Winter asked.

"Foo was not meant to mix with Reality," Lilly said soberly. "My people were supposed to be the last and final stand."

"I think somehow you and I were involved in giving them the key," Winter said.

"I was," Lilly admitted. "I took it to punish everyone."

"I was told I buried it to hide it from you," Winter informed her. "Then Leven found it. So let's just say it's Leven's fault."

Lilly let out a sigh four times bigger than her actual body. "Thanks, Winter."

"You know, I'll probably call you Clover by accident a lot," Winter informed her.

"Sycophants are not supposed to grow attached to their names anyhow."

Winter reached out, and Lilly jumped onto her arm. "You're lighter than Clover."

"What a nice thing to say," Lilly smiled. She then flipped up the hood of her small white robe and disappeared.

"Should we get Geth?" Winter asked.

Lilly giggled.

"And Phoebe?" Winter added.

"I guess, but what's with those two?" Lilly asked.

"I know, tell me about it."

Winter smiled.

CHAPTER TWENTY-FOUR

IT'S RAINING CONFUSED MEN

T he glass path was wide and dirty, and thick runs of red grass grew between the shattered shards. Plus, the right side of the path was beginning to be pushed up by growing tree roots. There were far more ruins on this side of the wall than Leven and Clover had passed earlier. Large castles were now nothing but weathered mounds of stone and growth. A row of seven small shops lined the path near an empty fountain filled with dirt. The shops were missing windows and doors, and the roofs of most of them had completely collapsed.

"What is all of this?" Leven asked. "Who lived here?"

"Who knows?" Clover said. "But, if you remember the history of Foo, it used to all be one big land mass with Alder at the center. These ruins are from a long time ago."

"I don't understand them," Leven said. "They look dead, but there is a feeling of life, as if the beings who once lived here still do."

"That's crazy," Clover said.

They checked the shops for any signs of life and then kept walking right through town. The glass path got even wider as it led to a small outdoor amphitheater with a covered stage up front and thick granite seats circling the other half. Fish and bird fossils were visible in the stone that was used for the seating. Leven could see the bones of small creatures and other long-dead animals. Two trees had burst through sections of the seats, and the stage was covered with moss-layered mounds of stone. Leven jumped down from the top ledge onto the upper row of seating.

"Cool," Leven said sincerely. "This must have been quite the place back in the day."

Leven hopped down another two rows and stopped to look around. From inside the amphitheater he could look out and see some of the houses and castles that had made up the town whose inhabitants had once lived and performed here.

Now it was nothing but a stone ghost town.

"Where does a person get something to eat around here?" Clover asked. He hopped off of Leven's shoulder and began jumping down the wide seats. Clover spotted a small bird fossil in the stone and scurried over to it. "Hey, look at—"

Blammt.

From out of nowhere a large, floppy body in a black robe fell from the sky and landed on Clover. Clover scurried to crawl out from under the moaning body as quickly as possible.

"What the—"

Whonnnt.

Another body smacked down two feet from Leven. Leven looked up at the gray sky and then ran to the aid of the individual who had just dropped in. He grabbed the being by the shoulder and turned him over. Leven was expecting to see someone he recognized, some person or being that he had unfinished business with, but it was just a very old man.

Dloopt.

Another being tumbled from above and onto the stone benches.

"What's going on?" Clover yelled as the sky opened up and body after body came crashing down. One landed on Leven and pinned him to the stone seating. Another landed on Leven's ankles, making it almost impossible for him to get up. Two came crashing down by Clover, but the small sycophant was able to dodge both blows.

Leven heaved the first body to the side and pushed the other one off of his ankles so he could stand up. "We should find cover," he called to Clover as two more bodies rained down.

"Where?" Clover asked as another black-robed old man landed facedown directly in front of him. Clover pulled out an old umbrella from his void. He popped it open just as another robed being crashed down onto it.

Leven checked the sky and then leaned down and propped the old man up, pushing back the hood of his robe so he could see him better. The old man moaned and opened his eyes.

For the moment the rain had stopped.

"Who are you?" Leven asked.

"Where am I?" the man demanded.

"I'm not sure," Leven said. "Who are you?"

"Syarm," he replied, looking around. "I am a Sochemist. I demand to know where we are."

The other old men began to sit up and check themselves for bruises and bumps. A couple hollered out to one another.

They had all survived the fall.

There were twenty-four of them altogether, and they wore heavy black robes and had gray hair that was either receding or gone. Around each of their necks was a thick leather band that extended into a strap attaching to the wrist on the left arm. Their right wrists were covered with gold bands of material.

"Where are we?" Syarm asked again.

"You're on the island of Alder," Leven answered.

"Alder?" They all began to chatter and moan.

"I've formed an opinion," a short man announced. "We are on the island of Alder. All those who agree say *aye*."

"Aye," all the others cheered.

"Are you together?" Leven asked.

A really tall old man in a black robe stood up and raised his right hand. "We are the Sochemists."

"From Morfit?" Clover asked, putting his bent umbrella back into his void.

The old Sochemist glanced down at Clover. "Typically we pay no attention to sycophants, but yes."

"Why are you here?" Leven answered.

"I have an opinion," Syarm said. "We were deciphering and translating a new batch of Lore Coils when, next thing I knew, I was falling from the sky."

"For the record," another Sochemist said, "let it be known that no Sochemist has ever traveled to Alder. All those in agreement say *aye*."

"Aye."

After they had dusted themselves off, they huddled together and whispered at one another. The whispering was soft and sober, as if the very next thing one of them said might possibly save them all. They debated what to say and what to ask and finally came up with something.

"We're curious as to who you are," Syarm wondered. Two of the other Sochemists patted Syarm on the back for expressing himself so clearly.

"I'm Leven Thumps," Leven answered.

The Sochemists went wild with the announcement—two fell backwards, one fell forward, and three gasped like timid women who had just seen a huge mouse. They righted themselves, huddled, and conversed.

"You're the Want?" Syarm finally asked.

Leven smiled. "I am."

They began to moan and chatter again. One started to cry, and another pulled his robe up over his head and curled up into a small, rocking ball. Yet another bravely reached out and touched Leven.

"Why are we here?" Syarm asked.

"I can't say for sure," Leven said. "Did we ever have any unfinished business?"

The Sochemists huddled and fiercely began to shout and yell at one another. "Unfinished business?" "He moves to the oldest tree." "How dare . . ." "The Want promised we would be done with . . ." "It wasn't *his* promise." "It is the end."

Leven held up his hand. "Be quiet!"

They shut up.

"What promise did my grandfather make to you?"

The fattest Sochemist stepped forward. "I have an opinion."

"Great, what is it?" Leven asked impatiently.

"Your grandfather promised to bring an end to us. He thought we were moved by darkness when he himself was touched in the head."

"You do confuse a lot of people," Leven pointed out.

They talked amongst themselves for three minutes and then Syarm spoke. "We disagree."

"I'm pretty certain people can think for themselves," Leven said.

"Foo would fall without us," the Sochemist shouted.

"Foo is falling because of people like you."

They huddled again. "We've yet to make a mistake," Syarm finally announced.

Leven just stared at them. "Who gave Sabine power?"

They all cleared their throats.

"Who eliminated the whisps, okayed the slaying of siids, allowed Jamoon to work with metal, used the Ring of Plague to support your agenda?"

"How do you—"

"Who buried and arranged the end of the lithens?"

"We serve because we care," Syarm said flatly. "Perhaps if the people worked harder."

"Really?" Leven asked in disbelief. "You make the rules and laws, create the stories, and spread the news that pleases only you."

The Sochemists all nodded, looking proud.

"Wow," Leven said sarcastically.

They huddled again, and then Syarm spoke: "Thank you."

Leven looked down at Clover and shrugged. "What do I do?"

"They seem slightly nuts," Clover said. "Maybe you're supposed to kill them."

"No way," Leven said. "I'm not killing a bunch of old men I've never even met before."

"Try telling them you love them," Clover suggested. "It worked with Amelia."

"You're absolutely no help," Leven sighed.

"Why are they your problem?" Clover asked.

"Geth did say they were part of the reason everything is so unbalanced," Leven reminded him. "And if my grandfather promised they'd come to an end, I guess I have to help finish them up."

Leven turned back to the Sochemists, who were still huddled together, debating all the reasons why none of the things that were going on in Foo should be blamed on them.

"Listen," Leven said. "I'm not sure what my connection to you is, but I know that there's something unfinished."

Syarm raised his hand. "I have an opinion."

Leven rubbed his forehead.

"My knees hurt," Syarm said. "And the weight of my body is pulling me down. All in favor of a brief reprieve say *aye*."

"Aye."

All the Sochemists began to lie down on the stone seating. They moaned and creaked as they tried to make themselves comfortable on the hard surface.

"A nap?" Leven snapped. "Fate dumps you down on me so that you can just take a nap? You're useless. I thought age brought wisdom."

Three of the Sochemists were already snoring.

"Look," Clover pointed.

The fattest Sochemist was asleep and slowly beginning to bleed into the stone he was resting on. His legs faded in first, then his head, and finally his torso. In under twenty seconds the fat Sochemist was nothing but a fossil in the stone. Two more started to fade.

"Should we wake them?" Clover asked.

"No way," Leven said.

Three more blended into the stone.

"Is this what normally happens?" Clover asked.

"How would I know?" Leven said. "I've never studied the sleeping habits of Sochemists."

The remaining Sochemists were waning, meshing into the stone like butter into warm potatoes. Syarm was the last to go. He opened his eyes as his body became one with the stone. He blinked, yawned, and then froze, becoming nothing but a fossil.

Leven looked around. He was now surrounded by the fossilized images of all twenty-four Sochemists. Like a carpet being rolled out, a thick layer of purple covered the sky, and the smaller sun jiggled just a bit.

"To be honest," Clover said, "they look much better like this. Did you see the chin on that one? It was all floppy, and now it's just a line. Of course, I don't think I would want to sit on any of these seats now."

"I'm worried," Leven said.

"Why?" Clover asked. "Those guys will never be able to bother anyone again. No more locust messages and new Lore Coil laws. Maybe Morfit will lighten up. Remember how dark that place was?"

"I'm not worried about the Sochemists," Leven said. "I'm worried about ever getting where I'm supposed to be. If *they* were unfinished business, there could be almost anything up ahead."

"You think more now that you're the Want," Clover said, hopping onto Leven's right shoulder. "What direction are we going?"

Leven pointed to the path of glass.

"Then all we need to do is walk," Clover said simply. "Who cares what's next—as long as there's the possibility of some food."

"We don't even know that," Leven pointed out.

"It's fun to pretend," Clover said.

Leven climbed up the amphitheater seats, got back on the path, and left the stone ghost town for good.

CHAPTER TWENTY-FIVE

PICKING YOURSELF OUT
IN A LINEUP

The population of the world is somewhere around six point four billion. That number is so large that it really is hard to comprehend. Let's see if this helps: If you took six point four billion ferrets and laid them end to end, you'd probably hear from some animal rights group and be sued for six billion dollars for being mean to ferrets.

Six point four billion is a huge number.

Of course, it seemed as if all six point four billion people were now gathered in Santa Rosa, New Mexico, and that wasn't including the population of Foo—the hundreds of thousands of refugees that had now successfully worked through the waterway and climbed into Reality. The highways were clogged, the skies were filled with helicopters and jets, and the sounds of engines and voices and sirens and tanks permeated the surroundings. There were thousands of RVs, dozens of news crews, hundreds of black limos containing hundreds of important people from all over the world, and two women with the exact same name, Ethel Lynn Lundburg, wearing the exact same outfit, who had never met before. What were the odds?

About one in six point four billion.

General Lank paced back and forth in one of the tents as Ezra slept on his pop-can throne and Dennis sat on a cot thinking. The steady stream of beings was still continuing, and all over the world the attacks by the buglike sarus and tornadolike telts were increasing. On the small TV in the corner of the tent, the news was reporting a herd of avalands that had been tearing up farms in Canada and a building that had walked into a nearby lake. In addition to the Eiffel Tower getting up and walking off, so had one of the pyramids and the Leaning Tower of Pisa. And as of an hour ago, large parts of the Great Wall of China were wriggling toward Mongolia.

General Lank stopped and looked down at a chart he had rolled out over a metal table. Other officials, including a jittery and sweaty Elton Thumps, were looking over the chart and talking on phones and radios. By now most of the world knew that telts could be destroyed with water, sarus hated fire, and avalands could be stopped by stone barricades. But even with that new knowledge, stopping these things was not easy. And now the U.S. military held in captivity things like black skeletons and rants and cogs and all manner of odd beings. To make matters worse, the Dearth had escaped and those in captivity were growing restless. Plus, the entire world was looking for answers, and so far the things that had crawled out of Blue Hole had only offered up more questions.

"We have doctors and scientists looking over the creatures,"

General Lank said into his phone. "No, so far there has been no real aggression. But I can't promise calm forever. There has been some protest over our examining them."

Dennis stood up. He walked over and looked down at the chart. General Lank snapped his phone shut and turned his attention to Dennis.

"Tell us something," General Lank said. "Anything."

"My head's so clear," Dennis said.

"Good for you," Elton snapped. "Mine's not. I say you send me in, general."

"There are still so many coming out," Lank replied.

"So what? I can push through," Elton argued. "I have been studying Foo for my whole adult life. It's time I see it for myself. America has to be the first to claim that land. I have to get in there."

"Who would you take?"

"Give me six men," Elton said. "Or give me none. I don't care. We'll be going against the current of refugees, but we can make it. We'll also be able to see if our equipment functions. If our radios and phones work, it will make things a lot different."

"I would wait," Dennis advised.

"No offense," Elton said dismissively, "but you're not being asked for your opinion."

"But my head's so clear," Dennis said again. "For the first time I think I can really see what is happening."

"What's happening?" General Lank said.

"All the messages from Sabine that have run across my brain and body for so long are clear."

Everyone just stared at Dennis.

"It's not good," he finally said. "They are planning to take over our world."

"What?" General Lank barked.

"See?" Elton snapped. "I must go in. I have to go in."

"Are you sure you're okay?" General Lank asked Elton. "You look horrible."

"I'm fine," Elton insisted. "My stomach hurts a little from being bitten, but I have to get in there."

"It's not that easy," Dennis argued. "The Dearth is already here. Why would—"

"Let me see the opening," General Lank interrupted. "If there's any slowing of those coming through, I'll send you in. Meanwhile, we need to resecure the fences and keep our troops on high alert."

General Lank strode out of the tent with an agitated Elton right behind him. Dennis picked up the sleeping Ezra and followed them. They walked through the troops and approached Blue Hole from the right side.

A whole family of cogs were currently climbing out of the empty lake, their orange foreheads and blue hands looking even more predominant in reality. They were crying and cheering and waving their blue hands.

Ezra slowly climbed up onto Dennis's left shoulder. He yawned and cursed the fact that even with everything going on he was still bored.

Two dozen rants clambered over the lake's edge. They were jumping and hollering and marveling over the feeling of Reality.

"Where's the bloodshed I was promised?" Ezra said to Dennis.

"You were never promised bloodshed," Dennis said.

"You have no idea what I promised myself," Ezra seethed. "Now, who can I set on fire?"

"You can't just set someone on fire," Dennis said.

"Wanna bet?" Ezra waved, and Elton Thumps was suddenly in flames.

Elton fell to the ground screaming and rolled himself out quickly as a nearby soldier patted him down. Elton stood back up slowly, his hair and eyebrows still smoking slightly.

"What was that?" General Lank asked.

Elton was glaring at Ezra.

"What?" Ezra said. "I needed to win a bet."

"You'd better knock that stuff off," Dennis whispered to Ezra.

"Why?"

"Because there's—"

"Who's that?" Ezra interrupted, pointing to a small group of beings climbing out of the lake.

The people being pointed at were two women and a man. The women were beautiful, both with long, flowing hair and deep-set eyes. They were wearing red robes and looking around in wonder. The man was tall and strong-looking, with long, dark blond hair. He was smiling as if he were completely happy with everything.

"The women are beautiful," Dennis whispered.

"This isn't the prom," Ezra roared. "I'm talking about the man. General, bring them over."

General Lank ordered two soldiers to intercept the trio of people.

"What's the matter?" Dennis asked Ezra.

Ezra was standing on Dennis's ear and shaking. "Can't you see it?"

"See what?"

"It's like looking into a mirror," Ezra seethed.

Dennis's eyes widened and he took a better look. "That's Geth?"

"Hot smack," Ezra cheered. "Thank goodness I sharpened my leg this morning."

"Are you sure?" Dennis asked.

"I've never been more certain of anything," Ezra quivered. "Now, flick me."

Dennis reached up and grabbed Ezra. He placed him between his thumb and forefinger. "Ready?"

"I've waited my whole life for this moment."

"You've only been alive a short while," Dennis reminded him.

"I can't believe I hang out with you," Ezra growled.

Dennis flicked Ezra as hard as he could.

CHAPTER TWENTY-SIX

AND THE WALLS CAME
TUMBLING DOWN

M ost everything fades—photographs, favorite shirts, hair. Many things that are bright and vibrant today will be muted and dull tomorrow. Even the things that seem still are fading. Memories fade. I remember . . . well, it'll come to me. Feelings fade. How many times have you been angry because somebody sold you a low-security secret at a high-security price? Only to have your feelings of betrayal fade away after that person is eaten by a shark while trying to escape the country.

Like I said, feelings fade.

Sometimes, recognizing that something familiar has faded is not easy. Those nice blue jeans you're wearing don't look so stiff and new when they're held up to a brand-new pair. And that clear, shiny whisp that you've been hanging out with for the last few days just might not look as shiny when you hold her up to the light of Reality.

The point is, Janet was fading.

"Are you all right?" Tim asked Janet.

"Fine," she replied, standing as close to Osck as she could.

The day was growing increasingly warm, and all four of them were crowded together in the large parking lot that had been fenced off. They were near the Porta Potties and behind the temporary first aid station. Tim was sweating profusely; his thinning hair was wet with perspiration. Tim fanned himself. "I miss Swig," he admitted.

A group of frustrated cogs shoved Tim and Osck as they tried to move by.

"Watch yourself," Osck said as one cog walked right through Janet.

"I'm not about to take orders from an echo," the cog said. "And I'm certainly not going to step around a whisp."

The cogs walked off laughing.

"It's so hot," Tim complained. "How long can they keep us here?"

"We can't last here much longer," Azure said weakly from beneath the hood of his robe.

Two nits who were fighting with each other ran into a large, overheated rant. The rant picked up one of the nits, cursed loudly, and then threw the nit into a line of beings waiting for the Porta Potty. Two soldiers grabbed the rant while others tried to help those who had been knocked down.

"This is bad," Tim said.

"What do you mean?" Janet asked.

"It's so hot and crowded. And Swig said that black skeletons and rants weren't designed to be cooped up with each other."

An official-looking military person was talking through a bull-horn, ordering everyone to stay calm.

Osck leaned over and put his hands on his knees.

"Are you okay?" Tim asked.

"I feel weak," Osck said. "Like after a long night with no reflec-tion. What are the large creatures up above us?"

Tim looked up. "Helicopters."

"There's so much metal," Osck said. "Is there killing?"

Tim nodded.

"That beast there," Osck pointed to a tank outside the fence. "It looks immovable."

"It's a tank," Tim said, wiping his forehead. "And they can actu-ally move quite quickly."

"I thought we'd be free," Osck said with a touch of panic in his normally stable voice. "Azure, you said we'd be free." Osck reached out and touched Azure on the shoulder.

Azure shook as long black strings whipped up from the soil and wrapped around him. It happened so quickly Tim could barely reg-ister it. Azure screamed and cried, his expression that of someone who knew better and was now getting his comeuppance. The black strands yanked Azure downward into the soil. Tim tried to grab Azure's arm, but it was no use.

"I was so wrong," Azure said as he was pulled completely under the soil.

Tim and Osck and Janet just stood there looking at the ground. A few others who had seen it happen looked on as well.

"Where'd he go?" Osck asked.

"The Dearth," Tim answered.

Janet shivered.

"We gotta get out of here," Osck said. "I feel like I'm fading. And look at the other echoes. Something is very wrong."

Tim looked around. All over, echoes were pulsating, their bright color fading in and out. Osck grabbed the fence near him and began to shake it. It rattled and swayed, but it wasn't until a couple of dozen other beings joined him that things really began to move. The tall fence teetered and rocked—and then in one smooth motion it tipped over, crashing down on top of tanks and soldiers.

The crowd cheered and swarmed the fence, scrambling up and over the tanks and soldiers trapped underneath.

Tim ran with the crowd, afraid to stand still and be trampled. "Stick with me, Osck!" he called over his shoulder.

Osck ran right behind Tim as they scurried up over the downed fence and into another parking lot filled with soldiers who now had their weapons out and were pointing them in their direction.

A huge rant knocked down a soldier and screamed triumphantly. That seemed to be all that was needed for everyone to forgo every ounce of restraint they had ever had. Fences from all over were pushed down as thousands of beings from Foo made it their business to free themselves.

The sound of shots being fired echoed off the pavement as megaphones screamed for everyone to please calm down. A troop of black skeletons tore apart a temporary shelter and were shot at with canisters of tear gas. The gas did nothing to the skeletons but make their bones shinier and their minds angrier.

Four rants mowed down a couple of soldiers and stole their rifles. One of the rants then accidentally shot himself, not knowing which end of the rifle was dangerous. The poor being fell to the ground moaning and was picked up and carried off by a chanting crowd of angry Foovians.

A tank fired a shot, taking out three small cogs who had been running.

"Keep moving!" Tim screamed. "Over behind those short trees."

Osck ran as fast as he could, stumbling with every other step and constantly turning around to make sure Janet was still there. "It's so hot here. My feet feel like they are falling apart."

"Keep going!" Tim yelled unsympathetically. "We're going to be trampled."

A huge purple bolt of light shot out across the sky as if heaven were shaking out a tablecloth, and birds began to drop from the air, flopping down against the ground.

"What's happening?" Tim yelled.

The ground shook, and then, as if the earth had slid off its axis, the whole landscape seemed to tilt, sending everyone to their knees.

"This is Reality?" Osck yelled to Tim as he got back on his feet.

"Normally it's calmer," Tim replied.

More fences came down as every Foovian who had come through the tunnels joined the movement to be free. The ground shook and the sky began to pulsate.

Soldiers didn't know whether to shoot at those escaping or run for their own lives. As most of them were trying to make up their minds, millions of thin black strings shot from the ground and began to wrap themselves around anything they could grab.

"It's the Dearth," Janet cried.

"Find a car," Tim yelled.

"What's a car?" Osck screamed back.

"Over there!" Tim pointed through the crowd to a blue jeep about a hundred yards away.

When they reached the jeep, they found the doors locked, but the windows were broken. Tim reached inside and unlocked the door. Osck crawled through the back window and took a seat next to Janet.

"Let's see if I can do this."

Tim was not a criminal. He was a garbage man with a great brain who had read a lot of books in his lifetime. Fortunately for the travelers, one that he had read and remembered dealt with what to do in an emergency—for example, if you were stuck in the woods and had lost your car keys. How would you get your vehicle started?

Tim reached down, pulled out some wires, twisted two of them and connected another, and the car roared to life. He took the briefest moment to smile proudly before throwing the jeep into drive and slamming his right foot down on the gas. The car bucked and then shot forward like a horse that had been stung in the rear. Tim plowed over a fallen fence, almost taking the life of a cog who was foolishly running for his life directly in front of the car.

Tim swerved and moved around the crowds of beings, finding brief open spots to drive on. He spun around a tank that was just sitting there and then headed for the far side of Blue Hole Lake, hoping that most people were going the other way. There were fewer people but more short, ugly trees and old houses.

Tim smashed a chicken coop and drove right through an empty garage that was attached to an old adobe house. He wound between the few houses, taking out mailboxes and trash cans and anything in his way. He worried for a moment that someone might be chasing him, but Santa Rosa, New Mexico, was one big, chaotic mess and there was no way, short of a miracle, that it would ever be anything else.

The world was officially off balance.

CHAPTER TWENTY-SEVEN

WAY TO WORSHIP

Sometimes we underestimate the impact we have on other people's lives. Everybody living, no matter how miserable his or her life may be or how glorious each day is, makes an impact on others.

Sometimes the impact is obvious.

Perhaps you're a plastic surgeon and you give someone a really big nose. That stands out; it is pretty clear what impact you had on that person's life. But sometimes the impact is less obvious—like when someone suggests a certain breakfast cereal and it lowers your cholesterol ten points. I mean, who's going to know unless you tell them? And sometimes you meet people so briefly, but in that brief moment they say or do something that sticks with you, and although you may never meet them again, your life is changed permanently because of it.

The journey to the oldest tree is not an easy one. In fact, it's quite challenging and draining on a person, because you never really know how much unfinished business might be lurking in the form of people you've somehow influenced. In the history of Foo, only a handful have ever walked through the ruins of what Foo once was and faced the things they had never finished. It's almost impossible to know who you might meet along the way or what bit of your past might be waiting up ahead to jump or drain you.

And that's before you ever even see the tree.

There were no pictures of the oldest tree, not even drawings, because so few had ever seen it—and those who had weren't exactly the type of people who were going to make postcards and sell them.

Of course, in the beginning, there were many who witnessed the tree. It was the center of Foo and of all activity. Great buildings and cities were built up around it. Many of the dreams that came in back then swirled through its branches and received inspiration from it. But as Foo changed, and as even the slightest imbalance occurred, fewer and fewer saw or experienced the tree. Towns and cities went to ruin as Alder eventually broke off and became an island in the center of the Lime Sea, a place only the Waves had access to. A place most of Foo could conveniently forget about.

Leven steadied himself—it felt as if the entire island of Alder was sliding around in the Lime Sea.

"What's going on?" Leven asked.

"I thought you were just walking funny," Clover replied.

"No more dreams?" Leven said. "And the ground's moving? And look at the color of the sky."

"Black's technically not a color," Clover said.

The bushes and trees were so thick that Leven had to stop every few feet and look for a clear place to step. He could still see bits of the glass trail under all the growth, but it was almost impossible to walk a straight line.

"Isn't it noon?" Leven asked.

Clover stared at him.

"Lunchtime?" Leven clarified.

"Feels like it," Clover complained.

"What's the deal with the sky being so dark?"

"It'll lighten up," Clover said. "It just looks like the suns are a bit confused. See, here comes one."

In the far sky the small sun rose up, as if peeking to see how bad things were. The light spread out across Alder and touched the path they were standing on.

"There," Leven pointed. "Look at that!"

In front of them a good way off stood a large chapel made completely out of wood. Its towers and roofs were ornate and massive. It was boxed in by trees, and there were bushes and branches shooting out of the windows and roof. Leven walked as quickly as he could, jumping over fallen trees and thick bushes. By the time he reached the chapel, he was short of breath. He looked up at it and walked around slowly.

"Wow," Leven said quietly. "I would have loved to see this thing years ago before it was so weathered." He made a complete circuit around the building and then climbed the seven steps up to the closed front doors.

"Are we going inside?" Clover asked.

"I am."

"What do you think is inside?"

"From the look of the windows, probably just bushes and trees."

Clover disappeared, and Leven reached out and tried the knob. The door was locked. Leven pulled out his kilve and slammed it down on the doorknob. The door made a snapping sound and then swung open, squealing as it moved.

Leven stuck his head inside.

The large chapel was completely overgrown. It looked like a bird sanctuary that someone had forgotten about and now it was nothing but growth and decay. There were a couple of very large trees that had actually grown so tall they were bursting through the ceiling, and all the windows had bushes around them that were thirsty for light.

Across the chapel, Leven could see what used to be a podium, and an organ with large wooden pipes sat silent.

Leven stepped in and walked carefully across the chapel and through the rows of decaying benches. It was deathly quiet. Even the air seemed to be holding its breath.

"Woooooaaammmmmnnnnnaaaa."

The organ played and Leven jumped half his height.

"Who's there?" Leven hollered.

"It's just me," Clover hollered back. "I wanted to see if this worked. Listen." Clover jumped all over the organ keyboard, making sounds no respectable organist would have approved of. He leapt onto the top keyboard and then bounced his behind down on the keys. It sounded like a circus who couldn't afford a real organist. The noise bounced off the walls and floors and made it difficult to think straight.

"That's enough," Leven called, holding up his hand.

Clover pressed one last note. "Sorry."

"What do you think this place was?" Leven asked.

"It was a church," a male voice answered him from behind.

Leven spun around, pulling out his kilve and slicing it through the air.

"No need for that," the voice said.

Whoever was speaking was sitting in one of the decaying pews and staring straight at Leven. Leven had walked right past him on his way across the chapel.

"Do you remember me?" the voice asked.

"I'm not sure that I do," Leven said, still pointing his kilve toward him. A tiny ray of light shifted to expose the right side of the dark visitor. Unlike the last time Leven had seen him, he was whole. "Jamoon."

Jamoon sighed. "There's no need to fear me. My body hardens even as we speak. My feet are stone and I can feel the rock creeping up my legs. This will be the last place I sit."

"I don't understand," Leven said, walking closer. "What unfinished business do we have? You were dead."

"You're right," Jamoon said. "Dreams have stopped. I suppose us rants are now whole. But what good is it? We will all harden, Foo is crumbling, and I helped make it happen."

"You had some pretty dark help," Leven pointed out. "Sabine—and Sabine and you were messed up by the Dearth."

"Don't make excuses for me," Jamoon pleaded. "I know what I did. I suppose that's why I'm here, to make something right."

"How did you get here?" Leven asked.

"I was working my way toward death when I was pulled here," Jamoon said. "When I fell at Morfit, I lay beneath the stones dying for days. As my life finally slipped away, I was stopped—by what, I don't know—but my fate was on hold until I came here."

Leven looked down at Jamoon and could see the stone creeping up his neck and beneath his chin.

"I'm sorry I chose the wrong side," Jamoon said.

"I've never needed your apology," Leven said sincerely. "In all honesty, you always sort of amazed me."

Jamoon smiled. "You are as remarkable as you were prophesied to be."

"I only wanted . . ."

The rock crept up Jamoon's face. His mouth and nose were now stone. He looked at Leven with his wide eyes and then shut them as the stone finished him off. Jamoon now sat there as a statue with closed eyes.

"Do you think that even looks like him?" Clover asked.

"It was him," Leven said quietly. "You saw."

"I know, but the stone makes him look like a woman."

Leven laughed softly.

"I'm just saying that someday someone might stumble upon it and think it's a statue of a woman and put it out in their garden."

"And you were complaining about me talking too much?" Leven asked.

Clover disappeared and they left the chapel.

"I feel different," Leven admitted. "It's like everyone we run into takes part of me."

"People can be so selfish."

"Seriously," Leven said. "Although maybe what they're taking are bits I shouldn't be holding onto anyhow."

Clover materialized and looked Leven up and down. "You look okay to me."

Leven walked faster, being careful not to trip over his own feet.

CHAPTER TWENTY-EIGHT

There's No Repellent
Strong Enough

Geth had just helped Phoebe up and out of Blue Hole Lake when something small and noisy smacked up against his left shoulder. Whatever it was bounced off and flew into a crowd of female cogs.

"What was that?" Phoebe asked.

"They have really big bugs here," Geth answered.

"There're so many people," Winter moaned.

Geth looked at the thousands and thousands of hot, unsettled, screaming people and strongly suggested to Winter and Phoebe that they still keep themselves hidden.

"You!" A heavy man with a square red face stopped them. "Come with me."

"Okay," Geth answered. "But . . ."

Apparently the red-faced man didn't have time to explain things. He waved frantically at Geth. "Come."

"What's this about?" Winter whispered out of the corner of her mouth.

"I have no idea," Geth replied.

Phoebe was mesmerized by all the cameras and flashbulbs. She stared at a tall reporter with red hair as he frantically clicked off hundreds of shots of her.

"Come on," Geth insisted.

"What are they doing with those sparkling lights?" Phoebe asked.

"They're taking your picture," Winter answered.

"What does that mean?"

"It means that millions of additional people can now drool over you," Winter explained.

The red-faced man waved at them to get them to run faster. In the distance they could hear crashing noises and the roar of a crazed crowd. The red-faced man stopped and looked in that direction.

"I knew it," he said, pressing a button on his walkie-talkie.

The sound of a gun going off cracked through the air.

"What was that?" Phoebe asked, plugging her beautiful ears.

"That was a gunshot," Geth said.

"I'm not sure I like Reality," she frowned.

The red-faced man seemed to lose interest in them; he stormed off as a tank fired out a shot and more fences started to come down.

"We've got to get somewhere safe," Geth said. "Follow—"

Geth flew backward, landing on his rear and slamming his head against the dirt.

"Geth!" both Phoebe and Winter yelled.

Winter knelt down next to him and tried to pull him up.

"Leave him be," a voice demanded.

Winter looked at Geth as he lay there. Geth's eyes were closed, and he wasn't moving. But there on his forehead, standing as tall as a fancy toothpick could possibly stand, stood Ezra. He was pulsating a muted purple color and had both of his fists up as if ready for a fight. Winter might have been surprised by a talking toothpick if it had not been for the time she had spent carrying Geth around when he was one.

"You must be—" Winter started to say.

But her words were halted by Geth as he sprang up, swiping Ezra into his right hand. Geth slowly opened his fingers and held up his palm. Ezra was not happy—small bits of steam were rising off of his purple tassel.

"You're Ezra," Geth said, holding him up close to his face.

"And you're Geth," Ezra spat.

Geth wiped the spit from his face with his other hand.

"You did this to me," Ezra raged. "Took all the pleasant and left me the rage."

"I don't know what you're talking about."

Two more tanks fired as the scene became complete anarchy. Dennis finally arrived and stopped to stare at Ezra in Geth's hand.

"Jealous?" Ezra snapped.

Dennis looked at Geth. "You must be Geth."

"I am," Geth answered kindly. "This is Phoebe and Winter."

Dennis looked at both of them and his bald white head went even paler.

"And this is, and this is, and this is," Ezra raged. "Who cares who anybody is? The only name that matters is mine because in a few moments you will be dead."

Ezra leapt from Geth's palm and slammed his metal leg directly into his forehead. The leg pierced the skin a good inch before Ezra pulled it out. Geth stumbled backwards but was able to pinch Ezra's tassel and fling him upward. Ezra flew up and then came right back down on Geth, pushing him to the ground and jumping up and down on his chest.

Geth rolled over, catching Ezra off guard and landing on top of him. All around, guns were going off and fights were breaking out.

"Run," Geth yelled to Phoebe and Winter. "Go with Dennis and get somewhere safe."

Geth could feel himself rising from the ground as Ezra lifted him from beneath. Geth began to spin as Ezra twirled him. He spun faster and faster until he flew up and into a platoon of soldiers. Geth knocked all the men and women down and landed on his stomach.

Ezra sprang up from where he was and perched on the edge of a fence, looking down at Geth.

"Had enough?" he screamed.

Geth was shaking his head, trying to regain his composure.

"Oh, really," Ezra said. "Excellent."

Ezra opened his arms and Geth was forced to the ground, unable to move. The deranged toothpick then shot off the fence, holding his arms and legs in and aiming directly for Geth's face. Geth pushed a fallen soldier off of himself and turned his head just in time to have Ezra miss his face and pierce his left earlobe.

Ezra was stuck tight.

Geth stood up, looking around, while Ezra was wedged in his left earlobe looking like a really tacky earring. Geth reached up to feel his ear.

"Hands off," Ezra screamed. "Get me out of here!"

Hordes of beings continued to flow over the downed fences. Some military members tried to stop the flow, but that only made things more heated. Geth was knocked over by a rant being chased by a soldier.

"Pull me out," Ezra screamed again.

Geth stood up. "Not here." He took off running with Ezra still in his ear.

"What are you doing?" Ezra yelled.

Geth leapt over a small concrete wall in the parking lot and up onto a tank that wasn't moving. He jumped off of the tank and over a half-fallen fence.

"What are you running from?" Ezra yelled. "I'm stuck in your ear."

"I'm running until you'll talk to me."

"What?"

"You need to talk to me."

"I need to kill you!" Ezra screamed.

"See," Geth said, "that's not really a motivation to stop."

Geth ran through crowds of protestors who had been picketing the whole idea of strangers coming in from another realm. One lady whacked Geth in the stomach with a sign that read, "Foo is for foo-ls."

Geth gently pushed her aside and jetted down a row of cars and media trucks. Two rows over at the end was a large black S.W.A.T. vehicle. Geth turned and headed directly toward it.

"Ewwww," Ezra yelped. "Ear sweat."

"Sorry," Geth said insincerely.

Ezra spat. "And I keep getting your hair in my mouth."

They reached the S.W.A.T. vehicle, and Geth pulled open the sliding side door and bounded up into the van. Two police officers were inside: One was looking at a computer screen and the other was on the phone. Geth grabbed the officer on the phone and tossed him out the door. Then, before the other officer could react, Geth yanked him up by the shoulders and threw him out the door also. Geth slammed the metal door shut and thrust the lock into place.

The vehicle was all stainless steel inside. There were a couple of computers and rows of empty lockers that had once contained weapons. Geth ran to the back doors and pulled the latch down to secure them. Someone was banging on the side door demanding to be let in.

"What are you doing?" Ezra demanded. "Where's Dennis?"

Geth moved up behind the front driver's seat and tried to lean in to see in the rearview mirror. He couldn't do it, so he pulled out his kilve. He knocked the side of the rearview mirror and sent it flying down into the driver's seat. Geth set his kilve down and picked up the mirror. He held it so that he could see Ezra stuck in his left ear. Ezra's arms were pinned to his side and he was desperately trying to kick at Geth's neck and face.

"Wow," Geth whispered.

"Take a picture," Ezra mocked. "It'll last dumber."

"You're different from what I was," Geth observed.

"You mean stronger?"

"Different," Geth smiled. "I didn't have the cool purple hair or body armor."

"It's nail polish," Ezra barked. "Now, pull me out so I can finish you."

"How come you can't get out yourself?" Geth asked. "You lifted me up."

"My arms are bound," Ezra yelled. "I need my arms."

"Well, then, we should probably work things out while you're still pinned in."

"Work things out?" Ezra gagged. "Unless you're talking about your funeral arrangements, that makes no sense."

Something huge slammed the outside of the vehicle, throwing Geth into the row of empty lockers. He fell to the floor, his head hitting a row of metal cabinets. He stood up, righted himself, and looked for the mirror he had just dropped.

"Looking for this?" Ezra asked.

Ezra was standing on the desk by the computer holding up the mirror.

"Thanks for knocking me loose," Ezra cackled.

"Trust me," Geth replied, "it wasn't on purpose."

Ezra punched the rearview mirror with his right hand. The glass broke into three pieces, and the pieces slid out from the plastic frame. Ezra dropped the frame and picked up one of the pieces of glass. It was twice the size of him. He looked at his reflection and smiled vainly.

"What are—"

Before Geth could get his question out, Ezra threw the piece of mirror at him. It whizzed through the air and lodged itself in Geth's left shoulder.

"Owww," Geth said with surprise.

He looked at the piece of mirror sticking out of his shoulder. A small stream of blood was dripping out from below it. Geth gently took ahold of the glass and slid it out. "What are you doing?"

A second piece of the mirror slammed into Geth's right arm. Geth pulled it out quickly and flung it back at Ezra before he could react. It flew past Ezra and shattered up against the front window.

"Worthless," Ezra screamed, throwing the third piece of mirror.

Geth turned, and the glass stuck into his right leg. He stared at the glass poking out of his leg and tried to look angry. He pulled the piece of mirror out and flung it at Ezra. He missed again, and glass sparkled all over the van.

"I hate you," Ezra yelled.

Geth lunged at Ezra, and Ezra lifted his arms and sent him flying backward into the back doors. Ezra jumped off the desk and onto Geth's neck. He then repeatedly pulled Geth's chin down and slammed Geth's head into the doors.

"You made me what I am," Ezra roared. "And I am angry!"

Geth reached up and wrapped his fingers around the deviant toothpick, trying hard to bind his arms, but Ezra bit back, taking a nice chomp out of Geth's left index finger. Blood squirted everywhere.

Geth reached for his kilve lying on the floor, but Ezra waved his arms and Geth flew to the ceiling as if his backbone was made of metal and the roof of the vehicle was magnetic.

"This is madness," Geth hollered.

"This is what I've been waiting for," Ezra replied, holding up one arm to keep Geth in place. Ezra waved his other hand, and Geth's kilve on the floor began to hover. Ezra waved some more, and the kilve rotated around so that the pointed end was aiming right at Geth's heart. Ezra lowered the kilve as far as he could and then he shot it straight for Geth. Geth twisted just enough for the kilve to miss his stomach and punch a hole through the roof.

"Can't we talk?" Geth yelled.

"No way," Ezra smiled. With a wave of his hand he pulled the kilve back down and shot it up at Geth's neck. Geth was able to bend just enough that the kilve only scraped the side of his neck while making another hole in the ceiling. Ezra pulled the kilve back down and aimed toward Geth's face.

"You shouldn't be doing this," Geth insisted. "What do you think will happen to you if I die?"

The flying kilve stopped short just inches in front of Geth's face.

"What did you say?" Ezra asked.

"What happens to you if I die?"

"I go on to rule the world," Ezra said seriously.

"I don't think so," Geth said. "You're a part of me."

"Don't say that," Ezra growled. "I am my own self."

"Maybe now," Geth said. "But you *were* a part of me, and if you kill me, you will perish."

"I don't believe it," Ezra said.

"There's one way for you to find out."

Something else large hit the side of the vehicle, and Geth wiggled like a piñata on the ceiling.

"We should be out there," Geth said. "We should be helping to bring this to an end. I need your anger."

Ezra put his hands down, and Geth fell to the floor.

"Thanks," Geth said sarcastically.

"You owe me," was Ezra's only reply.

"For what?"

"For not killing you yet."

Geth stood up and dusted off his chest and knees. Somebody else was now banging on the door and there were two cops jumping up trying to get a look through the front window.

"We have to stop this," Geth said, "or in a little over two days everyone will be dead. Including you."

"I can't die," Ezra said.

"You're wrong. Our lives are hooked together."

"I'm tempted to shoot you just to find out," Ezra moaned.

"I need you."

"Save your mush for the ladies," Ezra sniffed.

A bullet struck the front window, leaving a tremendous spider-web in the bullet-proof glass.

"They're trying to get in," Geth said.

"You're as bright as Dennis."

Geth was quiet as what sounded like a dozen people began to bang on the back doors.

"What do you know, anyway?" Ezra asked as if this were a drug deal and knowledge was the drug.

"I know what I've told you," Geth said. "In two more days this will all be over. Every creature will fade and every person will begin to wither away. Four days from now—five, tops—there will be nothing alive but the trees and plants in the ground."

"How do you know?"

"I'm a lithen," Geth said proudly. "We have been taught the consequences since birth."

"And if we do things your way?"

"We travel as fast as we can to meet up with Leven."

"Thumps?" Ezra spat.

Geth nodded as the vehicle rocked back and forth.

"His father's a generic noodle," Ezra observed.

"You know his father?"

"He's not far from here," Ezra sighed. "He's probably in the scuba shop. Wait a second; I was going to kill you."

"But you changed your mind," Geth reminded him.

"You left me with nothing but anger and confusion," Ezra wailed over the sound of some sort of saw cutting through the lock. "I hate everything, and my mind never stops buzzing."

"I'm so sorry," Geth said. "It wasn't me who chopped us up. But if it makes you feel any better, my body fluctuates. I get bigger and smaller, and at certain times my fingers and toes don't match my feet and hands."

"Really?" Ezra smiled. "You're just saying that."

"Not at all," Geth smiled back. "I'm incomplete without you."

"Okay," Ezra said, disgusted. "I'll see if what you're saying is correct. But there's still a good chance I'll kill you in the end."

"Fair enough," Geth agreed. "Now, how do we get out of here?"

"Why get out?" Ezra asked. "The keys are in the ignition."

Geth smiled. "I've never driven."

"How hard can it be?" Ezra asked. "I've seen Dennis do it."

"I'd never pass up the chance to try something new," Geth said.

"I like that about me," Ezra said happily.

Geth jumped behind the wheel and looked for the keys. He put his hand around them and turned as hard as he could. The huge engine roared to life and the banging and screaming on the outside increased.

"Push that stick," Ezra ordered.

The large vehicle jumped forward two feet.

"Now press that skinny pedal. Hard."

Geth jammed his foot down on the gas, and the massive vehicle seemed to fly forward. Geth plowed into the back end of an expensive-looking car and then swerved to avoid running over two hundred people.

"Is there a way to stop?" Geth asked.

"Yes," Ezra answered. "But why would we want to? Go that direction, to that white building—and keep your foot down on the pedal."

Geth kept the vehicle pointed toward the scuba shop. He moved around cars and rioting creatures. He made it around two news vans and straightened out.

"The building's coming," Geth yelled. "How do I stop?"

"Hold on," Ezra insisted.

The scuba shop was getting closer and closer. It was ringed with tanks and soldiers.

"I don't want to run anyone over, or run into a tank."

"Hold on," Ezra ordered.

"It's right there," Geth motioned. "In front of us."

"Hold," Ezra said.

The scuba shop was one hundred feet away.

"Now," Ezra said calmly. "Push the other pedal as hard as you can."

Geth took his foot off of the gas and slammed it down on the brake. The gigantic vehicle squealed and then spun in a circle, throwing dust up in nuclear-sized clouds. Geth could feel one side of the vehicle lifting up and the wheels chirping madly as they came to a stop. The vehicle shook for a few seconds and then settled.

Ezra nodded toward the lock on the front door. Geth pulled it back and the door opened. There was a tank two inches away.

"Driving a car's even more fun than I thought it would be," Geth said happily.

"Yeah, it looks easy," Ezra replied.

Ezra jumped from the back of the seat onto Geth's right shoulder. "I still might kill you," he said honestly.

"I appreciate the warning." Geth stepped out of the vehicle and headed into the scuba shop.

CHAPTER TWENTY-NINE

THE RESIDUE OF A
LIFE WELL LIVED

Nighttime on Alder was as spectacular and scary as one might imagine. The sky was very dark despite there being two moons out. And every sound seemed bigger and more ominous than the last. Leven and Clover had been walking the entire day and now had decided to stop and get some sleep.

They had set up camp near a small lake on the side of a mountain. Clover was in charge of gathering wood, but he kept becoming attached to the sticks and logs he found and he wouldn't let Leven burn them. So Leven gathered some wood himself while Clover fished around in his void for something for them to eat.

Leven came back to the camp with an armful of logs.

Clover "ahhhhed."

"Don't look at them," Leven insisted. "Because even if you fall in love with those logs, I'm burning them."

"Fine," Clover said. "I hope you're hungry."

"Starving."

Clover handed Leven two Filler Crisps and a small white stick. Leven looked at the stick and waited for an explanation.

"What?" Clover asked. "Finish that and I'll get you more."

"Finish what?"

"Just lick it," Clover insisted.

"No way."

Clover sighed. "Look." Clover began to lick the end of the stick as if there were a sucker there. "It doesn't do anything; it just tastes like whatever you're hungry for."

Leven stuck the stick in his mouth and sucked. "I don't taste anything."

"You don't suck the stick," Clover laughed. "You have to pretend there's candy on the end."

Leven put the stick in his mouth and pretended it was a sucker.

"They're good, aren't they?" Clover slurped.

"I still can't taste anything," Leven complained.

"Try the other end."

Leven tried licking the other end of the white stick. "Nothing."

"That's weird," Clover said. "Here, let me see yours."

Leven handed Clover his sucker. Clover looked at it and took a pretend lick.

"Oh, this is just a stick," Clover said. He then reached into his void and finally fished out another Phantom Pop.

Leven reluctantly grabbed it and took a small lick. His gold eyes went wide and he smiled tall. "Not bad."

Leven built a big fire and the two of them lay back on their robes looking at the stars and sucking on their suckers.

"I'm worried about Geth and Winter."

"They're probably worried about us, too," Clover pointed out.

"Two days left and I don't feel like we're anywhere closer to saving Foo," Leven complained. "It's like we've been placed aside while my body goes whacky."

"Maybe it's not you that saves Foo," Clover sucked. "Maybe fate just needed you out of the way."

"So all this was for nothing?"

"Even nothing's for something," Clover said wisely.

"What?" Leven questioned.

"I don't know," Clover shrugged. "It just sounds like something Geth would say, doesn't it?"

"Go to sleep."

Thirty seconds later Clover was snoring.

Leven listened carefully to the night, his mind refusing to shut off. Every noise and breeze caused his heart to beat a little bit faster. He shifted up onto his elbows as his feet burned. He felt like he wanted to run fast, to see how far he could go without stopping.

The trees in front of him rustled.

"Who's there?"

There was no answer, just the sounds of Clover snoring and the small crackle of fire. Leven sensed something brush over him, and suddenly the orange fire was burning blue. The change of color made the small campsite feel closed and secure. Leven looked at the fire and was reminded of the den of the dead and his visits from his mother and Antsel.

"Mom?" he whispered, and instantly small flecks of light drifted down from the dark sky and began to cluster near Leven. "I know

I'm supposed to speak of you, but I know so little. You were named Maria." The soft bits of light stacked up higher and higher.

Leven sat up completely and babbled on about anything he knew about his mother, knowing that in the den of the dead, people only appeared if you spoke of them.

"I think you had dark hair," Leven went on. "And Addy was your half sister but you never really lived with her. And you married my father, but something went wrong."

The bits continued to build. The shape wasn't as clear as before, but Leven could make out that it was a person in a robe. More lights floated down as the head took shape. She was turned away from Leven, but as the last bits settled she began to spin and face him.

Leven's heart was beating so quickly he thought it was going to splatter internally.

"Hello, Leven." It wasn't his mom.

"Antsel?"

Antsel nodded and reached out to touch Leven's shoulder.

"I wasn't talking about you," Leven pointed out.

Antsel smiled. "This may feel like the den of the dead, but it isn't."

Clover snored loudly and turned over.

"What're you doing here?" Leven said, feeling disappointed.

"I came to warn you."

"Of what?"

"Between ten and eleven, he will attack."

"Who?"

"It will be the last stand for him," Antsel said.

"I don't understand."

"You're almost there," Antsel said. "What an accomplishment you are."

"I've done nothing," Leven said angrily. "What I want is to get off this island and to be with Geth and Winter."

"You'll understand," Antsel said kindly.

"I've been shelved."

"Look how passionate you are," Antsel observed. "From a boy to a warrior—perfect."

"Let me fight," Leven begged.

"Clear your life and you will fight," Antsel insisted. "You have no idea how powerful a settled soul is. It is necessary that you have no inner conflict. Now, between ten and eleven."

"Tonight?" Leven asked desperately.

The flame flickered back to orange and the speckled outline of Antsel was gone.

Clover mumbled in his sleep, "I'm a lot taller than I look."

"Ahhh," Leven said to himself, lying back down. "If I ever get off this island, I'm going to have it buried."

Leven closed his eyes and tried to see the future.

CHAPTER THIRTY

KARMA

There are few things more miraculous than a new day. Nothing wipes away the concern of yesterday like a good sleep and the promise of tomorrow. It's amazing how heavy and impossible something might be at night, but the next morning you're wondering why you ever worried. It doesn't matter where I am or what I'm doing, there's always something magical about starting again.

I remember when I was in China once, I had spent the night answering questions that I didn't want to answer and being treated as if I were a spy. That was a dark night. But I also remember the next morning, when I was escorted out of my cell and taken to a bus, how the sunlight shone off the front of the bus and the smell and sounds of a new day almost made everything better. Of course, getting free also required a pair of smuggled tweezers, a car filled with priests, and one well-timed train accident. But I'm not sure I would have felt so happy if it had not all gone down during the dawning of a new day.

Well, unfortunately, Reality had seen its last regularly scheduled dawn for a while. Our single moon couldn't decide if it should go up, down, or sideways, and the sun was acting sluggish and depressed.

"What's up with the sky?" Janet asked.

"What's up with the world?" Tim countered.

They were currently in their stolen blue jeep going over a hundred miles an hour down a road heading north. The highway was filled with other cars whose occupants had long given up on the speed limit.

Thick patches of sarus flew across the sky, and Tim watched as one of those patches descended on a car and lifted it right up off of the road. The sky behind the sarus was changing different colors and appeared to be rolling from side to side.

Tim looked in his rearview mirror at Osck and Janet. He wanted so badly for it to just be the lighting, but he could tell they were fading. Janet caught him looking.

"What?" she asked.

"Are you two okay?"

"I feel sick," Osck said. "I move my arms, but they don't feel like they belong to me. And my body hurts because Janet's changing shades. They were right, weren't they?"

"What are you talking about?" Tim asked. "Who was right?"

"Those who fought against Azure," Osck said. "We shouldn't be here. We're dying."

Tim was silent as the car continued to race forward.

"We could go back," Tim suggested. "But I'm afraid we would

never get through the entrance. There are probably still hundreds coming through."

"I can't go back," Janet said. "I have to see myself."

"But . . ." Osck started to say.

"I have to see myself before I fade," Janet insisted. "I need to tell myself what I've learned and make sure that I understand about Winter."

"I don't know how much time we have," Tim said.

"Then I want to die trying." Janet looked at Osck.

"It's a fair plan," he said, smiling at her.

Tim pulled off the road and raced into a service station. Two short men inside were intently listening to a radio. They looked at Tim as if he were a salesman peddling something they didn't want any part of.

"Stay in the back," Tim whispered to Janet and Osck. "I'm not sure what these people will think of you."

Tim stepped out of the car and in through the open door. "Hello."

One man nodded.

"Would it be possible to buy some gas?" Tim asked.

"You got cash?" the fatter one asked.

Tim nodded.

"Where you heading to?" the other asked. "There's a war going on."

"I know," Tim said. "I'm just trying to get home before it gets messier."

The radio was talking about windy telts messing with the Golden Gate Bridge. All three of them listened for a few moments and then shivered.

"Well, then, help yourself," the fatter man said. "I ain't going to charge a man trying to get home to his family during the end of the world."

"Yeah," the other one agreed. "What if that karma stuff's for real?"

"Then this should cover me," the fatter clerk smiled.

Tim filled up the car and sped off. As he was making his way to the main road, a giant avaland tore across the opposite road and missed hitting Tim head-on by two feet. The avaland wiggled under the road, sending another car rolling.

Tim swerved and drove faster.

"Did you see that?" Tim asked. "I hope we make it."

Tim looked at Osck and Janet in his rearview mirror. They were huddled together and trembling.

"I must be on drugs," Tim said to himself. "The world's falling apart, and here I am chauffeuring a ghost and a man made of fire."

"What about me?" Swig asked, materializing in the passenger's seat.

Tim looked down in amazement.

"Swig," Tim cheered. "I thought you were out."

"I was," Swig answered. "But I got to thinking how helpless you all were without me and I thought it just might be the right decision to tag along."

"You've been here the whole time?"

Swig nodded while reaching up to put his seat belt on. He clicked it and smoothed out his fur. "Can't this thing go any faster?"

Tim pushed the gas pedal all the way down and flew.

CHAPTER THIRTY-ONE

MAYBE JUST A BITE

This day looks better than yesterday," Clover said cheerfully as he hopped from moss-covered stone to moss-covered stone.

"Really?" Leven replied. "That's because you slept well. All I see is trees and rocks and . . . oh, look, there's some more trees."

"Where?" Clover asked, excited.

"Seriously," Leven said. "It's beginning to feel a little hopeless. I'd give anything to see Geth and Winter and have them point the way."

"They're not the Want," Clover pointed out. "And you have a path to follow. I bet even if they *were* here pointing, you would stick to the path."

Leven stopped and stared at Clover. "When did you get so wise?"

"Probably school," Clover answered. "I had a really good

teacher—Professor Winsnicker. He said he was the smartest teacher Foo's ever had."

"Wow," Leven said, smiling.

"So who do you think's up ahead?" Clover asked, springing from the ground to Leven's right shoulder.

"You know, I've thought about it, and I kind of never really squared things off with that Phoebe girl."

"Oh," Clover cooed. "Nice one."

"What?" Leven said defensively. "I'm not kidding. I mean, I unlocked her cage and that was it."

"And how would you finish that?" Clover asked. "With a big kiss?"

"Forget it," Leven said, frustrated. "I was just saying."

"No," Clover replied. "I can't wait to tell Winter about what you were just saying."

"I take back everything I ever mentioned about you being wise."

The glass path widened as they came to the edge of a massive river. Leven could barely see across to the other side. He stood there with Clover on top of his head staring at the swift-moving water.

"I still don't like water," Leven said.

"Really?" Clover asked, surprised. "It's so refreshing."

"I like to drink it," Leven clarified. "But I don't like to be in it."

"Well, that is a lot of water," Clover observed.

"Thanks."

"And look," Clover pointed. "There's a bunch of oaf fish."

"Are they bad?" Leven asked, trying to see what Clover was pointing at. "You mean those huge black things?

Clover nodded.

"They look like whales."

"Well, do you think any of your Wave friends are in this river?" Clover asked.

Leven called out, but nobody answered.

"Interesting," Clover said.

"What is?"

"Well, it's just interesting how those Waves aren't here but I am," Clover said.

"Interesting and lucky," Leven replied, lifting Clover off of his head.

"So," Clover asked, "how are we getting across?"

"Maybe we're not supposed to cross it," Leven suggested.

"Nice try."

"How deep do you think it is?" Leven asked.

"I have no idea," Clover answered. "You could wade into it and find out, but stay away from the fish." Clover paused to stare at Leven's hands. "Are you okay? Does the water really make you sweaty?"

"I don't know," Leven said, wiping sweat off his forehead. "I don't feel right. My hands feel all tingly—and look at my fingers."

Leven held up his hands and showed them to Clover. There was a strange sharpness to his mitts. Whereas his fingers were normally round on the edges, they now had sharper, squared-off corners and ends.

"Weird," Clover said.

"It started this morning," Leven admitted. "I was kind of hoping it would wear off."

"You don't want that to wear off," Clover said kindly. "We

sycophants are supposed to help you develop your gifts. The thing is, you have so many gifts I forget that more could be coming."

"This is a gift?" Leven asked, holding up his hands.

"You'll learn how to control it," Clover said. "So your hands won't look like that when you don't want them to, like when you're at the prom. You can make them normal."

"Again with the prom."

"You only get one," Clover said defensively.

"So what kind of gift is this?" Leven asked.

"Remember when you were fighting the Ring of Plague and that one nit fell off the onick and then dug himself into the soil and popped back out at you?"

"Kind of," Leven admitted.

"You can burrow," Clover said. "Try it."

Leven bent down and thrust his hands into the ground. Large swatches of dirt effortlessly twisted around his hands and arms as if he were a drill bit.

"Now pull back," Clover instructed.

Leven pulled his arms back and there, with almost no effort, was a nice round hole big enough for him to crawl through.

"Wow," Leven whispered. "Are you thinking what I'm thinking?"

"About the prom?"

Leven's eyes glowed gold. "No, we could just tunnel under the river."

Clover liked the idea. So much so that he smiled and began to dance anxiously on Leven's left shoulder. "Do it."

Leven stepped off the path and bent down at the side of the river. He thrust his hands into the dirt as deep as he could. The soil seemed to magically twist up around him and gather behind. He shifted his position and dug deeper. The movement was new to him, but it felt natural. His ability to see through soil made it possible for him to see where he was going and just how deep the river was. Unfortunately for Leven, just because he had the gift of burrowing didn't make him an engineer. And any self-respecting engineer could have seen that Leven was burrowing way too close to the river.

Leven burrowed ten feet down and started to angle farther.

When he got twenty feet down, the weight of the water against the walls of his tunnel became too great. The walls began to crack and water crashed in, filling the tunnel and sucking Leven out into the river.

"I hate water," Leven gagged as he was swept up into the heart of the river.

Leven heard Clover hollering something about how the world needed water to live. He also felt the pull of water carrying him deeper down into the river. Fat oaf fish smacked up against him, and his arm scratched against a large, jagged rock. Leven tried to relax, hoping he might have the gift of breathing underwater, but his lungs began to burn violently. He clawed his way to the surface, got two breaths of air, and was pulled down under again.

Leven kicked and pulled at the heavy robe he was wearing. It felt like a mushy chain pulling him down. He pulled out his kilve and wriggled out of his robe.

He let the robe go as his lungs began to burn again. He pushed his head above the water and sucked in air as quickly as he could. In his mind he pleaded for the Baadyn to come save him, or for

Garnock to wash up underneath him and carry him to safety. But nobody came to his rescue.

Leven hit a huge rock and was propelled upward. His body shot out of the water, and he was able to gulp down some air before he was slapped back into some surging rapids. The river became deeper, and there was no sign of any sides or bottom.

Another huge fish bumped into him, biting his right side. He couldn't see the fish clearly, but it looked like a big, dark ball. A different and even larger fish came up from below and completely swallowed Leven's legs.

Leven kicked as hard as he could and stabbed the fish with his kilve. The fish let go, and Leven sprang to the top of the river, desperately gasping for air. As soon as his lungs were filled he was pulled back under by a twisting current.

Two huge fish squeezed around him as he moved into the middle of a school of whale-sized oaf fish. Leven stabbed one that was coming at him and punched another as his lungs began to scream for air again. Leven kicked off a particularly huge oaf fish and paddled for the surface.

He was too slow.

The large fish opened its mouth and with one smooth gulp swallowed Leven.

Leven's eyes glowed strong. It was suddenly quiet, and he could see he was inside a large stomach. There was some air to breathe, but it wasn't the kind of fresh air you joyfully suck in. It was more the rotten, foul, Dumpster kind of air that you desperately try to blow out. Leven wobbled about as the fish swam up and down in the river. He tried to pry open the fish's throat or mouth with his kilve, but the opening he had come through was sealed shut.

A trickling, hissing sound could be heard.

Leven looked down to see that small holes in the bottom of the fish's stomach were beginning to ooze. Leven touched some of the ooze with his right foot, and instantly the plastic on his shoes began to melt. The smell of hot plastic added to the other unpleasant aromas.

"I'm going to be digested," Leven moaned, banging hard on the inside of the fish.

The hissing got louder and stronger as the bile filled the stomach from the bottom up. Leven jammed his kilve into one side of the fish's stomach and then pushed it so that it was wedged up against the other, creating a bar across the whole stomach. Leven lay across that bar watching the bile rise.

"Clover?"

There was no answer.

Leven foraged frantically in his pocket. His fingers brushed up against the Filler Crisps Clover had given him earlier.

Leven smiled.

He took the two crackers out of his pocket and crumbled them in his hands. He then dropped all of the crumbs into the bile. Instantly the crackers began to whine and expand, and foam pressed up against Leven.

"Open your mouth," Leven yelled at the fish. "Open your mouth!"

The foam pushed up and around Leven.

"Spit me out!"

The foam filled Leven's nose and mouth and ears, pressing in on him tightly and squeezing him up against the inside of the fish.

Once again Leven couldn't breathe, but this time it was because of foam.

The Filler Crisps continued to expand.

Leven could feel his nose being pushed inward and his body being crammed into one tight ball. The pressure against his ears was so great that his head began to pound and ring. It took all the strength he had to move his hands over his ears. He wanted to scream, but there was no room for it. It felt as if his entire body were being pumped like a blood-pressure test.

The pressure was too great.

Leven's eyes were pushing in, his stomach was being shoved up into his ribs, and he had foam in places where foam should never be as the Filler Crisps filled the fish's stomach well beyond capacity.

Four seconds before the pressure would have collapsed all his organs, a tremendous explosion rocked his ears and Leven felt himself flying through the air. His body slammed down against something hard, and then there was nothing but sweet relief and a dizzying unconsciousness.

ii

"You're off course," a strong voice said.

"Is he?" another voice questioned. "Or is this how it was meant to be?"

"You might want to get up," Clover whispered into Leven's right ear.

Leven blinked and then coughed. He pressed his palms into the dirt and pushed his chest up off the ground. His long, dark hair hung down in front of his face and covered his glowing eyes. Leven got onto his knees and then sprang up as if he were a child. He pushed back his hair and partially smiled. The landscape was covered with snow, and Leven brushed some of it off his arms.

"We were just talking about you."

Before Leven stood the Ring of Plague—twelve nits, each with a different one of Foo's twelve gifts. The last time Leven had seen them he had been fighting them from the back of an onick outside of Cork. Now they were standing still, almost as if waiting for him to say something.

"You're shorter than I remember," Leven finally said, standing up straight and measuring at least two inches taller than the tallest ring member.

"You've become legendary," one of the Ring members said. "I don't suppose you remember me, but you left me floating in the maze of air in Fissure Gorge."

"Sorry," Leven apologized.

"No apology necessary," the Ring member insisted. "I'm just happy that fate has pulled me out so that we can finish our business."

Leven reached for his kilve, but it was not there. He also wasn't wearing his robe.

"Wait a second," Leven said. "How did I get here?"

"Um, the tunnel you were digging collapsed," Clover said. "And you were taken downriver. I couldn't find you, but then there was this huge explosion and foam was shooting up everywhere and I saw you get blown up out of the river. After that it was pretty easy to find you."

Leven looked down and for the first time realized it wasn't snow he was standing in and brushing off, it was foam mixed with what looked like fish bits.

"I was inside a huge fish," Leven said, disgusted.

"Is this him?" Clover asked, picking up a scaly piece of skin.

"You have a strange life, Leven," one of the Ring members observed.

Leven felt an odd pang of pride from such a comment. If someone from Foo thought he had an unusual life, that was really saying something.

"And now you are my unfinished business?" Leven said. He spotted his kilve five trees over in the top branches of a tree. "Clover."

"I'm on it," Clover replied.

A Ring member with a long, braided beard saw what Leven was looking at and held up his palm. "You won't need that with us. Were we to have met three days ago, we might have desired to fight you, but we know now that you were right."

"I was?" Leven asked in amazement.

"Can't you feel Foo failing?" Beardy asked.

"I thought it was just me," Leven said. "I've been going through a lot of changes."

"No dreams come in any longer," Beardy said.

"That, I've noticed."

Clover knocked Leven's kilve from the tree and it came crashing down.

"And so many are leaving that we fear there will be nobody here to sustain Foo," Beardy added. "Even those who believed in Foo are making a run for it. Beings from the farthest corners of Foo are figuring their only chance is to make it to Reality. The Sochemists are gone, Cusp and Cork have no law, and the siids are dying—fading away, actually. Can you imagine a being so big fading away?"

Leven shook his head as Clover dragged his kilve over to him. Leven bent down and picked it up.

"You've been washed downriver," Beardy said. "We were to meet near the path of glass. Now you must move that direction and make up time."

"What about you?" Leven asked.

"The Dearth still holds us," Beardy said. "I speak for myself, but my soul is soon his. Look: We are bound to him."

Beardy held up the hem of his robe to expose his feet meshing with the soil. His ankles looked like mossy stumps.

"Can't you stop it?" Leven asked.

"We have given away all our freedom by pretending that we had nothing to worry about," Beardy said. "We were supposed to be an indestructible force, but in the end we have changed nothing for the better, and our souls belong to the soil."

"No," Leven insisted.

"What do you mean *no?*" Beardy said, confused.

"There's always a chance to turn from what you've become. I've seen people become better seconds before their dying breath."

"It is not our fate."

"Then let's change things," Leven urged.

Leven lunged forward with his kilve. Then, with one swift move, he spun and smacked Beardy on the side of his right shoulder. Beardy flew sideways as Leven charged him. Leven threw his weight into him and hoisted him off the ground, ripping his feet from the soil. Beardy screamed, but Leven jumped up on top of a large, flat rock and held him there. He kicked and hollered for a while, but eventually he stopped wailing and lay still.

Leven looked down at the other eleven Ring members. They were trembling, but they hadn't moved.

"He was our leader," one with blue stripes on his cheeks said.

"Well, he wants you to stay still."

They all just stood there as Leven climbed down from the rocky shelf. Leven then wrapped his arms around the one with blue stripes and, with one terrific pull, tore him from the ground. He screamed louder than the last one had. Leven carried him up onto the rock and held him down by Beardy, who was passed out. Once he was subdued, Leven turned and looked down at the remaining ten.

"He was second in command," a Ring member with really bad teeth said.

"Can none of you think for yourself?"

They all shrugged.

"It's hard to believe anyone ever feared you."

Leven tore out another, and another, and another, and another. He then took a break so that Clover could show him an odd-shaped bickerwick. Leven then went back to plucking up Ring members. Each one screamed louder than the last, and in the end Leven was exhausted, but he had before him a row of twelve beings with raw, swollen feet and clear souls. Most of them had passed out due to the pain of being ripped from the soil.

"We'll let them rest," Leven said. "So let's sleep here."

"That will leave us just one day," Clover said casually. "And you're off track."

"I'm exhausted. Besides, I want to make sure these twelve are clearheaded."

"You're the boss," Clover said. "Hey, do you think if you ever left me that I would just stand around like that not knowing what to do?"

"I'd never leave you," Leven smiled.

Clover did a little jig and then disappeared while Leven quickly bound the hands and feet of each Ring member to make sure they stayed in place.

CHAPTER THIRTY-TWO

OKLAHOMA BOUND

S anta Rosa, New Mexico, was a mess. All over there were fires and fights breaking out. Some vehicles were racing to get to the scene; others were racing to escape it. The air was filled with twice as many helicopters as before, and there was no semblance of law down below. Every fence and tent had been torn down while jeeps and cars had been tipped over or torn apart.

The government had tried to stop the flow of Foovians coming in, but that had just created panic, and greater numbers were spilling out mad and ready to fight. And on top of that, all the commotion had attracted any avaland or telt from miles away to come join the party.

It was complete chaos, and there was no sign of it slowing.

Dennis had taken Winter and Phoebe to the secured scuba shop, where they had waited for Geth to return. When Geth did come in with Ezra on his shoulder, only Dennis was surprised.

"I thought you were going to kill him," Dennis said to Ezra.

"Has your face always been so bland?" Ezra asked Dennis.

"It was your plan," Dennis said boldly.

"Well, maybe I'm just drawing them in to my confidence," Ezra whispered.

"Are you?"

"No," Ezra said.

General Lank looked about as desperate as a man can look. What was supposed to be his big chance had turned into the beginning of the end of the world. He kept asking Ezra and Dennis what he should do and radioing important people who were dealing with things falling apart in their own parts of the world.

"What do we do?" Lank said as he paced the room. He stopped in front of Geth. "Well, what do we do?"

"I know what *we* have to do," Geth said. "We're going to Oklahoma."

"The play?" General Lank asked.

Elton Thumps hit his head with his palm and screamed.

"See what I've been dealing with?" Ezra asked Geth. "Total and complete incompetence."

Ever since Geth and Ezra had returned, Ezra had begun to see the value of having part of him be a big man. He was also quite impressed with how handsome he was. And when Phoebe held onto Geth's arm and looked him over to make sure he was okay, Ezra kind of felt like she was talking to him.

"Dennis," Geth said kindly, "will you come with us?"

Dennis looked at Ezra. "Are we on the good side now?"

Ezra screamed, "Can't you think for yourself? Your brain's as smooth as your forehead."

"All right," Dennis said, embarrassed. "We'll come with you."

"We'll?" Ezra questioned. "You got a gimped-up monkey in your pocket? There's no 'we'll' any longer. I'm with me."

"Okay," Geth said nicely. "But 'we'll' need everyone."

"Not me," Elton insisted. "Don't count on me."

Geth didn't have the heart to tell him he wasn't really invited anyhow.

"I'm going down through that empty lake and into Foo if it kills me," Elton announced.

"Let's hope it kills you," Ezra said.

"You won't succeed," General Lank said. "There are just too many still coming out, and the tunnel's probably packed with thousands behind those thousands."

"I'll go by myself," Elton growled. He grabbed his stomach and mumbled something about Leven.

"Suit yourself," General Lank moaned. "Your presence has always been a joke."

"What?" Elton said angrily.

"This mess is because of you," General Lank accused. "You were supposed to understand what was happening."

"I do understand what's happening," Elton replied. "You're looking for a scapegoat, you old fool."

"You're useless," General Lank said. "They needed you because of your son and now you have no way—"

"Hold it," Winter insisted. "This isn't helping anything. You two can argue later if you want, but for now Geth and I are going to Oklahoma."

"I don't understand, but fine," Lank said.

"So," Geth asked, "where's Oklahoma?"

Lank reluctantly pointed east.

"And do you have a helicopter we can borrow?" Geth added.

General Lank put his head in his hands and began to sob.

"I like my style," Ezra cheered.

Phoebe gazed up at Geth and smiled. "Is Reality always this exciting?"

Geth, Dennis, Ezra, General Lank, and Elton all began to answer Phoebe's question as she sat there looking beautiful.

Lilly sighed and whispered into Winter's left ear, "Is she for real?"

"She gets worse," Winter whispered back.

Geth stood up and picked up his kilve. He slipped it behind his back. "Now, about that helicopter, General."

General Lank waved a tall soldier over as Lilly continued to whisper in Winter's ear. "I've never flown before," she said excitedly.

"Me neither," Winter said back.

Lilly wrapped her arms around Winter's neck and smiled for the first time in a very long while.

ii

Elton Thumps was sick of it—sick of it. His whole body burned with the feeling of hate and darkness. He had spent his entire adult life studying, investigating, and wondering about Foo, and still he had nothing to show for it. He was bitter and resolved to the fact that if it had not been for Foo he would have still had his wife, his child, and possibly his self-respect.

Now he had nothing but a blackness in the gut.

General Lank had finally said what everyone was thinking: Elton Thumps was a joke and a failure. The government had used him for their purposes and now, when the chips were down, they were ready to leave him by the side of the road and pretend he had never happened.

Elton unbuttoned his shirt and looked at his stomach. Large black scratches were pulsating and oozing. He looked away and quickly buttoned his shirt back up.

Elton rummaged through the scuba shop and found a couple of guns. He then threw on a military jacket, a helmet, and the most rugged boots he could find. He loaded the jacket pockets with food and ammo and left without saying a word to General Lank.

Once outside the scuba shop, Elton moved through the rings of guards and tanks and worked his way over to Blue Hole Lake. The empty lake was still spewing out hundreds of strange creatures and beings like a volcano. Elton worked his way to a steeper spot where there wasn't anybody climbing out at the moment. It worked for a little bit and he was able to climb down the back wall of the empty lake. Then the flow of refugees was just too great and too strong for him to continue forward.

Hundreds of beings were crawling over each other frantically trying to get out. Those climbing out seemed to realize that things were falling apart. Many had weapons ready and were already looking for someone to fight.

Elton turned around and moved in reverse. Walking backwards, he squeezed himself down through the opening and into the cavern, but a huge woman carrying a crying child in her right arm pushed him back out and kicked him down.

Elton tried again, but there were too many people and odd-looking beings coming out. He tried to be forceful, ordering those who were about to trample him to make room for him to climb down.

Nobody was listening.

Elton attempted to dive between people and crawl his way into the watery cavern, but he was forced out again by a thick group of huge rants who had linked arms and were plowing through everyone.

Elton pulled out his gun and waved it around. Nobody seemed to care—the refugees just kept coming and coming, wave after wave of frantic and excited beings. Some looked scared, some looked anxious, and others looked as if they were out for blood, here to fight for their place in Reality.

Elton fired his weapon into the roof of the cavern. Everyone in the cavern stopped, while those already in the empty lake scrambled out.

"That's better," Elton said. "I've got to get back behind you all. Now, move!"

Apparently no one was in the mood to cooperate. They surged forward again, trampling Elton, walking over him as if he were a rug. He dropped the gun and it slid to the far side of the cavern. Elton tried to reach for it, but it was no use.

Feet rained down on him in the face, the neck, the stomach. Elton tried to scream, but nobody cared. Feet just kept pounding down on him. Then, as if someone had pulled the plug on the tunnel, the walls of water collapsed inward, washing over everything and pushing out all the air. Deep in the tunnel the door slammed shut, and everybody unfortunate enough to still be in the passageway was enveloped in water and darkness.

Working toward Foo had been a really bad idea.

CHAPTER THIRTY-THREE

FAIR FIGHT

Leven tossed and turned, trying to catch a few last minutes of early-morning sleep. The bed of leaves he had made up on a rock shelf was not half as comfortable as he wished it would be. Each time he turned over, it sounded like someone or something was creeping up on him.

Clover was bothered as well. "Can't you stay still?" he whispered. "You're making me jumpy."

"You're always jumpy."

"Still," Clover insisted. "This is different."

The members of the Ring of Plague had initially all passed out from the pain of being ripped up from the contact with the Dearth. But as they had come to, they had begun to complain and fuss over Leven's insisting that they stay on rock. They were like some horrible drug addicts who were bad at lying; they kept making up stories to get a chance to reconnect with the soil. Leven had kept them tied up through the night.

Beardy, it turned out, was named Glen, and was originally from Canada. He had been snatched into Foo over thirty years ago and had been made a member of the Ring of Plague about ten years back.

Now that Foo was falling apart, he was confused and worried and aware that those he had worked with had been wrong. But they had spent so much time being influenced, mindlessly doing as they were told, that they now felt a bit adrift. After being detached from the soil for a number of hours, however, they all began to feel incredible. Their heads were clear and they could think for themselves for the first time in a while.

Leven and Clover had slept thirty feet away, but they could now hear the Ring members talking. Leven staggered up and wordlessly untied them, then dragged himself back to his leaf bed.

"You were pretty cool with them," Clover said softly to Leven.

"What?" Leven asked.

"I mean, the way you ripped them out of the ground last night and threw them over there. I wish Winter and Geth had been here to see that."

"I just lifted them up," Leven said modestly.

"Listen to you," Clover waved. "So humble."

"Look at the air this morning," Leven whispered. "There're no dreams at all anymore. I barely got a chance to start seeing them and now they're gone. It sort of makes me mad."

"Yeah, you said that in your sleep."

"I did?"

"That and some stuff about Winter."

"I don't believe you," Leven smiled.

"It's true," Clover insisted. "Of course, maybe you were talking about winter, the season."

"Maybe," Leven laughed. "Do you see how the horizon is slanted?"

Clover nodded.

"So many of our inhabitants have left Foo."

"And that's why the ground is kind of tipping?"

"Yeah, and it's going to get worse," Leven predicted.

"Do you think Geth and Winter made it out?"

"I hope so," Leven said. "They should be on their way to Oklahoma by now."

"It's a nice place," Clover remembered. "I like those burgers from that one store."

"Now all we need is to be there," Leven said. "It's weird, when I close my eyes I can see myself fighting there, but I have no idea how *that* future is going to come about. I'm here."

"Well, you're almost to the tree," Clover tried.

"How do you know?"

"Look at the sky," Clover pointed. "If you squint, you can almost see a center of it where everything radiates out. The oldest tree stands directly below that center."

Leven looked carefully. "That's not too bad. We should get going."

"Fine with me," Clover said. "I can sleep a bit more on your head." He turned to the twelve nits, who were still discussing their options. "What about them?" he asked.

"Their future is theirs," Leven said.

"You think they'll keep to the stone?"

Leven nodded and sat up as the Ring of Plague began talking louder. Something was bothering them.

"Hey," Glen said, "where'd you come from?"

Leven stood up and listened.

"Who do you think we are?" another Ring member said. "We used to be respected."

Leven walked around the trees that divided their camps and up to the stone ledge. He could see a middle-aged man being taunted by the Ring of Plague. The man's clothes were soaked.

"This is our space," Glen insisted.

"I'm . . ." the man tried to say.

"You're what?" Leven asked.

"I'm trying to figure out how I got here," the man said angrily, turning to face Leven. "I was working my way down into the cavern when suddenly I was swirling though the air and slammed down here. So this is Foo? Or am I still in Reality?"

Leven looked closely at the stranger. He saw the dark hair and the strong chin and the eyes and knew exactly who he was talking to.

"And why were you working your way toward Foo?" Leven asked, his body shaking slightly.

"I had to see it," the man insisted. "I'm somewhat of an authority on it."

"Really?"

The man stood up and straightened his wet shirt and tie. He held onto his stomach as if it were a package.

"Listen," he demanded, "I've got important business here. I insist you take me to someone in the know."

"Someone in the know?" Leven questioned.

"Like your king, or your president."

"We don't have any of those," Leven said.

"So who runs this place?"

"Well," Leven said coolly, "dreams used to. But now that so many of ours have slipped into Reality, we're in chaos."

"And who are you?" the man asked snidely.

Leven looked at him and let his gold eyes shine. "I'm your son, Leven."

If Leven was thinking something wonderful was going to happen, he was dead wrong. If he suspected that his father might open his arms and embrace him, he was misguided. And if he thought his dad was going to begin crying and beg for forgiveness—well, he must have been really surprised when Elton jumped forward and hit him as hard as he could beneath the jaw. Leven teetered and then righted himself. He rubbed his jaw and looked at his father.

"Nice to meet you, too."

Elton Thumps just stood there flexing his fists and staring directly at Leven. His face was red and he looked like he could bite through metal. The Ring of Plague sat there watching in shock.

"What was that for?" Leven added. "*I* should be hitting *you*."

Elton took another swing, his body shaking. Leven ducked and punched him right in the stomach. Elton screamed. He bent over and then spun around, kicking Leven in the side of the head. Leven shifted and missed the brunt of the blow. Elton spun again, and this time Leven intercepted his foot as it was coming around to kick the other side of his face. Leven squeezed Elton's foot and pushed him back. Elton had to hop on his one foot trying desperately to pull his other one free.

"What are you doing?" Leven demanded.

"You've ruined my entire life," Elton shouted, his body sick from the Dearth's bite. "You killed Maria and left me for dead."

"What?" Leven asked, confused. "I was a baby."

"It makes no difference."

"I think it does," Leven said. "You abandoned me."

"They took me from you," Elton said. "They took me from you and made me spend the next fourteen years of my life trying to figure you out."

"Well, then, attack them," Leven said adamantly.

Elton twisted his captured foot and his shoe popped off, freeing him. He charged toward Leven and slammed into his waist. The two of them flew backwards and onto the ground. They rolled twenty feet before Leven's head hit a square stone that stopped them.

Elton jumped up and kicked Leven's rear, sending his face down into the dirt. He was about to kick Leven again, but suddenly he was flying. Glen had Elton by the shoulders and was carrying him off.

"What are you doing?" Elton screamed.

"You can't kick a man when he's down," Glen insisted. He dropped Elton back onto the ground about thirty feet from Leven.

Leven jumped up and looked at his father. "This is crazy."

Elton grabbed his stomach and ran toward Leven again. This time Leven yanked Elton's wrist and bent it back under his chin, holding him in a headlock.

"We should talk this through," Leven said. "Because this will—"

A good-sized stone smacked Leven on the side of his head. He let go of his father and stumbled backwards. Another rock hit him in the stomach.

"It's those Plague guys," Clover whispered to Leven. "One's lev-
itating and throwing rocks."

"Well, could you stop him?" Leven asked, just as Elton was leap-
ing on top of him.

Elton had grabbed Leven's kilve and was now banging it on the
right side of Leven.

"You killed Maria," Elton screamed.

"She was my mother," Leven yelled back, deflecting the blows
the best he could. "You left me with horrible people."

"I didn't do anything," Elton said stubbornly. "I was ripped from
everything I had."

Leven stood up as tall as he could and faced his father. He
walked slowly backwards, trying to stay out of the reach of the kilve
that Elton was now swinging.

Swish.

The kilve missed Leven and he stepped back farther.

"We can settle this," Leven insisted. "We were both used. Why
can't you see that?"

"They didn't want me," Elton seethed. "Your grandfather didn't
think I was the one. I was defective and lacked what was needed. So
they waited for you, the great Leven, while I was stuck in an office
trying to make sense of something that is impossible to make sense
of. Now where are you? Are you going to save the world, Leven?"

"Not if you kill me first."

"Good," Elton said, his brain mad. "Then maybe it'll be me that
saves them all."

Elton stepped forward and swung the kilve as hard as he could.
He would have hit Leven for sure except that Leven, stepping back,

fell into a newly burrowed hole that one of the Ring members had just dug.

Elton swore.

Using his own new ability, Leven dug quickly under his father and popped up behind him. Elton turned just as Leven wrapped his arms around his father. He lifted him up, and Elton screamed and bucked.

"I didn't ask to be picked," Leven pointed out. "You're my father. I'm your son."

"Big deal," Elton screamed. "We know nothing of each other."

"That could change, couldn't it?"

Elton threw his head back, cracking his skull against Leven's nose. Blood began to squirt all over as Leven hollered.

"This is ridiculous," Leven said angrily. He opened his mouth and fire shot out, wrapping around Elton's legs.

Elton jumped up and down screaming as lightning ripped through the sky, striking the ground directly in front of Leven.

Leven flew backwards and landed on his rear, tangled in ivy.

Clover materialized and began rubbing his shoulders. "It's those guys. One threw the lightning," Clover said, sounding like a coach giving his fighter instructions. "It's the Ring of Plague."

"Whose side are they on?" Leven asked.

"I think they're just keeping the fight fair," Clover said.

"I'm not going to fight my father," Leven argued.

"That's obvious," Clover said, embarrassed.

"What's that supposed to mean?" Leven said defensively.

"I mean, you're the Want—and you're getting your butt kicked."

Leven looked at Clover. He then jumped up. He could feel all the changes and storms inside himself. He could feel the abilities he was growing into and begged his body to work right.

He had forgotten who he was.

Elton was standing and holding the kilve, his eyes bouncing back and forth. Leven marched toward him and then faded, only to reappear closer to him. Leven waved his hand, and the kilve flew out of Elton's hands and into the bushes.

Leven stared at his father, his gold eyes sweeping up and down him like a scanner. One of the Ring members came from the side to interfere; Leven simply turned and lit the guy on fire.

Leven then returned his gaze to his father.

Elton backed up as Leven pushed him down with his eyes. His father was now sitting on a round stone, trying not to cower. Leven shoved up the sleeves on his shirt and growled slightly.

One of the Ring members came running in at super speed to knock Leven down. But Leven stepped back and extended his right leg. The Ring member tripped over the leg and went flying.

"Knock it off," Leven yelled to any listening Ring member. "I don't care if you think you're making it fair. You're making me mad!"

A couple of members mumbled something about just wanting to keep things even, but they all retreated into the background.

"Now," Leven said to his father, "I suppose if you had asked me before this all happened if I had father issues, I would have said *yes*. I wanted nothing more than for you to be alive and to come save me. But you're not a father, and there are others in my life who I look to now for love and wisdom. So I suppose you were unfinished business, but not any longer. You're a man who was mistreated and who is too stubborn to ever get over it. Don't look for me. Don't send me cards on my birthday. And don't forget that it was you who wanted it this way."

Leven motioned to Glen. Glen walked over, looking like a child who had been busted.

"We were just making it interesting," Glen said defensively.

"I don't care about that," Leven smiled. "Do you mind doing me a favor?"

"Not at all," Glen said.

Leven gave Glen a few simple instructions, and then Glen wrapped his arms around Elton. Both Leven and Clover watched as Elton was lifted up and carried far, far away.

"So that's your dad?" Clover asked.

"I guess," Leven answered. "In title."

"I don't see much of him in you."

"Thanks," Leven said.

"Do you think *that* business is finished now?" Clover asked.

"Definitely," Leven said, picking Clover up and placing him on his head.

"He wasn't a very nice dad," Clover observed.

Leven was quiet.

"Hey, if you need someone to play catch with, or toss around a ball, I'd be happy to help."

"I'm a lucky guy," Leven smiled.

"I'll say," Clover agreed.

CHAPTER THIRTY-FOUR

You Don't Know What You've Mocked Till It's Gone

L ook over there," Geth pointed.

Winter looked down out of the helicopter and saw herds of avalands busting through a small town far below. She and Geth could also see a bunch of firefighters spraying their hoses, trying to subdue a telt. And, of course, they saw cows and other livestock being pulled down beneath the soil by black strands of the Dearth.

"Where are we?" Winter yelled.

"Someplace over Texas," Geth yelled back.

Geth, Winter, Phoebe, Ezra, Dennis, and Lilly were being flown by two pilots to Burnt Culvert, Oklahoma. One of the pilots, Captain Coin, had skin so white you could see his veins beneath it. The other was just plain white; he had been introduced as Captain Bubble. General Lank had arranged the ride but had stayed back at

Blue Hole Lake to fight there. The helicopter was large and army green, with open sides. Everyone was strapped in tightly.

Lilly materialized in Winter's lap behind the seat belt. "Is Texas a good place?"

"I think so," Winter said. "But we're not stopping there."

Lilly disappeared.

Ezra was riding in Geth's hand. He hopped forward to Captain Bubble's shoulder and started bossing him around because he had been on a helicopter before and felt that made him an expert. After explaining to the pilots what he felt a certain button did, he pointed out the front window and asked, "What are those?"

The pilots looked out the window at the large, gray clouds that appeared to be racing across the sky toward them.

"Those clouds don't look right," Captain Coin said.

"Those aren't clouds," Geth hollered. "They're hazen."

Both pilots swore, apologized, and then told everyone to hang on. The hazen had been giving people grief all over the world. They had been messing with planes, tall buildings, kites, windmills, and even one blimp at a sporting event in Cairo. They looked like thick, gray clouds, but they had facial features and arms that became better defined when they were attacking. In Foo the hazen were sort of shy and reserved, but those here in Reality were mischievous and territorial.

"Maybe they haven't seen us?" Dennis hoped.

Ezra slapped his own forehead. "That's Dennis's solution to everything: hope they never saw us."

"Well, it's possible they haven't," Geth said, trying to be kind to Dennis.

"Now that you put it that way," Ezra agreed, "maybe they haven't."

Dennis and Winter stared at Ezra. It seemed pretty obvious that he was enamored with his human counterpart. Just a few hours ago, he had been vowing to find and kill him, but now he was kissing up to himself more than he was hating Geth.

The hazen shifted their course a tiny bit and began charging.

"They've seen us," Phoebe said.

Ezra lifted his hands and waved, but he had no effect on the hazen.

"Let's see if we can outrun them," Captain Coin said with enthusiasm.

Captain Bubble pulled the helicopter to the side, racing at an angle away from the clouds. The hazen saw their movement and picked up speed.

"They're coming faster," Dennis said.

The helicopter pushed forward.

Winter heard it first. "Are they yelling?"

The speeding hazen were screaming as they drew closer. Their words were ominous and vulgar.

The wind in front of the hazen rocked the helicopter violently.

"Hold on," Captain Bubble commanded.

The helicopter tilted sideways and blasted out across the sky. Large hazen swiped at the copter as it moved away.

More vulgarity.

Captain Coin pushed forward at full speed.

"You can't outrun it," Geth yelled.

"We're gonna try," Captain Coin yelled back.

As if on cue, one huge hazen reached out and wrapped itself

around one of the landing skids on the helicopter. The poor machine whined and screeched as it tried to move forward.

"How do you fight hazen?" Winter yelled to Geth.

"I have no idea," he yelled back. "In Foo they behaved."

The helicopter tilted to the side and its blades sliced right through the dark cloud. The hazen released its hold and the copter lurched forward, jerking its passengers around.

"Go," Captain Coin yelled at his copilot. "Go!"

"I'm going!" he yelled back.

Phoebe looked out the side to witness the entire west sky turning dark and moving toward them. "There are thousands of them now."

Dennis looked down at the robe he was wearing. "Can this robe do anything?"

Ezra looked embarrassed to know him. "Yeah, jump out and it will act as a parachute."

"I was just trying—"

Thick, dark hazen crowded around the helicopter and pushed in the open sides. They batted around the passengers, pushing and pulling at them. Gray, swirling strings of cloud grabbed Winter's and Phoebe's hair and yanked hard.

Both women screamed with equal volume.

Geth tried to tear at the hazen, but they had no real substance. "Land this thing," he yelled to the pilots.

"We're trying to go down," Captain Coin yelled back. "But they seem to be pushing us up from below."

A thin string of black cloud reached in and pressed the release on Dennis's seat belt. The belt flew open, and Dennis was thrust forward and halfway out of the helicopter door. Geth reached to grab him and got ahold of the robe.

"What are you doing?" Ezra yelled, as if Dennis had chosen to fall out.

Dennis was too busy trying to find something to hold onto to reply. Geth lost his grip, and Dennis slid all the way out. His face slammed against the edge of the copter and he fell onto the left landing skid. Dennis shifted and was now hanging by his arms as the helicopter whizzed back and forth.

"Do something!" Ezra commanded.

Everyone looked at the toothpick, wondering if he had a suggestion.

"He's not completely worthless," Ezra added.

Geth unbuckled his own belt and fell to the floor of the helicopter onto his stomach. He scooted to the edge and looked out and down at Dennis. Winter unbuckled and grabbed Geth's legs.

"Dennis!" Geth yelled down. "Don't let go!"

The hazen wrapped around Dennis and batted him back and forth like a pale punching bag.

"Do something," Ezra yelled again.

Geth tried to scoot forward to reach Dennis's hand but the distance was too great. He couldn't reach him.

Dennis couldn't hold on any longer.

He looked at Geth and halfway smiled. He then let go and fell down into the belly of the dark clouds.

"No!" Ezra wailed.

Ezra jumped out of the helicopter, diving down into the clouds. Geth reached out and grabbed the small toothpick and pulled him back in. Winter and Geth rebuckled as Ezra kicked and screamed.

"Cowards!" he yelled. "I could have caught him."

The hazen pushed up against the front windows and sides, making it almost pitch black. They rocked the helicopter in all directions.

Winter looked up at the only source of natural light. She could see through the two small windows in the ceiling that there were no hazen up above. They had surrounded the sides and bottom of the craft, but the top was clear.

"Tilt the helicopter again!" Winter yelled.

The pilots, desperate to try anything, threw the controls to the side, and the helicopter leaned sideways. The hazen on that side of the copter did not like the rotors chopping through them and pulled back.

"Can you spin around in a circle?" Winter hollered. "I think they hate the blades."

The captains spun the helicopter around in a full circle, cutting away the hazen. Those bits reaching in pulled outward and the helicopter spun faster.

"I'm going to be ill," Phoebe said.

"Now go after them," Winter yelled to the pilots. "If they grab us from below, spin in a circle again and cut them off."

The copter tilted sideways and moved in a straight line across the sky. The hazen came around the opposite side, but the pilots just spun, cutting at them with the helicopter's rotors.

"Brilliant," Geth said, smiling at Winter.

The sky began to lighten as the hazen grew frustrated and moved away. In a few minutes the horizon was hazen free.

"Should we land?" Captain Coin asked.

"No," Geth replied. "Keep going."

"What?" Ezra roared. "We've got to get Dennis."

Nobody could make eye contact with the single-eyed toothpick.

"Turn this thing around!" Ezra yelled.

Phoebe reached out to touch Ezra and he screamed at her.

"It's no use," Geth said.

Ezra looked at Geth. "I hate me."

And then, for the first time ever in the history of man, woman, or woodenkind, a toothpick produced a real tear. Lilly clung to Winter's neck and shivered, Phoebe held Geth's hand, and they sadly moved on.

CHAPTER THIRTY-FIVE

JUST ADD WATER

Swig peered over the back of his seat and gazed at Janet and Osck. He made some sort of sad noise and then turned back around.

"The lady one's not doing too well," Swig told Tim.

Tim looked into his rearview mirror. He could barely see Janet up against the vehicle's black leather seating. What he could see of her looked weak and thin enough to simply blow away. Osck didn't look that much better. His flamelike body seemed dim and he smoldered as if he were just minutes from burning out completely.

"Hold on, you two," Tim said as cheerfully as he could.

"We should never have left Foo," Osck moaned, looking at Janet.

"Hurry," Janet said. "I have to tell myself about Winter."

Tim's foot had been pressed down on the gas pedal as hard as it would go. He pushed even harder, knowing it wouldn't make a dif-ference. The highway was a crazy mess. There were some sections where the roads had been demolished by avalands burrowing under them or telts blowing across them. Some cars had been unable to make it over or around the mess. Luckily for Tim and his group, he had hot-wired a vehicle big and strong enough to make it over the torn-up roads.

"Where are we?" Swig asked.

"Someplace in Kansas," Tim replied. "Almost to Wichita."

"So, how much longer?"

"About five hours," Tim whispered, not wanting to alarm his passengers in the back.

"And this beast is fed?" Swig asked.

"Not enough," Tim answered. "We're going to have to get gas one more time."

The highway was empty at the moment. In fact, it looked like they were the only vehicle in the world. The landscape was covered with farms, and the sky was filled with bright streaks of color. Tim spotted a small gas station off the interstate and took the next exit heading toward it.

The gas station stood alone and closed. Tim pulled the vehicle up to one of the pumps and got out. Nobody was around. Tim stepped over to the small store and banged on the door.

Nobody answered.

Tim walked back to the pumps and looked around. He then pulled open the front of one of the pumps and messed with the insides.

"What are you doing?" Swig asked.

"Seeing if I can get this to work," Tim answered.

"You're very ingenious," Swig said, patting Tim on the head.

Tim jimmied the pump and got the gas flowing. He filled up the tank and then shut the pump off.

"This should be enough to get us home," Tim said.

"Good," Swig replied. "To be honest, I don't feel well. It will be nice to rest."

Tim wiped his own forehead.

"How about you?" Swig asked. "Are you okay?"

"I'm fine," he lied. Tim was not only ill at ease, he was sick in the stomach. He could tell something was wrong with him, but he had no desire to worry those he was with.

Tim got back into the jeep and started it up.

"You two okay?" he asked Osck and Janet.

"Please hurry," was Osck's only reply.

Tim turned the jeep around and headed toward the highway.

"What's that?" Osck asked nervously.

Tim looked around but couldn't see anything. "What's what?"

"I think he's talking about what's behind you," Swig said politely.

Tim turned his head around. All he could see through the back window were multiple mounds of dirt.

"Go!" Osck screamed.

Tim pressed on the gas like it was a lump of coal that needed to be squeezed into a diamond. The jeep growled and surged forward like a boxy bolt of lightning. In his rearview mirror, Tim could see the avalands barreling directly toward them.

"How many are there?" Tim asked.

"Eight, nine . . . I don't know, at least twenty." Swig's small voice was loaded with panic.

"Let's see if we can go faster than they can," Tim hollered.

The jeep curved onto the highway and took off. From the new angle, Tim could see the avalands much better through the rearview mirror. The beasts were as large as small hills, their backs covered with crops and grass. He could see their dirty eyes and their massive mouths that chomped through the dirt as they moved.

The avalands dipped and twisted below the highway, popping back up on the other side. New ones were racing in from the other direction.

"They're all over," Janet cried.

"Are they getting closer?" Tim asked.

"What do you want me to say?" Swig asked.

"The truth, remember?"

"Yes," Swig answered. "They're getting much closer."

Tim glanced in the rearview mirror and saw dirt and debris flying everywhere. Large chunks of soil and stone were beginning to pelt the back of the jeep.

"Honk the horn," Janet suggested.

Tim honked, but nothing happened.

"Go faster," Osck begged.

"I'm going as fast as I can," Tim hollered.

The back of the jeep began to lift as the avalands caught up. Tim turned the wheel and flew off the side of the highway and into a field of dead cornstalks. The jeep burned through the field as the avalands hurried to make a wide turn and keep after it.

A large avaland with a back full of grass moved alongside the jeep and thrust its head into the side of the vehicle. The jeep bumped sideways as Janet and Swig screamed.

Another even larger avaland galloped along the other side and butted its huge dirt head into the jeep. The vehicle bounced back and forth between the two beasts as it raced over the rutted field.

Tim wound through two small mounds of earth; the avalands just burrowed through them as if they weren't there. He then made the mistake of looking into the rearview mirror again. He could see a massive avaland inches behind them. The beast opened its mouth and chomped down on the spare tire attached to the back of the jeep. The avaland ripped the tire off and bucked wildly. It took everything Tim had to keep the vehicle under control.

"They're all behind us," Swig said.

The avalands had bunched together as a mammoth herd. They were in a triangle formation, the front one right on the tail of the jeep.

Swig began throwing anything he could find out the shattered back. He nailed one avaland with a tire iron and smacked another one with one of the headrests that had come loose. The attack did nothing to slow the avalands.

The jeep burst out of the cornfield and onto a narrow highway. A large sign in need of repair read *Cheney Reservoir*. Tim drove off the other side of the road and toward the reservoir. An earth-fill dam sloped up to the highest point where the water was.

Tim drove up the sloping dam as fast as he could.

"Do you know what you're doing?" Swig asked.

"Nope."

Janet began to wail louder as the avalands pushed from behind, causing the jeep to jump forward.

"They're all behind us?" Tim asked, his forehead dripping with perspiration.

"Every one of them," Swig cried.

The jeep skidded and roared as it climbed the earth-fill dam.

"Is there water up ahead?" Swig asked.

"I sure hope so," Tim yelled back.

"Osck can't get wet," Swig said urgently.

"I know."

The jeep crested the top of the dam, flying over the lip of it. The avalands simply pushed through the earth dam after it. The jeep came down on the top of the dam, and Tim pulled the wheel to the right as hard as he could. The jeep flipped and rolled two complete times as the avalands shot through the dam and blew out into the reservoir. At their speed and with their size, they had no chance. Some blew hundreds of feet into the water.

Long swatches of dirt floated to the top of the reservoir as the avalands all dissolved, one after another, in an explosion of dirt and water. Heaps of muddy waves and ripples washed up against the side of the dam.

The jeep came to a stop on all four wheels. As dust settled around the vehicle, Tim caught his breath. He looked back at Janet and Osck, amazed that all of them were still in one piece.

"These things are helpful," Swig said, stretching out his seat belt.

"Wow," was all Osck had to say.

"You're okay?" Tim asked.

Janet and Osck nodded.

"Let's see if this still works," Tim said, pressing on the gas.

The jeep was beat up, but it moved forward. Tim turned the wheel and headed toward Iowa as the sky turned an uncomfortable shade of brown.

"I hope we make it," Swig said calmly.

"Me too," Tim replied.

The jeep shook violently as they drove.

"Are you doing that?" Swig asked.

"No," Tim yelled. "I think the jeep's broken, or—"

"They're still after us," Osck said dryly.

Tim looked in the rearview mirror. "I don't see anything . . . I . . . oh, no."

"What is it?" Swig asked, interested.

"The dam's breaking," Tim yelled. "The avalands must have weakened it."

"Is that bad?"

"It's worse than bad," Tim moaned, pressing on the gas as hard as he could. In the rearview mirror he could see the top of the earth-fill dam breaking up as water began to push through.

"Osck can't get wet!" Janet yelled.

"I know!" Tim yelled back.

The jeep raced along a high road that stretched out from the far side of the dam and ran alongside the river where the dam released water. Tim could see that the dam was continuing to crumble from the top.

"Look," Swig shouted, pointing in front of them.

Tim was not fond of vulgarity. He had always thought that there were far better ways for people to express themselves than to swear. Many times he had told his sons, Rochester and Darcy, that if a man can't find a clean word to properly express himself, then he is not very imaginative or bright.

Apparently Tim was a bit dim at the moment.

"That's a fancy word," Swig complimented. "What's it mean?"

"It means we're in trouble."

What Swig had pointed out for Tim to look at were more

avalands. They were coming from the south, and there were hundreds of them.

"Wait," Tim said nervously, wiping more sweat off his head. "I have an idea."

"Osck can't get wet," Janet reiterated.

"I know," Tim yelled.

The dam was spilling over in huge, spastic waves now, water washing away the earth that had successfully held it back for so many years. Tim could hear the howling of air. The water tearing out of the dam was pushing a massive body of wind in front of it. The water was rising up out of the riverbed, wiping out the banks and creating a noise so terrible it made the jeep shiver.

"Tell me how far away the water is," Tim hollered, looking in his rearview mirror.

"But all I can see is water," Swig cried.

In front all Tim could see was the mass of avalands. They were racing from the side and almost directly in Tim's path. The jeep screamed as it flew. Osck and Janet were huddled together moaning, and Swig was holding onto the seat and looking out the back.

"The river's rising," Swig cried.

The noise of the approaching water was deafening. And now Tim could hear the roar of the avalands.

"This better work," Tim screamed.

Tim turned sharply and headed up the steep side of the small gorge. The jeep cried and sputtered as it tore up the rocky incline, the tires throwing dirt and stones everywhere. The water was only inches away from the back tires.

The front tires of the jeep caught the top of the gorge, and the jeep hopped up on top of the ridge just as the water roared by below.

"You made it," Swig said proudly.

The landscape opened up below and the water from the reservoir spilled out, flooding over the entire valley and washing away every avaland. The beasts screamed and protested, but once surrounded there was nothing they could do but turn to mud. Tim and his group watched the water spread out for miles from safely up above.

"Wow," Swig said. "That's a lot of water."

"It's like we planned it," Tim said.

"You really are good with this thing," Swig said. "What's it called?"

"A jeep."

Osck cleared his throat.

Tim pushed on the gas and tore off, heading north and leaving a giant mess behind him.

CHAPTER THIRTY-SIX

STANDING BEFORE BOTH THE PROBLEM AND THE ANSWER

L even was tired. Every bone in his body ached and screamed for him to rest awhile. He felt sick in the stomach and worried in the mind. He could feel Foo falling apart and knew very well that it was only a matter of hours before it was completely finished. Despite his pain, Leven kept putting one foot in front of the other, working his way up the dirt trail toward the tree.

"Good or bad?" Clover asked him.

"What?" Leven replied, his thoughts elsewhere.

"Good or bad?" Clover said again. "Is the next thing good or bad?"

"All of them are draining," Leven replied. "I'm not sure I'm up to it. I can't see straight."

"So you feel that too?" Clover asked.

"Feel what?"

"Sick," Clover said softly. "Geth used to say that in the end we'll all feel ill and then fade away."

"I wish he were here," Leven said seriously.

"But then he'd be making some of the decisions that you should."

"That's why I wish he were here, to make some of the decisions."

"You know who's good at making decisions?" Clover asked.

"Who?"

"My brother Pebble," Clover answered. "No matter what's going on or who's in charge, he's always trying to make a decision."

"Hmm," Leven replied. "It'd be kinda cool to meet some of your family."

"There's a lot of them."

The ground became harder as they marched around a massive statue of a siid. The statue was covered in moss and bird droppings, and the back third of it had cracked off and fallen to the ground.

"It's almost as big as a real siid," Clover whispered.

"I wonder how old it is."

The forest surrounding the statue creaked and moaned like a wooden ship in a choppy sea.

"I've never seen so many trees," Leven observed. "Everywhere you look there're hundreds of trees hiding hundreds of ruins. I would love to have seen this place when it wasn't a grown-over wasteland."

As if they had heard Leven, the trees thinned just a bit and the overwhelming sweet perfume of flowers filled the air. Large orange flowers carpeted a small valley that was thick with long grass and animals.

"What is that?" Leven asked, pointing to a tiger-looking crea-ture with horns.

"That's a lorn," Clover said. "She'll eat the flowers and then throw them up."

"Let's go around," Leven suggested.

The path of glass wound around the valley up through some thick trees and over a bridge that spanned a weak mountain stream. The sound of some sort of monkey could be heard screaming in the distance.

On the other side of the stream was a tremendous monastery-style building. It was five stories high and as wide as a football field. Its roof was made of thick yellow thatch, and there were dozens of windows and chimneys. Myriads of colorful flags hung from the edge of the roof.

From where Leven stood he could see five sets of doors, all equally spaced apart. The side of the great building was white, but dark beams ran through it, making Leven feel like he was back in Germany. The whole thing looked ancient, and it was covered with great cracks as well as decay and rot.

"Unbelievable," Leven whispered, starting to walk again.

"You're not going in there, are you?" Clover asked nervously.

"Of course," Leven said. "The path leads right to it."

"But can't you feel that?"

Leven stopped again and contemplated what he could or couldn't feel. He could hear Tea birds singing and the wind playing with all the trees. He could see that the sky was still off color and something was wrong with the smaller sun—it was drooping in the center like a fat, middle-aged man. He could see the snow-covered mountain peaks above the monastery. And he could feel the temperature trying to make up its mind, and the soreness in his feet and legs, but he was pretty sure Clover wasn't talking about that.

"Feel what?"

"It's heavy," Clover said. "Something is in that building, and it isn't nice."

"I feel fine," Leven insisted. "And we certainly didn't come all this way to turn around when we felt scared."

"Not scared," Clover said, clinging to Leven's right arm. "Wrong."

Leven walked straight to the middle set of doors and stopped. He looked down at the wooden doorknobs; carved on each one was a figure of a key. He reached out and turned the right knob. The knob turned and the door clicked open.

Leven looked down at Clover and shrugged.

He pushed the door open further and it squealed like a pig with a complaint. Leven stopped pushing and Alder was quiet once more.

Leven stepped inside.

"Hello," he hollered out. "Is anyone here?"

There was no answer, only the sound of Clover, who was trying to be brave by listing things that made him happy.

" . . . cold pickles, red shoes, pants with lots of pockets . . ."

"Shhh," Leven insisted.

" . . . not being told to be quiet, daytime television . . ." Clover said softly.

"Seriously," Leven said.

Clover shut up.

Just inside the door there was a wide hall with numerous doors leading off of it. Leven opened the first one and saw a bed with a moldy, straw-stuffed mattress, a small table, and a wardrobe. He checked the next door and found the same.

"So was this like a boarding school?" Leven asked.

"You told me not to talk," Clover said, hurt.

"Not to talk *needlessly*," Leven clarified.

"Then yes," Clover said crisply. "I believe it was a school of some sort."

Farther down, another wide hall intersected with the main one. It too was loaded with doors. Some of the doors were shut, but a number were hanging open, exposing empty rooms similar to the ones they had already seen.

"I wonder who lived here," Leven whispered, continuing down the main hall. "Should we check all the rooms?"

"Why?" Clover asked.

"What if what we're looking for is in one of them?"

"It isn't," Clover said.

"How do you know?"

"Because look." Clover hopped down to the floor and stood in front of Leven. He pointed down the long hall to where the back doors would have been if they were still there. Through the open space Leven could see the base of a very large tree.

"Do you think?" Leven whispered reverently.

"I wouldn't point at just any tree."

Leven ran, swooping up Clover with his left hand as he passed him and tossing him up onto his right shoulder. He sped down the hall and out the opening.

Leven stopped and took it all in. He was in a giant courtyard. On all sides there were buildings just like the one he had burst out of. The courtyard they surrounded was overgrown, and there were brick paths crisscrossing it. There were also many spots where thick tree roots shot up straight or arched up and back into the ground. But the most prominent feature was the tree. A single tree stood four stories tall right in the middle of the open space. It had long, knobby, leafy branches that twisted queerly out from the trunk and up into the sky. The bark of the tree looked almost gold, and the odd-shaped branches outlined shifting objects.

It wasn't the biggest tree Leven had ever seen, but it was the most impressive.

The path of glass wound right up to it and circled its base.

"So do you talk to it?" Clover asked.

"I've never done this before," Leven said. "Remember?"

The two of them walked slowly down the broken glass path. There was no wind or noise in the courtyard; the massive buildings blocked off all such things.

"I mean, do you bow?" Clover asked. "Or curtsy?"

"Isn't curtsying what girls do?"

"Great," Clover blushed. "No wonder they always made fun of me."

Leven stood beside the tree. Its trunk was at least ten feet in diameter, and the gold bark looked fuzzy close up. Dark ivy was woven into the bark, some strands climbing all the way up into the branches.

"Does it talk?" Leven asked.

The tree just stood there, its branches creaking.

"Maybe this isn't the one," Clover said. "I mean, it looks old, but *oldest?* I'm not sure."

Leven walked slowly around the tree, glass crunching beneath

his feet. He looked up and down at the markings and branches on the tree and at the soil it was stuck in.

"The roots are huge," Leven said, bending down and touching one of the protruding roots.

The tree's roots shot out from its base and then turned straight down into the soil. Each one looked to be at least three feet in diameter.

"Do we chop it down?" Clover asked.

Leven leaned in and touched the bark. The tree felt warm, like the hood of a vehicle that had just been running. Waves of energy passed from his hand to the trunk.

"I don't think so," Leven said.

"Maybe we climb it," Clover suggested. "We could make an amazing fort in this tree."

"Shhh, quiet," Leven requested. "Let me think."

"That's the second time you've 'shhhhed' me," Clover pointed out. "I know I'm not exactly the perfect sycophant, and I probably deserve it, but—"

"Shhh."

"Third time," Clover said, and he disappeared.

Leven rubbed his right hand on the tree. He looked for an opening or some other indication of what he was supposed to do. He had no doubt about it being the right tree. Standing there beneath its branches, Leven felt as if the tree were part of him. Something on the tip of one of the low-hanging branches shimmered under the afternoon sun. Leven walked over and touched the tip of the branch. A hard silver drop was pushing out of the end of the branch like a leaf.

Leven twisted the drop, and it popped off. He tried to bend it, but it was solid. He bent down and tapped it against the glass on the ground.

"A tree that grows metal," Clover said from on top of Leven's head.

The tree creaked and crackled some more.

"Do you think it's trying to say something?" Clover asked.

"I don't know," Leven replied. "I don't speak tree."

"I bet their language involves a lot of clicking and snapping."

"Shhh."

"It's beginning to hurt," Clover complained.

"Sorry," Leven said. "But I'm having a hard time thinking straight. I kind of feel like I'm going to throw up."

The tree creaked loudly, followed by a pop. Instantly roots shot up from the ground and twisted around Leven. Leven hollered as the roots lifted him up a few feet and turned him around as if examining him. Leven felt exposed and helpless. No gifts came to him, and his body grew cold. After a couple of minutes the roots set him down and disappeared back under the soil.

"What was that?" Clover asked.

Leven was standing and dusting himself off. "I have no idea."

The tree creaked loudly again, as if telling someone something.

"Okay, okay," a strange voice said. "I'll show myself."

Leven looked up into the branches of the tree and saw a long, fat, sage-green sycophant sitting there. He was wearing a shimmering green robe and small gray moccasins on his feet. His eyes were bright red and glowed slightly in the afternoon light.

"Hello," Leven said. "I'm—"

"Be quiet," the sycophant said impatiently. "I know who you are. We've actually talked before. But I had my foot on your head that time, and you were less than interesting. I'm sorry to see you've made it."

The tree creaked.

"Sorry," the sycophant apologized to the tree. "I dealt with him the best I could. I didn't want to talk to him in your presence."

"I don't understand," Leven said, looking at the sycophant and then back at the tree.

"Most nits don't. I am Frond," the sycophant said pompously. "And I speak for the oldest tree."

Leven just stared, his gold eyes letting off light.

"Okay, then," Frond said, clearing his throat. "You've made it back."

"I was here before?" Leven said, confused.

"In one of those rooms way over there," Frond said.

"When I traveled through the puddle I came *here?*" Leven asked angrily. "And I wasted all that time coming back?"

The tree creaked.

"That voice was you?"

"Yes, it was me," Frond said to Leven. "You had to finish some things up. Nobody just approaches the tree without being in the right mind. Besides, the tree wasn't sure you were the one."

The tree smacked Frond in the back of the head with one of its low branches.

"I take it back," Frond said. "He was sure; I wasn't—*Alderam Degarus.*"

Clover appeared, hanging on the back of Leven's left shoulder.

"You shouldn't have brought your sycophant with you," Frond said. "This was a journey to make alone."

"You never mentioned that," Leven pointed out. "And Clover goes wherever I go."

The tree creaked, and Frond turned to argue with it. "I'm getting to the point. Do you not wish me to use my own words?" The tree creaked again. "Okay, give me some credit."

"Are you okay?" Leven asked.

"Don't interrupt," Frond insisted. He then patted the tree and looked at Leven. "Go ahead."

"Go ahead what?"

"You must have questions."

"What am I doing here?" Leven asked impatiently.

Frond swung down from the branches and dropped to the ground in front of Leven. "Since the creation of Foo, a sycophant has been assigned to speak for the tree. I have held the position longer than any. The language is old and complicated."

"No offense," Leven said, "but that doesn't answer my question. Besides, what does the tree want with me?"

"It's an honor just to gaze at him," Frond said with affection. "An honor."

"I'm sure it is," Leven admitted. "But Foo is falling apart. What does he want from me?"

"He wants you to leave," Frond said impatiently.

Again the tree smacked Frond and they argued like two old women. "I don't want to do this. It's not right. Do you know what it means?"

"Should I give you two some time alone?" Leven asked.

"Yes," Frond said quickly.

He was smacked again. Frond breathed in deeply and tried to compose himself. He smoothed out his little robe and sighed.

"Do you know about duty?" Frond asked.

"What kind of duty are you talking about?" Leven questioned.

Frond sighed. "Sometimes one is forced to do things because of duty. I've always done as I was told, but this is the one time I wish I could stay quiet. You understand that I speak for the tree but not for me."

"Nice to know," Leven said, looking at the tree.

"Do you know where you're standing?" Frond asked.

"Before the oldest tree."

"Yes, but look at the soil."

Leven looked down at the soil and glass and grass. He toed the dry dirt and small bits of dead grass broke off.

"I can see the soil," Leven said.

"Of course," Frond continued. "Do you know where the roots of this tree reach?"

The tree creaked, and Frond argued with it for another couple of seconds.

"Geth is the lithen?" Frond finally asked.

"Yes," Leven answered. "What's—"

"His roots intertwine with those of the oldest tree," Frond said reluctantly.

Leven looked around at all the roots running through the courtyard.

"Had that tree just been planted, and the seed pure, it would have secured the desolate fate of Foo forever," Frond said. "But Sabine was foolish enough to curse Geth, placing him in the very seed that otherwise would have ended it all. His act was more foolish than he can ever know."

"Sabine's dead," Leven said. "He's dead like six times over, so I don't think it really matters to him."

"Had that tree grown to fruition, it would have held Reality to Foo by the roots of this tree. No need for dreams to bind us together."

"So you're with the Dearth?" Leven said angrily.

"No," Frond snapped. "I speak for the tree. And the tree believes that Foo must be restored, no matter the cost. The Dearth wishes for the end of everything—nothing but soil."

"So why am I here?" Leven asked.

"You're Leven Thumps." Frond began to cry. "You're from the line of humans who were directly woven into the fabric of Foo from the beginning. You're the last, save your father, who apparently was too weak from the beginning."

"How do you know?" Leven asked.

"Foo has been aware of his dreams," Frond said. "They are as weak and selfish as the Dearth's. You, despite your age, have thought only of others since the moment you were chosen. Foo must have that, and your father lacks it even until this day. I saw how he treated you just now."

"That was you following us?" Leven asked.

Frond nodded and scratched the back of his right ear with his left foot.

"So what do I do?"

"I have protected this tree for hundreds of years," Frond said sadly. "As did my father before me and his father before him. My grandfather was alive when they built these great buildings, cutting the tree off from all wind. His branches hear no Lore Coils, and the wind delivers no news of trouble or pain. He has stood here holding the soil of Foo taut and keeping things in place. But now the balance is too far gone; the siids wobble and fade, and even the sky grows mushy. The Dearth has stolen all sustenance from the soil, and the tree has fed off of nothing but dreams for the last many years. Now even the dreams have stopped. Look at his leaves."

Leven and Clover looked at the leaves of the tree, which began to curl and yellow as they stared.

"In another day, his branches will be completely bare and his trunk will begin to harden. It's over." Frond began to sob, looking and sounding like a completely different sycophant from the one they had first met.

"This is uncomfortable," Clover whispered into Leven's right ear. "Maybe we should just back away slowly."

"I still don't understand why I'm here," Leven pressed.

"The tree produces metal," Frond said, drying his eyes. "It is a miracle if you believe in those things, or a marvel, if you prefer. The seven keys that were designed to protect Foo were fashioned from the metal this tree made. He has also produced the metal that will finish him off."

Frond looked up at the tree. After a moment of silence, an axe dropped from the leaves. Frond picked up the axe and reluctantly lifted it toward Leven. The tree pushed the sycophant forward with the end of one of his branches.

"What?" Leven asked. "I'm supposed to chop it down?"

Frond handed him the axe.

"This tree wants me to chop it down?"

"It is the only way," Frond cried. "Foo will be restored once the tree is gone and a new one is planted."

The tree shivered, and a large seed fell to the ground in front of Leven. Leven leaned down and picked up the seed.

Leven hefted the axe. "I chop down this tree and Foo is restored?"

Frond nodded.

"That's it?" Leven asked.

Frond nodded again.

"The Dearth will be pulled from the soil?"

"Yes."

"The balance will be restored and the dreams will re-commence?"

"Plant the seed and Foo will be as it was in its beginning days," Frond wailed. "Clean, with no darkness."

"And Reality?"

"They will never know what happened," Frond said. "But their dreams will be stronger and more powerful than they have been in a long time. You will have saved them all and they will have no knowledge of it."

"All that by just chopping this tree down?" Leven asked, confused. "There has to be a catch."

"There is," Frond said. "You and all those you've traveled with will die."

Clover gasped. "Does that mean me too? 'Cause technically I haven't 'traveled with' him; I've led the way."

The tree poked Frond. "All right," he admitted, "those you've traveled with won't die. I made that part up."

"I take it you don't want me to chop down this tree," Leven said compassionately.

"Don't try to understand me," Frond shrieked, baring his teeth. "I do as I'm told, but only if I am told by the tree."

"What about Geth and Winter?" Leven asked. "They're in Reality."

"They will stay there," Frond said. "The exits will be closed and new keys will be required."

"So I die and they're trapped there?"

"I didn't say it just like that," Frond argued.

Leven looked at the axe. He looked at the tree and saw age and softness and wisdom.

"I still don't understand," Leven said.

The tree creaked and moaned.

"It's not an end," Frond said sadly. "It's a beginning prophesied from the creation of time—a renewal. Everything decays, and it is time to clean the rot. And you're the only person alive who can do it."

Frond sobbed.

Clouds moved in above the tree and great bolts of pink light flashed over the tops of the mountains. Leven wobbled as the ground rolled.

The tree moaned loudly.

"What did it say?" Leven asked.

"Nothing," Frond lied. The tree poked him from behind. "I can't say it," Frond cried and then disappeared.

Leven looked at the axe in his hands.

"It's a beautiful tree," Clover said reverently.

Leven threw back the axe and swung.

CHAPTER THIRTY-SEVEN

EXPLAINING TO YOURSELF

The town of Dependence, Iowa, was as scared and crazy as all of the other towns and places Tim had just driven through. The only difference was that this was home. Tim's heart raced and his hands became sweaty. He had honestly thought that he would never make it back. Now here he was with Janet, Osck, and Swig.

"It looks like the city has been picked up and shaken," Janet said weakly.

All over there were cars overturned and stores with broken windows. Three police cars passed them going south while two passed them going north. Tim looked at the gas gauge.

"We barely made it," he said to Swig.

"I know," Swig replied. "She's hardly there anymore."

Tim looked in the rearview mirror and his whirling heart fell.

Janet was fading fast. He pushed on the gas and exited the highway, flying down into their old neighborhood.

Tim knew the city of Dependence well. He had picked up trash at almost every home there. And he knew the street he was now on particularly well. He could see his home at the end with the red door, but he turned into the curb instead, coming to a stop in front of Winter's old house. Tim could see the curtains move as somebody peeked out.

"Hurry," Tim yelled.

Osck tried to help Janet out of the jeep. There was even less for him not to be able to hold onto than before. They stepped along the very same uneven sidewalk that Janet the whisp had been created on and up to the door. Tim reached out and rang the doorbell.

There was no answer.

"I know someone's in there," Tim said, ringing the bell again.

"There's a key beneath the rock," Janet said weakly.

Tim picked up a big rock near a dead shrub and pulled out the key. He stuck it in the lock and opened the door.

"Hello," Tim yelled out. "Janet?"

"Who is it?" the fleshy Janet yelled back from somewhere in the house. "I have a gun."

"It's me, Tim Tuttle. I live down the street. I was here about Winter."

"So what?" Janet yelled back. "What'd you want? My money? My food?"

"No," Tim hollered, stepping into the house.

"How'd you get in?" the fleshy Janet demanded, still not showing herself.

"It's complicated," Tim answered.

He motioned for Osck and wispy Janet to follow him. He then positioned wispy Janet in front of a white section of wall where she showed up best.

"Get out of my house," fleshy Janet yelled.

"No," Tim said back.

"Janet," wispy Janet said to herself. "Come out, it's me."

"Who said that?"

Fleshy Janet slowly emerged from the kitchen holding a baseball bat. She was wearing the exact same yellow housecoat as her whisp version, but her eyes were puffier and her hair was as ratted and messed up as a crow's nest.

Janet looked at her whisp self and gasped. "What is this?" she asked, frightened. "Is it a trick?"

"No trick," Tim said gently.

"What's that?" she asked, pointing at Osck.

"That's Osck."

"This isn't right," she insisted. "Get out."

Tim ignored her request and kept talking. "A couple of weeks ago when you walked out to get the mail you accidentally stepped where you shouldn't have and part of you was taken to Foo."

"Foo?" fleshy Janet asked. "The place they keep talking about?"

Wispy Janet nodded.

"That's me?" she pointed.

Another nod.

"I don't believe—"

"Shut up," wispy Janet ordered. "Just be quiet for a second. You—we—always did have a hard time letting anyone else speak. But I'm dying. In a few moments I'll be gone. And I don't care so much about that as I do about dying without you realizing how wrong we were. We had Winter for almost thirteen years and we treated her like garbage. No offense, Tim."

"None taken," Tim replied.

"Still, somehow she turned out to be a remarkable person who is at this moment trying to save the world."

"Winter?" fleshy Janet said.

Wispy Janet nodded. "I—you—were wrong. So wrong to have treated her the way we did."

"I did my best," fleshy Janet said indifferently.

"We did our worst," fading Janet cried. "We should have loved her. I know . . ."

"She's going," Swig said with alarm.

Osck tried to grab at her, but it was useless. Wispy Janet pulsated lightly and then faded, and faded, and faded.

"Be sorry," she mouthed to her bulkier self as she disappeared completely.

Osck fell to his knees crying.

"No," he wailed.

He turned over and over on the rug, writhing in agony. He then stopped, arching his back. His body flared a bright red; then, like a cold brick of coal, he dimmed to nothing but white ash. His form collapsed on fleshy Janet's floor in a small pile of grey dust.

Janet looked at Tim, her eyes as wide as Frisbees. "That was real?"

"Very."

"I came back to tell myself I was sorry?"

Tim nodded.

"I've not been feeling well for weeks," she cried.

"You weren't completely yourself."

Fleshy Janet stepped over to her couch and sat down. Then, in a display of mucus, tears, and old makeup that might never be duplicated, she began to sob.

"I can't believe anyone ever wanted to leave Foo for this," Swig whispered reverently.

At the moment Tim had no rebuttal.

CHAPTER THIRTY-EIGHT

CLOVERINE

The axe swung swiftly and silently through the air. The tool felt like an extension of Leven's body. The act felt so natural, which is why what happened next was such a surprise to Leven.

Frond pounced from the tree and onto Leven's arm, throwing his swing downward and into the ground. Bits of glass and soil shot up as Leven fell to the ground rolling. The axe bounced and flew across the courtyard while the clouds above began to rain blue streaks down.

"What are you doing?" Leven yelled.

"I won't let you do it," Frond screamed, baring his small white teeth. He leapt up from the ground, aiming for Leven's neck.

"No way," Clover hollered, moving in from the right side and knocking Frond down. "Nobody bites my burn but me."

293

Frond and Clover rolled across the ground swatting at one another.

Foo shifted, and Leven had to brace himself against the tree to keep from falling. The tree moaned and creaked.

Frond disappeared.

"Alderam Degarus!" Leven yelled.

Frond reappeared midleap, diving for Leven. Clover sprang up and grabbed Frond by the ankles, causing both of them to hit the ground inches away from Leven.

"This isn't about you," Frond yelled. "You filthy sycophant."

"Do you sing to your mother with that mouth?" Clover yelled back.

Frond looked confused. He grabbed Clover's arm and yanked it backwards. Clover yelped and twisted, falling onto his back against the ground.

"Chop the tree," Clover yelled out.

Leven scrambled onto his feet and ran for the axe. He picked it up, spun around, and got a face full of Frond. Frond was on his head scratching away at his hair and pulling clumps out.

"Stop!" Leven screamed.

Clover scurried up Leven and attacked Frond from behind, desperately trying to pull the sycophant off of Leven.

"I speak for the tree," Frond screamed.

"Who cares?" Clover screamed back. Clover ripped Frond from Leven's head and the two of them flew to the ground, crashing into a protruding root. Clover cried out and tried to twist out from under Frond, but Frond was kicking madly. He grabbed Clover's ears and pulled.

A high-pitched screaming, like that of a yodeler being branded, rang out.

"Clover!" Leven yelled.

"Just chop the tree," Clover yelled back.

Leven looked at the axe in his hand and then swung. Frond barreled into Leven's left leg, causing him to flip forward and land on his face.

The axe slid up against the tree.

Clover jumped onto Frond's shoulders, grabbed Frond's eyebrows, and yanked up as hard as he could. Frond screamed and threw his head forward, propelling Clover down hard against the ground.

"Stay out of this," Frond demanded.

"No way," Clover yelled.

"You have no idea what's at stake!"

"I don't think I'd act any differently if I did," Clover smiled.

"I speak for the tree," Frond insisted.

"I speak for myself," Clover insisted back.

The two of them leapt forward simultaneously, smacking into each other and tumbling to the side. Frond wrapped his right leg around Clover's waist and spun him like a top. Clover whirled away yelping.

Leven got up and looked around for the axe. Frond spotted it first. He picked it up and hurled it across the courtyard.

"What are you doing?" Leven hollered. "You told me to cut the tree down."

"I changed my mind."

"What does the tree think?" Leven asked. "Foo is falling apart."

The clouds above broke up just enough to show the smallest sun falling from the sky. The wind up above the monastery was swirling madly and pushing down into the courtyard.

"The tree will live," Frond said.

Clover dashed in from the side, wrapped his arms around Frond, and tackled him. Leven didn't waste a second. He ran to the axe, picked it up, and threw it at the tree. The axe whirled through the air but was stopped by Frond, who had pulled away from Clover just in time.

Frond threw the axe away as the tree smacked him from behind. The axe flew across the courtyard and through one of the windows.

"Get it," Clover yelled. "I'll hold him off."

Leven scrambled to his feet and raced across the courtyard and into the building. The axe had flown through a third-story window, so Leven had to find some stairs. He spotted some at the end of the hall. He ran quickly, took the stairs three at a time, and spilled out on the third floor.

The axe was in the third room he checked. He picked it up and shoved the handle down the back of his pants. He then ran down the stairs and outside. Clover had just thrown Frond down against the glass path, and Frond was now picking glass from his fur and calling Clover names.

"Nit lover," Frond yelled. "We have served for too long. Our moment is now."

"I don't even really know what that means," Clover admitted, jumping on top of Frond and punching him directly in the face.

Frond's small nose began to bleed. Clover looked at his fist, amazed by what he had done. Frond used the moment to flip Clover back over and pin him to the ground.

"No axe?" Clover yelled out as Leven came running up.

"I couldn't find it," Leven lied. "You're faster."

Clover rolled out from under Frond's hold and shot toward the building. Frond followed after him. Leven moved to the tree and pulled the axe from the back of his pants.

The tree moaned deeply.

"Man, I hope you're telling me to chop you down," Leven said seriously. He then drew the axe back and with all his strength threw his arms forward. Leven spun in a circle and stumbled to the ground.

Frond had stolen the axe from his grip at the last moment.

"I'm not stupid," Frond wailed.

Leven leaned up on his hands. "Well, you're confusing."

Clover was back. "I couldn't find . . . hey, I thought you . . . oh."

The sky turned red.

"I have obeyed every wish this tree has ever whispered," Frond said. "But I've decided that I can't let you chop it down. I love this tree."

Leven closed his eyes. It had been some time since he had felt the kind of calm he needed to rest his eyes and look to the future.

There was nothing there. It reminded Leven of the scene he had witnessed when the Dearth had shown him the future. It was so dark and depressing Leven could barely breathe.

"Are you okay?" Clover asked. "Your eyes are wigging out."

Leven stood up and looked down at Frond. "Give me the axe."

"No."

The tree jabbed Frond hard enough in the back to cause him to throw the axe forward. It landed at Leven's feet. Leven picked it up and turned it in his hand.

"Move," Leven commanded.

"I won't let you do it," Frond raged. He sprang toward Leven's arm with his teeth bared. It was greatly forbidden for one sycophant to bite another sycophant's burn—especially if it was out of anger.

But Frond's mind was warped, and the bit of his brain that showed him right from wrong was buried by a much larger, angrier bit that was looking to protect the tree.

Clover pulled one of the sticks he had refused to burn from his void and, holding it with both hands, shoved it toward Frond. Frond's teeth bit down, hit the stick, and snapped it in two.

"How dare you?" Frond screamed. "If you had any idea of position and rank, you would bow to me and do my bidding."

"Well, I guess I'm lucky I have no idea," Clover yelled back.

Frond jumped forward and pushed Clover's shoulders back down and against the ground. "This isn't your fight."

Clover closed his eyes and threw his hands to the side as if to deflect the blows. No blows came.

Clover opened his eyes.

Frond was sitting on him looking baffled. There were dark red marks across Frond's chest, and the marks seemed to be oozing. Clover looked at his hands and marveled.

"Finally," Clover whispered.

Leven looked down at Clover and smiled. "You got your claws."

Most sycophants' claws grew in when they were posted as guards on the shores of Sycophant Run. The claws would stay for the few years they served and then fall off. Clover, however, had never gotten his claws. It was a source of great embarrassment to him. Now, right when he needed them most, they had finally appeared.

"Claws?" Frond said, confused. He jumped off of Clover as quickly as he could.

Clover sprang to his feet and swiped his claws though the air. Frond looked like he had just swallowed something disgusting.

"Leven," Clover said calmly, "chop down that tree."

Frond turned as if to make a move, but Clover simply scraped his claws together. The sound was full of pain and portend. Frond began to sob.

"Do you cry for the tree as well?" Clover asked.

Leven gripped the axe, stepped forward, and swung. The axe sliced into the tree's trunk, sending out sparks of fire from bits of metal in the wood. Leven fell down unconscious next to it.

CHAPTER THIRTY-NINE

HURRY UP AND WAIT

There are people who believe in you. You might not always believe that yourself, but there are—parents, teachers, neighbors, relatives, me. I know that no matter what is thrown at you, you'll recover amazingly.

Leven lived the first thirteen years of his life surrounded by people who didn't believe in him. They may have stunted his growth or knocked him down a hundred pegs or so, but they couldn't erase the fact that he was something much more than they believed. Every time they told him he was nothing, they simply made it that much more difficult for him to believe he was something. But once the darkness of their influence and attitude was removed from his life, Leven truly began to understand that he was much more than he had ever thought. And part of the reason he felt like he did now was because of Geth.

Even as a toothpick, Geth had made sure that Leven understood what he really was. And as a man, Geth had followed through, never wavering in his belief in Leven.

Never.

Geth knew that in the end Leven would not only become what he must, he would believe wholeheartedly in what he was doing.

"I hope Leven comes through," Winter said.

"Don't worry," Geth smiled. "He will."

The helicopter settled onto the ground and the rotors instantly began to slow. Geth, Winter, Phoebe, Ezra, and Lilly jumped out.

"I can't believe we made it," Winter said.

"Not all of us did," Ezra said angrily.

"Sorry," Winter tried.

Ezra crawled under the collar of Geth's robe.

"Where are we?" Phoebe asked.

"Burnt Culvert, Oklahoma," Geth answered.

The helicopter had landed in the field just next to the Rolling Greens Deluxe Mobile Home Park. They had seen the rubble and debris from the air and decided it would be best to land outside of it. The weather was calm at the moment, but they had seen avalands and telts not too far away while flying.

"Come on," Geth waved.

They trudged across the field and into the mobile home park. Trash and pieces of building were strewn everywhere. A couple of tractors were moving stuff around while residents were shifting through the wreckage looking for personal belongings or valuables.

"Reality is messy," Lilly observed.

"It's not always this bad," Winter said.

They all followed Geth through the devastation and back to

1712 Andorra Court. That piece of property was completely cleared. All the topsoil was gone, and all that was left was the stump sticking out of the ground.

"There it is," Winter smiled.

Geth stared at his old bottom half as Ezra crawled out from beneath his collar.

"That's us?" Ezra asked.

Geth nodded.

The stump was wide and hardening already. Ezra jumped down and felt it.

"It's cold," he said. "We came all this way and killed Dennis for a cold stump?"

"We came to wait," Geth said calmly.

"For what?"

"For Leven."

"You're kidding, right?" Ezra barked. "We're not just going to wait."

"I suppose we could help people clean up a bit."

"Girl!" Ezra called out. "Big eyes!"

Winter turned from what she was looking at. "Are you talking to me?"

"Well, I'm not talking to the pretty one," Ezra snapped. "Did you know that we came all this way and killed Dennis just to wait?"

Winter nodded, and Ezra swore accordingly. "Pretty one!" he then yelled.

Phoebe floated over.

"Did you know that we were coming all this way and killing Dennis to sit here and wait?"

Phoebe looked sad. She reached down toward the stump to touch Ezra.

"Don't touch me," Ezra hollered. "You'll just make me angrier. Listen, I don't know how the soft half of me operates, but I don't fly across the world and kill somebody harmless just to wait. That is a sorry plan even if part of me did make it up. Now we're here— why?"

"To wait," Geth said.

"Not you, you big sack of moisture," Ezra ranted. "Why?"

Winter sat down on the ground leaning against the stump.

"Sorry about Dennis," she said.

"What?" Ezra growled.

"Sorry about Dennis," Winter said again. "I know how much he meant to you."

"Where's this coming from?" Ezra demanded. "I could care less what happened to . . . Dennis." Ezra began to sob. He lay down on the stump and cried his eye out while Winter gently patted him on the back with her index finger.

"He was so stupid," Ezra wailed. "But he had a sort of janitorial smarts."

"I know," Winter soothed.

"He saved my life," Ezra admitted. "And his pants were always so neatly pressed."

"He did look clean," Phoebe tried.

"And now that big lumpy part of me," Ezra turned over just enough to point up at Geth. "That big lumpy part just wants to sit here waiting—or, worse yet, wants me to help clean up. I hate cleaning up."

"How about you just rest here on your stump?" Winter suggested. "We shouldn't have to wait long."

Ezra turned over and lay flat on his crooked back. With his one eye looking up and his arms stretched out, he looked just about as pathetic as a fancy toothpick could.

"He really was a decent person," Ezra sniffed.

"Just rest."

"He didn't say a lot, but when he did talk it was so funny."

Winter looked at Phoebe and Geth, not knowing how to respond to that.

"He . . ."

Ezra passed out from exhaustion.

CHAPTER FORTY

STICKS AND STONES

The English county of Wiltshire was normally quaint and serene. Thousands of tourists traversed its roads, but most of them were polite and simply in search of a photo op. You see, the county of Wiltshire is home to Stonehenge, one of the world's most famous landmarks—earthen ditches built around large, oddly stacked slabs of stone sticking up from the green countryside. Yes, normally it was quite a nice place to visit, and certainly the sort of place you would want to bring your camera.

But things weren't normal.

The Dearth had been showing up all over North America. He had moved through the soil at lightning speed, capturing any dark, dead souls long buried there. He had also reached above the soil in over a thousand places, pulling unsuspecting animals or people down into the earth.

He had shown up in Portsmouth, Maine, at a petting zoo. Children were simply petting and playing when thousands of thin, dark strings had shot up and dragged every last animal down into the soil.

The Dearth was enjoying the freedom and the seemingly limitless amount of soil in Reality. He had pushed under the Atlantic Ocean, and bits of him had begun to show up all over Europe.

The world was scared to death.

In Wiltshire County, not far from Stonehenge, the first signs of darkness had just appeared. A farmer was moving his sheep out of a pasture and into a barn with a solid floor when all of a sudden the ground began to rumble and crack. Innumerable tentacles flashed upward, wrapping themselves around the sheep and farmer.

Currently dozens of police cars were racing to the scene, not having any idea what they could actually do to stop the phenomenon.

"Do we shoot it?" one officer asked as they drove. He was sitting in the back of a white van filled with six other police officers.

"They say bullets go right through," the lead officer said.

"Tie it up?" another questioned.

"I don't think that'll work; it's just a bunch of black strings."

"So why are we racing there?" a third one asked. "This is mental. Maybe we should be racing home to our families."

"I agree," another officer said. "The world is a mess. What good can—"

The police officers' complaining was temporarily halted. And two of the officers swore—which of course is wrong even though when someone swears with an English accent it never sounds quite as bad.

The driver slammed on the brakes. There before them, rising out of the green countryside, was what looked like a black, bubbling mountain. It looked almost as if someone had struck oil and now it was shooting out of the earth. Except for the fact that this blackness had a face and arms and was moving forward.

"I never," one of the officers whispered.

The rest began to pray or chatter.

The Dearth pulled himself up, standing two hundred feet out of the soil. The bottom of him rippled and flowed into the ground while his top half bubbled and popped. His head was gigantic and round, with bits of earth all over it. On his face were two deep pits for eyes and a large, gaping mouth. Long gone was the quaint little friendly Englishman. The true Dearth was alive and huge.

The Dearth opened his mouth and screamed.

Millions of tiny stones and bits of earth flew out from around him. A helicopter half a mile away fell from the sky.

"Turn around," one of the police officers yelled. "Get us out of here."

"But we've got to stop it," another more valiant officer said.

"How?" six officers screamed in unison.

The Dearth shuffled toward Stonehenge and picked up one of the massive rocks with his long, sticky right arm. He heaved the rock, and it blasted into one of the police cars, sending it flying hundreds of feet.

"Get out of here," those in the van yelled.

The Dearth grabbed another stone and threw it into a small house, obliterating the two-hundred-year-old structure and creating a crater in the ground.

The sound of jets approaching from the south grew louder and

louder. Then, almost magically, the planes appeared, firing at the Dearth. The Dearth just stood there absorbing every shot that hit him. The jets circled back and fired heavily at the Dearth again. Once more the Dearth just stood there absorbing their shots.

As the planes were circling around for a third time, the Dearth began to swell and expand. Then, just as the jets reached him, the Dearth expelled every shot that had been fired into him. The sky was filled with shrapnel flying in all directions. Two jets exploded and a third flew into the ground.

Some of the police officers were actually crying now.

The Dearth roared, and any trees within a mile in front of him were stripped of their leaves. The black monster picked up another piece of Stonehenge and threw it toward the police van. It missed, but the vibration from the stone hitting the ground caused the van to jump three feet before settling back down on the road.

"Get us out of here!" one police officer yelled.

The van raced down the street with its siren blaring as stone after stone smacked down next to it. The driver swerved and dodged as best he could, believing the next one would destroy them completely.

A stone came down two hundred feet in front of them on the road, creating a huge divot in the earth. The van swerved and drove out over the countryside.

"This isn't good," one of the police officers said, sweating.

More jets arrived on the scene, and through the rear windows of the van the officers could see the Dearth sinking back into the earth.

"How do we beat that?" one cried.

"I'm not sure we can," another replied.

The van sped as quickly as it could away from the action.

CHAPTER FORTY-ONE

ALL TOGETHER AGAIN

There's nothing like coming home after being gone a long while. There's just something you can't duplicate about walking down the street you once lived on and stepping up to the door of the house you call home. But imagine that feeling if you had been gone for weeks. Or what if you had been taken to another realm and told you would never get back to see the ones you loved and left behind? What if you believed that you would never again touch the dishes you once set the table with or drink from the cups you once drank from or slept in the bed you once slept in? What if you had a husband or a wife and children waiting for you, but you had no way of telling them that you might never make it back? But then, what if you made it back?

That would be a pretty nice feeling.

Tim had stayed with Janet for a short while more. He had

explained a number of things, told her all he knew about wispy Janet and Osck, and filled her in on Winter. Janet had cried and nodded the whole time, staring at Tim as if he were a ghost himself. At one point she had stopped him and told him she didn't believe it, that she had just imagined her wispy self. At that point Tim had let Swig materialize and tell her she wasn't imagining.

Janet had touched Swig and cried.

Now Tim was running down the street heading toward his home. He could see that a light was on in the kitchen window and that the grass needed mowing.

"Which one is it?" Swig asked.

"The yellow one with the red door," Tim replied happily.

They ran up the sidewalk and straight to the door. Tim tried the knob, but it was locked. Fighting the urge to pound the door down, he reached over and pressed the doorbell.

A polite chime sounded.

Tim stood there with his heart in his throat and his feet begging to move.

"Who is it?" Tim's wife, Wendy, asked through the door.

"Tim."

Never in the history of mankind had three little letters evoked so much happiness and joy. Never had they announced so clearly that things, although bad, were about to get better. And never in the span of time had the name *Tim* been so wonderful to hear.

The door flew open, there were screams, and then the kind of hugs that happen when you thought your children were missing and then you found them were given all around.

"How?"

"Where?"

"Winter?"

"Why?"

"Foo?"

Wendy had her red hair down, and her eyes, which had been heavy with sorrow and care just moments ago, now shone with light. She kissed her husband repeatedly on the face and neck. Tim's two boys, Darcy and Rochester, wouldn't let go of him. He finally had to fall back into a chair and pull them both onto his lap.

"You went to Foo?" Darcy asked.

Tim nodded.

"No way," Rochester said.

Wendy clung to Tim's right arm as he sat there, as if it were the last life preserver in the time of Noah.

Swig cleared his throat, and all of them looked around.

"What was that?" Wendy asked.

"Oh, yeah," Tim smiled. "I brought you something from Foo. Swig?"

Swig materialized on top of Tim's left shoulder—posing in such a way as to look slightly majestic. All three of them jumped back. Wendy screamed.

"What is it?" Darcy asked in amazement.

"He's a sycophant," Tim said. "His name is Swig."

"Pleased to meet you," Swig said, bowing just a bit.

All three of them let their jaws drop to the floor.

"Will he bite?" Rochester asked.

"Not unless you wish me to," Swig said.

"You know, Swig," Tim said, "we're not in Foo anymore. You're welcome to think for yourself."

Swig smiled. "Well, then, I don't bite."

The whole family gathered around the small, furry creature, marveling over him and over the fact that they were all together again. In a world where everything was wrong, it was nice to feel right, even if for just a moment.

CHAPTER FORTY-TWO

THERE'S NOTHING
BETTER THAN BRISKET

The Rolling Greens Deluxe Mobile Home Park was none of the above. It was more like Burnt Culvert's newest landfill. Like the rest of the world, it had been picked on by strange things and left for dead.

Dooley Hornbackle had brought in a number of tractors to remove debris and help clear things out, but so far they hadn't made a dent. Had the Rolling Greens Deluxe Mobile Home Park been torn apart during an average time in history, its inhabitants might very well have been able to roll up their sleeves, work hard, and one day restore the place. But the park had been torn apart during one of Reality's most trying and difficult times. There were thousands of places in need, and nobody knew when their needs would be met.

The only structure still standing was the cement shelter in the middle of the park. Most of the residents had found other places to stay, and only a few were bothering to come back and search the wreckage for salvageable items or personal mementos.

Geth and Winter and Phoebe and Lilly had left Ezra to sleep it off. They were walking around the park helping anyone who wanted help. But soon the sky began to turn white and red, and what sounded like vulgar thunder rang though the air. The thunder had evidently taken on the bad habit of the thunder in Foo and was calling people names.

"Pathetic," the thunder cracked.

Mr. Hornbackle spotted them and asked Geth to help him lift a bed off of a car. Geth helped, and Mr. Hornbackle then offered them brisket sandwiches and remarkably cold root beer. They sat under a sturdy tent out of the wind, near what used to be the entrance to the park.

"Oh," Phoebe said after taking her first bite and sip. "Now I see why people like Reality."

"It'll never be the same," Mr. Hornbackle said with a loud sigh.

"What won't?" Geth asked.

"The world," he replied. "It's been a long time coming. I always suspected things would fall apart; I just didn't think it would involve a whole other world."

"Foo, you mean?" Winter asked.

"Foo," he echoed softly. "You know, I was a pilot in World War II. We chased some lights over Germany one time that later became known as Foo fighters. That was a scary time, but now I fear Foo even more."

"You shouldn't," Geth said. "There's nothing to fear but selfishness."

"Another sandwich?" Dooley offered.

As Dooley handed Geth his second sandwich, Geth noticed the old man leaning to one side. "Are you okay?" he asked.

Dooley didn't answer but continued to tip until he was lying on his right side with his eyes wide open.

"Dooley!" Winter said.

He didn't blink or move in the slightest.

"It's happening," Geth said.

"What's happening?" Winter asked.

"Everything's changing," Geth answered. "We're moving into the third day. Those who are older will fall first. Dooley might never get up again if Leven doesn't come through."

"My wings don't work," Phoebe revealed. "I didn't want to alarm anyone, but they stopped working a while ago."

"I don't understand how Leven can affect any of this," Winter said. "He's so far away. We should never have left him in Foo."

"Don't say that!" Geth snapped, banging the picnic table. The reaction was so unlike Geth that both Phoebe's and Winter's jaws dropped. "Those who doubt fate will be among the first to go. Leven will come through."

"Are you okay?" Winter asked.

"I don't know," Geth answered honestly. "I need to talk to Ezra."

Dooley groaned.

"Do you think he would mind if I took another one of those sandwiches?" Phoebe asked.

"I don't think he's going to mind anything for a while," Winter replied, grabbing another sandwich herself and handing it to Lilly.

Once they were out from under the tent, a timid rain began to fall and the thunder picked up its insults.

"Flightless," it mocked Phoebe.

"It's so personal," she said.

"Hurry," Geth urged.

They worked their way back to 1712 Andorra Court. When they were about a hundred feet away, Geth ran to the stump. There was nothing there besides the purple tassel and the bent paper clip. Small flecks of green nail polish lined where Ezra had once lain.

"Where is he?" Lilly asked.

"I don't believe it," Geth said, kneeling next to the stump.

"He soaked in?" Phoebe asked innocently.

"He's gone," Geth said sadly.

"That's a good thing, right?" Lilly asked.

"I don't know," Geth answered honestly.

Winter put her hand on Geth's back and rubbed it as the rain picked up. The small bits of green nail polish ran off the stump, followed by the purple tassel. All that was left was the bent paper clip. Winter picked it up and put it in her pocket.

It is only appropriate to point out that, despite his anger and hatred, Ezra had done his bit to fight for Foo. His life was also a fantastic reminder that even the smallest bit of anger can cause damage and unnecessary drama in our lives.

"It's getting close," Geth said seriously. "I have been alive for a long time and I'm not sure I ever thought this time would come."

They all just stood there getting wetter and wetter and staring at the stump. They might very well have stood there all day if it had not been for the loud cracking noise that shot through the air and shook the ground.

Geth and Phoebe fell down.

"Look," Winter yelled, pointing at the stump. "Look."

Geth and Phoebe watched the stump as it raised up two feet into the air.

"Is that because of Ezra?" Phoebe asked.

"Leven's knocking," Geth smiled. "Are you two—"

Lilly cleared her throat.

"Excuse me," Geth said. "Are you *three* ready?"

Nobody answered; they just stared at the stump, waiting. Had they turned around and looked all the way down the road back toward the entrance to the mobile home park, they might have been able to see long strands of black shoot up into the air and pull Dooley Hornbackle down into the soil.

CHAPTER FORTY-THREE

OUTTA WHACK

Get up," Clover pleaded.

Leven just lay there on the ground, his body completely limp and his arms spread to his sides. The axe he had hit the tree with was lying on the ground next to him. Clover looked at the damage the chop had done. There was a good-sized gash in the trunk of the tree. Frond was rubbing something on the gash and crying.

"Get up," Clover yelled to Leven.

"He's probably dead," Frond said coldly.

"He's not dead," Clover replied, flashing his claws.

Foo rumbled and the oldest tree's branches shook and trembled. It moaned and creaked.

"What did it say?" Clover asked.

"It said to get out of here," Frond answered.

The tree bonked Frond on the head.

"I'm trying to save you," Frond told the tree.

Leven mumbled and began to stir. He rolled over onto his right side and opened his eyes.

"Are you okay?" Clover asked.

"Ouch," was all Leven could answer.

"You can lie there for a bit," Clover said. "But I'm kind of worried we're running out of time."

Leven sat up. "How long have I been out?"

"Just a few minutes," Clover answered.

Leven saw the axe lying there and looked at the tree.

"You didn't tell me it would hurt so much," Leven said to Frond. "I feel like a giant bruise."

"I was hoping you weren't the one," Frond said. "A normal person wouldn't have felt anything."

"Well, then, let's get a normal person to chop the tree down," Leven insisted.

"I tried to stop you," Frond said hotly. "I warned you. Now leave."

Leven stood up and dusted off his palms on the legs of his pants. He looked down at the axe and nonchalantly reached out his hand. The axe lifted from the ground and flew to his hand.

Leven was as surprised as the rest of them.

"I couldn't do that before," Leven said as a strong wind began to tear at the outside walls of the monastery. It sounded as if the wind wanted desperately to get into the courtyard.

"What are you doing with that axe?" Frond demanded.

Leven stepped up to the tree and winced. Frond looked as if he were going to pounce, but Clover proudly flashed his claws.

"This is the only way," Leven said. He pulled the axe back and, with twice the force of before, he swung at the tree.

There were more sparks as the metal sank deep into the tree's trunk. Leven fell to the ground on his knees, screaming. He arched his back, howling into the air like a wounded coyote. His body lurched and trembled and he fell forward onto his stomach.

Time stopped momentarily, and then the sun rolled completely across the sky and the wind tore harder at the monastery walls— wood beams and mortar were being pulled away and dropped down into the gorge Leven had crossed. The ground shook and the oldest tree quivered spastically.

"Leven's not going to make it," Frond screamed. "He'll be dead by the fourth whack."

"You don't know him like I do," Clover argued.

"I don't care how well you know him," Frond said. "You will still have a dead burn. Think about it. You want to kill him?"

Clover knelt down by Leven's head and gently shook his shoulders.

"Come on," Clover whispered. "Get up."

Clover pulled a leather bladder from his void and unscrewed the top of it. He poured water onto the right side of Leven's face, drowning his right ear and hair.

Leven coughed and sputtered like a dying engine; then his eyes flashed open. He lifted his head and looked at the tree. The gash was bigger, but the tree was still standing.

"Shoot," Leven complained. "How many was that?"

"Two," Clover answered.

Leven moaned like the wind. He lay on the ground with his face in the soil and then pushed himself up and back onto his knees, groaning. He looked at the axe and raised his hand again. The axe floated nicely into his grip.

"You don't have to do this," Frond argued.

"You said I did," Leven replied, not fully paying attention to the desperate sycophant.

"It was the tree," Frond yelled. "He's old and he's not thinking . . ."

The wounded tree still had the strength to smack Frond.

Leven looked at the axe and shivered. He could see his reflection in the metal and was surprised how wounded his eyes looked.

"What are you waiting for?" Clover asked as the wind howled outside the courtyard.

"It hurts," Leven said honestly.

"What good things don't?" Clover pointed out.

Leven looked at Clover. "You're amazing."

Clover blushed and jumped onto Leven's right shoulder. "Well, I figure this is that part you were talking about where I save everyone. I know sycophants are supposed to listen and take orders, but I'm telling you to hit that tree."

Leven smiled as best he could and then swung. The axe hit its mark and sent every nerve ending in Leven's body into a spastic convulsion. Leven stood there shaking as if he were a cartoon character who had foolishly put his finger into a light switch. His hair smoldered and his chest flexed violently. He tried to say something but instead tipped backwards wordlessly, falling to the ground.

Frond looked at the deepening gash in the tree. He picked up some of the chunks of wood that had been chopped out and frantically tried to put them back in the cut.

"Are you happy?" Frond screamed at Clover.

Clover just stood there looking at Leven as he was lying on the ground. Clover had only belonged to two beings: first Antsel and then Leven. And, to be honest, as much as he had loved Antsel, he now cared for Leven ten times more. Clover looked at Leven as he lay there and couldn't decide if he should cry or be angry.

On the other side of the monastery the island of Alder was drift-ing toward Morfit, creating new mountains and rivers and flooding once-dry shores. The Waves of the Lime Sea had begun to retreat to the Green Pond, and the animals that populated Foo were losing their minds. Avalands were driving themselves into the seas; onicks were attacking nits and cogs; and the Cinder Depression was rising like a mountain.

The ground shook and Clover jiggled.

"What kind of sycophant lets his burn die?" Frond hollered, still trying to patch up the tree.

Clover's mind was a mess. He kept trying to think of the things he had been taught, hoping they would help him know what he should do. He remembered his mother telling him that he would do great things, and his father reminding him that "without sycophants, Foo would fall." But Clover couldn't decide if he would be best serv-ing Foo by stopping Leven or by keeping him going.

Leven sat up and looked around. He looked like a kid who had just been awakened from a long nap and now had no idea where he was.

Frond swore.

"Are you okay?" Clover asked.

"No," Leven mumbled. "My head feels like it isn't even attached."

Clover looked Leven over. "It is."

Leven could barely lift his arms and he had to sit still for a while before his legs would work again.

"This might kill me," Leven said groggily.

"Frond said it would," Clover reminded him.

"I wish Winter was here," Leven slurred. "I think I'm in love with her."

"That's great," Clover said, trying to prop Leven up.

"Don't you care if I die?" Leven asked.

Clover stared at him. "Of course. But there are worse things than death."

Leven stood up and reached for the axe. It flew to him again. "It's a pity. I would have liked to have lived with this ability for a while."

"Yeah, it's pretty cool," Clover agreed.

Leven stumbled forward and struck the tree for the fourth time.

ii

The stump continued to rise. Long shoots shot from the sides of it and up into the air. The roots beneath the stump began to churn and burrow.

"What's happening?" Winter asked.

"Leven's doing it," Geth said. "I can't believe it."

"Doing what?" Phoebe asked.

"You'll see."

An older couple who had been across the street rummaging through their ruined home stopped to look at the rising stump. The woman pointed and the man fell to the dirt. Two seconds later she joined him.

"People are dropping off," Geth said needlessly.

In the far distance, an entire mountain range moved across their view. The old people who had just fallen were sucked into the soil by long strands of black.

"Shouldn't we be standing on stone or something?" Winter asked.

"It's too late for that," Geth said. "The Dearth's reach is as wide as the world."

Hail fell from the clear sky, pelting them on the head.

"So we just stare at this stump?"

"Remember what Leven said," Geth said seriously.

"Leven's said a lot of things," Winter pointed out.

Geth smiled. "In the end you might save us all."

Lilly stroked Winter's hair.

"How?" Winter questioned. "By staring at this stump?"

There was a tremendous rap, and the stump shot up two more feet. The sun circled around the earth and Phoebe fell to the ground. Geth ran to her and knelt beside her. He laid her head in his lap.

"Phoebe," he said calmly, "are you there?"

Phoebe just lay there looking as beautiful as ever. Her white skin glowed and her body trembled slightly.

"She's going," Geth said. "Going . . ."

Her body began to fade and then pulsate. Winter tried to pull on her arms and stop it from happening, but Geth did nothing.

In less than a few seconds Phoebe's body blinked and then was gone.

Winter looked at Geth in disgust.

"What?" Geth asked.

"You didn't do anything!"

"There's no way to stop it."

"How romantic," Winter snapped. "She loved you."

"I love her," Geth said coolly.

Winter couldn't decide if she should slap or punch Geth. She went with punch. Geth stumbled back and grabbed his chin where she had struck.

"What was that for?" he asked.

"Way to fight for her," Winter growled.

"You know I have fought for a lot of things in my life," Geth said kindly. "And I would have held onto Phoebe forever if I believed it would help, but it wouldn't have made a difference. What will make the difference is Leven."

"I don't understand," Winter said, trying not to cry.

"You will shortly," Geth said. "And you will help Leven restore everything as it should be. I'll see Phoebe again, and you'll get a chance to give her a hard time about how beautiful she is."

"She *was* overly attractive," Winter complained.

Geth smiled. "This is it. Now, if it had been you who was taken, I would be worried."

"Really?"

"There's nobody I'd rather have here as fate's about to mess with us."

Winter straightened her shoulders.

"So you love Phoebe?" Winter said, trying to lighten the mood.

"Very much," Geth replied. "And she told me how you felt about Leven."

Winter's green eyes burned. "I'm almost glad she's gone for the moment."

Geth smiled as the stump shot up three more feet.

CHAPTER FORTY-FOUR

YOUR NAME HERE

I t took more than twenty minutes for Leven to come to. In that time the back half of the far monastery wall had been torn apart by wind, the moon had passed over twice, and Frond had fetched some dark herbs and was rubbing them on the tree.

Leven got up on his hands and knees and threw up. Thunder above roared, calling him a wuss, and he shook his head and wiped his mouth with the back of his hand.

With Clover's help he was finally able to stand.

"Stop this madness," Frond pleaded.

"I'm trying to," Leven replied. He stuck out his hand, and as the axe flew to him he strode and used the forward motion to chop the tree once more.

The tree moaned and shivered as Leven collapsed against it. Frond began kicking Leven and Clover jumped over to take a swipe at him. Frond fell to the ground. Before he could hop back up, Clover was wrapping a long rope around him.

"What are you doing?" Frond frothed.

Clover bound Frond like Gulliver and then tied the rope off tightly. Frond sat on the soil crying and pleading.

"You don't care?" Frond asked.

"Oh, I care," Clover replied. "Wait . . . about what?"

"Can't you see what's happening?" Frond said. "Foo is trying to cleanse itself of every nit that ever stepped in here. It'll be just us."

"You and me?" Clover asked awkwardly.

"Not just *us,*" Frond said. "We sycophants. Never will we have to take an order from a nit again. No more fighting over the right to serve. Just us. No stupid commands or selfish wishes. Just us."

"You said 'just us' four times," Clover pointed out.

"Well, I meant it five," Frond argued, fighting at the ropes that bound him.

Clover looked at Leven as he lay collapsed against the tree. "So why do you want to save the tree? It looks like it gives you a lot of orders."

"Don't be a child," Frond said. "The tree keeps things as they are. It guarantees our comfort."

"Foo's falling apart," Clover said.

"And the tree pins us down," Frond said. "As everything is blown away and destroyed, we sycophants will live on."

"I'm not sure I believe that."

"Then you're a fool."

"Don't call Clover a fool," Leven insisted. He pushed himself up against the tree and stood straight. His mind was confused. "Do you think Winter will call me?"

Clover stared at Leven. "Um, maybe you should just work on the tree."

"What tree?"

"The one you're leaning against."

Leven looked at the tree and winced. "Where's Geth?"

"Waiting for you," Clover answered, handing Leven the axe.

Leven looked at it and began to shake. His legs and arms cracked and burned like dry wood.

"Leave now," Frond said.

"Just let me finish one thing," Leven said. He bent his knees and put his whole body into it, swinging the axe as if it were a baseball bat and this were the one chance he had to win the game. The axe sunk into the trunk ten inches and a wedge of wood the size of a toaster tumbled out, surrounded by sparks. Leven dropped the axe and put his head in his hands. The wind seemed to stop and then go in reverse, pulling all daylight with it. Instantly the monastery was filled with people, all looking out the windows and pointing toward the tree. The scene wound further back and the monastery buildings were being erected by thousands of cogs.

Leven screamed, tearing at his own face and beginning to weep. The scenery around him stopped moving and the half-built monastery sat there empty. For the first time in many years, wind blew in from the sides and pushed through the oldest tree's branches. The leaves of the tree turned all different colors and then one by one flew off into the distance.

"Don't let him die," Frond begged.

"I don't care about the tree," Clover said, jumping up onto Leven's shoulder and gently patting the back of Leven's head.

"I wasn't talking about the tree," Frond said. "Lead Leven away—let him live."

Clover looked at Leven and cocked his head. "Had enough?"

"No way."

The axe flew into Leven's hands and he swung once more, driving the head of the axe a foot into the trunk. Then before his body could register the pain he yanked the axe back and swung again.

The tree seemed to scream as a piece of it the size of a basketball flew out. Leven fell to the ground unconscious as time ran backwards and the monastery buildings completely disappeared.

CHAPTER FORTY-FIVE

RECORD PLAY STOP
FAST-FORWARD REWIND EJECT

Winter watched the clouds and the sun move in reverse. The piles of torn-up mobile home blew away like sand in the wind and in a few movements they were standing in an untouched prairie staring at the trunk. She felt dizzy and tired and wanted desperately to lie down on the soil.

"Don't do it," Geth said, watching her lean toward the ground. "I can feel it too, but we have to keep standing. The Dearth is everywhere, but he's so consumed with taking over that he's not paying attention to us."

The sound of a record being played in reverse scratched out across the landscape as the roads and buildings in the distance became overgrown and then disappeared completely.

"What's happening?" Winter yelled, her voice competing with the screeching. "Where is everything going?"

"It never was," Geth said, taking Winter's hand.

The soil around the stump began to churn and pop. Large dirt clods shot up into the air as the roots of the stump twisted in the soil.

"The Dearth will catch on soon," Geth said. "But if Leven can fell the tree before he even realizes we are right here, we might not have to fight."

"Where's the fun in that?" Winter asked.

Wind blew back and forth across the prairie. Large herds of buffalo could be seen running in the distance. And then, in the blink of an eye, they were gone.

"Is this happening all over?" Winter yelled.

"At different speeds," Geth answered. "Time as we know it is no longer a factor."

The wind became so strong that Winter could feel herself being pushed backwards.

"Hold onto the stump," Geth ordered.

Winter crouched down beside the stump and threw her arms around one of the roots. She locked her fingers together and held tight. Geth was right beside her hanging onto his own root.

"Don't let go," Geth yelled.

"I wasn't planning to."

"And don't drift off."

The stump pulsated as it was sucked up and down like a plunger. It pounded against the earth and dug in with its roots.

"Are we going to die?" Winter yelled.

"Maybe," Geth yelled back.

Dirt and rocks and debris blew up against them like angry, supersized rain. A small branch whipped Winter in the face, drawing blood on her right cheek. As she turned her head, she saw a massive wall of dirt rolling across the prairie. The dirt lifted up and came crashing down toward them.

Without even thinking about it, Winter froze the dirt. Flakes of snowlike ice crackled and drifted down on them.

"Did you see that?" Winter asked, dumbfounded.

"I was wondering when it would come back," Geth yelled happily, a large fist of snow filling his mouth. "It's like your gift was never stolen."

Winter smiled, showing off her own ice-filled teeth.

"Lilly!" Winter yelled. "Are you there?"

"I'm here," Lilly said from the side of Winter. The small sycophant was tucked up under Winter's arm and holding on for dear life.

"I can freeze things again," Winter said.

"I'd clap, but I'd probably blow away," Lilly yelled back.

The ground shook and the wind stopped completely. Every bit of dirt or rock it was blowing around dropped instantly to the ground. The scene had become a vacuum.

Winter tried to speak but no sound came from her voice. Geth was no more successful. Lilly tried to scream. The three of them began to grasp at their necks for air.

As their faces turned red, a large "Pop!" sounded and a rush of air flooded back into the prairie like a tsunami.

All three gasped for air.

"You're sure we're going to make it?" Winter screamed.

"I'm still sticking with maybe," Geth answered.

The two held onto the roots of the tall stump as the world continued to fall apart.

"So if I can freeze things again, how come you're not turning back into a tree?" Winter yelled.

There was no answer.

"Geth, can you . . ." Winter turned her head and saw that Geth was gone. "Geth!"

The root she was holding onto began to warm, and Winter looked up at the huge, swaying branches and millions of leaves above her.

ii

Clover continued pouring water over Leven's face. He had been out cold for almost fifteen minutes, and in that time the scenery surrounding them had completely changed. Gone was the monastery, the three mountain peaks behind them were now four, and the soil on which Leven lay was growing darker and richer.

The oldest tree stood by itself being beaten by the wind. The tree leaned well to the left, its branches drooping.

Frond lay on the ground, bound and shivering.

"You're going to drown me," Leven said to Clover. "Where are we?"

"Same place," Clover told him. "Everything keeps changing. I think I actually saw a siid flying overhead."

"The monastery?"

"Gone."

Leven turned himself over and got up onto his knees, holding his right side. He winced with pain and closed his eyes. Unlike before, when he could see nothing, now he saw light and out-of-focus images. He waited for the images to come into focus but they just faded away.

Leven stood hunched over and gazed at the tree. The poor thing was creaking loudly.

"He's suffering," Frond cried.

Clover handed Leven the axe.

"Everything comes from the soil and air," Frond wailed. "Let it return."

"I believe in mankind," Leven said.

"Why?" Frond argued. "I know your history. You were abused by mankind from the beginning. Why have faith in them?"

"It can be better," Leven said.

Frond began to laugh. His laugher grew until he was shaking and his teeth were showing. "Do better? The one thing men have proven is their inability to learn from their mistakes. They strive only to be comfortable and then let the world slide away for the sake of a soft seat. Do better? Men will do only what they can to believe they have some control. They are experts at reacting and champions of selfishness."

"Well, then," Leven said, "just chalk this up to me *reacting*."

Leven took another swing at the tree. The sparks were bright and the gash was now halfway through the huge trunk. Leven's arms contracted and his legs felt like stone. He gasped for air as his chest tightened like a drum. His shoulders dropped and his knees collapsed, sending him forward onto his face. He dropped the axe and his forehead scraped against the path of glass—blood began to run down and into his glowing eyes.

Clover watched Leven suffer and shivered.

"You can't let him go on," Frond said. "He'll die, and what then? Look at him—such pain."

"It's not my decision," Clover said softly. "If he wanted to stop, he would."

"That's where you're wrong," Frond said. "He's obsessed. I watched him hike up Alder never caring about anything but doing as he was told."

"So?" Clover said slowly.

"He doesn't make his decisions, which means you too are just toeing the line," Frond said sinisterly. "Now look at him. He'll die and leave you to be blamed for all that has happened. You're the only one who can stop him from completely destroying Foo *and* Reality."

Clover turned to look at Frond. He looked back at Leven. Leven was spitting and coughing up blood while on his knees. The moon moved backwards across the sky again and the roots of the oldest tree wriggled throughout the now-empty courtyard.

"I'll make sure they know," Frond said desperately. "It's your choice. Every remaining sycophant will know that you saved us all."

Clover looked at his own hands. His razor-sharp claws extended from the backs of his knuckles and looked impressive under the swift-moving moon. He watched Leven pick the axe back up and then stumble toward the tree. Clover could see quite clearly that there was no turning back. Foo was completely changing and would never be the same.

Leven stood up straight. His body faded in and out like a neon sign on the fritz. He touched his chin and wiped his free hand on his shirt.

Leven stepped up to the dying tree.

"I'm not sure what's happening," Leven wheezed. "Why I'm connected to all this . . . I'm not sure. But when I close my eyes, I know I have to do this. And I know it sounds nuts, but I'd rather be dead and right than alive and all wrong."

The tree creaked.

"I thought you'd understand."

Leven screamed in agony before the axe head even hit the tree. His body was a bruise on top of a bruise on top of a bruise on top of a throbbing wound. He let the pain bounce around inside of himself and followed through with the tenth chop. A tremendously large wedge of wood flew from the tree, missing Frond by a couple of inches.

Leven dropped the axe and closed his eyes, begging his body to absorb the pain and then get rid of it. He couldn't feel his fingers or toes and there was no separation between his arms and legs. He felt like a solid brick of sorrow. His heart shifted inside his chest and blood began to ooze out of the corner of his mouth. He was standing, but not because he had the strength. It was more like he was a statue on the verge of imploding.

Stars spread out overhead, spelling messages of doom and finality. The ground dropped three feet and then settled with a tremendous click.

Leven still stood.

He tried to close his eyes but he didn't have the energy. He could see Winter and Geth and Amelia. He could sense that Clover was on his shoulder and patting his head, but he couldn't feel it. More than anything, Leven wanted to be done—and if it took death to do it, then so be it.

Leven stood still.

"You have to stop him," Frond pleaded.

"He looks pretty stopped," Clover answered.

"Our fate will be your fault," Frond yelled.

As Frond argued his point, large roots began to spring up around the tree. The roots shot up ten feet, curling at the ends, and were lighter than those of the oldest tree. On the ends of the roots were wicked-looking weeds.

One root shot up directly in front of Leven, catching the attention of both Clover and Frond and sending Leven toppling to the ground.

The soil around the tree bubbled and surged. Frond disappeared, and the dark sky became wet and heavy.

Clover picked up the heavy axe and looked at it. Thunder screamed, "Sheep!"

The oldest tree moaned and screeched as it leaned forward. It used one of its longest branches to take the axe from Clover.

"You going to do it yourself?" Clover yelled. "I'm not sure he has it in him."

The oldest tree bent his branch back and then catapulted the axe into the air. It flew miles and miles away.

"I'm not getting that," Clover said.

The tree then reached out and picked up Leven. He hoisted Leven up into his highest branches and then threw him as hard as he could back down against the soil.

Clover disappeared.

CHAPTER FORTY-SIX

TO BE OR NOT TO BE

Geth!" Winter yelled, clinging to one of his roots and not knowing if he could even understand her. "Geth!"

The wind blowing across the prairie was so forceful that Winter knew she couldn't hold on much longer. The sky rolled backwards again and the sound of some eerie music filled the air. The music stopped, the sun turned green, and the wind blew even harder.

"Lilly?"

There was no answer.

"Geth!"

Geth reached down with two of his limbs and pulled Winter up into his branches. The wind was tearing off his leaves and screeching through his limbs. Winter stood on one of the high branches and wrapped her arms around the trunk of the tree.

The wind stopped.

"Please, Geth," Winter pleaded.

A fantastic sucking sound rumbled across the Oklahoma prairie. Winter looked to the north and watched as the ground about a mile away began to buckle and rise. She thought at first it was just an avaland, but the soil was too dark, and the mound rose hundreds of feet into the air.

Winter had never seen the Dearth in all his dark glory. She had seen him as a kindly old man, but something was different about him now. It very well could have been the fact that he was taller than a twenty-story building, as thick as a mountain, and bubbling like black tar. Winter could see his round head and watched as he opened his mouth and blew out enough dirt to fill the Grand Canyon.

"He's coming this way!" Winter yelled.

Dark roots shot out of the dirt and up toward Winter. She looked down from Geth and could see dozens of those dark roots popping up from the soil and wrapping themselves around Geth.

Geth shot his own roots downward, mixing with the roots of the oldest tree. The two trees stiffened and clung, each trying to pull the other under.

"What are you doing?" Winter screamed. "The Dearth."

The Dearth rose even higher, pushing across the prairie like a filthy flood. His bulk absorbed everything in his path. He threw his face down into the soil and took a massive bite out of the ground.

He spat and for a number of minutes it was raining dirt.

Winter clung to Geth, crying as the Dearth moved closer. She felt like a sacrifice waiting to be devoured.

"Leven!" she yelled. "Where are you?"

The wind began again, and the ground felt like it dropped ten feet as Geth wrestled with the roots of the oldest tree.

"Leven!"

The Dearth moved ever closer as the sun and the moon appeared to bump up against each other and then roll backwards.

Winter closed her eyes and froze the Dearth. The black beast stood still for almost a full second and then dropped back down into the soil, leaving its icy shell to shatter and fall.

Instantly the Dearth was back up just like before, except now he was bothered. He shot thousands of dark strings up out of the soil and into the branches, reaching for Winter. Winter moved through the branches like a cat, freezing the strands and breaking them as she pushed upward.

The Dearth roared and took another bite out of the ground.

"Please, Geth," Winter pleaded, frightened by the desperation in her own voice.

More dark roots shot up and coiled around Geth's trunk. Winter could feel the entire tree being pulled down into the dirt. She climbed madly to the highest branches.

It was no use. The Dearth loomed larger than a mountain up above, and she and Geth were being dragged down below, where Winter knew the Dearth had even greater power.

The tree dropped ten more feet. It was being sucked into the soil.

"Come on, Geth," Winter begged as she held tightly to the tallest point of his trunk. "Come on!" Geth was pulled in further.

The Dearth shot out more thousands of tiny black strings that wrapped around Geth's branches and pinned Winter to the tree. She froze them and then busted out of their grasp, sending shards of ice into the surrounding dirt.

The tree dropped again. Winter's legs were now under the soil. "Anyone!" she cried.

Again Geth sank; he was now completely buried under the earth. The Dearth thundered and shot upward like a dirty gusher. He then slammed down against the ground, chasing after Geth.

ii

Clover had no idea what to do. He looked around him as mountains pushed up from the soil and then leveled out. The air was as thick and sticky as maple syrup and it took three breaths to equal just one gulp of air.

His tiny body shivered as he tried to pull Leven away from the tree. It was a lesson in futility. The oldest tree had drastically changed his mood. It was as if self-preservation had kicked in. He was clacking and hollering and pounding the ground with his branches. His roots were whirling and slithering through the soil so heatedly that the ground looked like it was boiling.

A thick branch shot out and wrapped around Leven's ankles. The tree then picked the unconscious Leven up and pounded him against the ground a few times. As he was about to toss him, the tree seemed to slip and sink into the soil a few inches. He dropped Leven and moaned, pulling himself back up.

"Leven," Clover pleaded. "Get up."

Leven's eyes flashed open and then shut.

"Get up," Clover begged.

"No," Leven whispered. "The tree doesn't wanna go."

"You have to," Clover yelled.

"I can't."

"I wish I were Geth so I could beat some sense into you."

"Geth's probably dead," Leven moaned. "I've failed."

Three volcanoes shot off in succession in the background. The sound rocked the ground as massive waves of ash blew toward them.

"I think Geth's alive," Clover tried. "I think those are his roots tugging on the tree."

"I can't do it," Leven pleaded, his body still lying motionless on the ground. "I've hit that thing dozens of times. He's not going down."

"Actually you've hit him ten times," Clover said. "The next one will be eleven."

Leven's eyes flashed open and stayed open. "Between ten and eleven," he mumbled. He screamed and ripped his body from the dirt to sit up. He looked toward the oldest tree and watched as the tree struggled with the roots beneath him. The tree would lift up and then be dragged under a couple of inches, only to lift up again later.

"Where's the axe?" Leven asked, wiping blood from his lips.

"He threw it that way," Clover pointed.

Leven coughed and turned onto his hands and knees. Then, like an elderly dog, he lifted his front hand. As if by magic, the axe returned.

Unfortunately, the oldest tree noticed.

The tree slammed a branch down against Leven's back. Leven collapsed against the ground and the axe flew from his grip. The tree reached for the axe while desperately trying to fight off Geth's root beneath him. Clover leapt from the ground and landed on the branch. With one swift move he sliced the branch off.

The tree screamed and Leven reached for the axe.

iii

Winter could barely breathe. Geth used his roots to pull at the roots of the oldest tree to keep creating small pockets of air. Winter could feel that the Dearth had now joined the fight. Blackness swept over her heart like a smothering plastic. She couldn't breathe, but, more depressingly, she no longer hoped. She let go of the part of Geth she was holding onto and just let herself be tossed around in the wriggling roots. She knew she needed air, but she didn't care. Her leg got caught between two fighting roots and snapped. The pain was horrible, but it didn't compare to the misery in her chest.

Winter believed all was lost.

The Dearth began to bunch up into the roots, pulling himself from all over the soil to smother the one thing that could stop him now. He was so huge that he no longer had any personality or thought, just a mission statement to destroy everything. Like a massive underground aquifer the Dearth flooded the tree roots, pushing Geth and the oldest tree apart.

Winter froze the black mass, but it simply shook off the ice and continued to smother. She kept thinking about what Leven had said and wondering where she had gone wrong. She could get no more air and her lungs were collapsing.

The Dearth pushed up out of the soil in Reality. He was larger than a mountain and covered in dirt.

He screamed and the whole world heard it.

The Dearth then arched his back and threw his head down to the earth. He pushed his entire mass into the soil, wedging the long roots of the two trees apart and pushing Winter up against Geth's roots. Her hair caught and she could feel her neck bending backwards. There was no clear thought in her head. All she could think about through the pain was stopping the Dearth from diving on them again.

Winter was ready to fade.

She pictured the surface of the earth being nothing but solid ice and then passed out.

iv

The Dearth screamed beneath the soil, fighting to keep Geth from pulling the oldest tree down. The ice Winter had placed over the soil of Reality scratched at him like a fatal sweat. His tarlike being bubbled and gasped for more air. The Dearth pried at the roots, wedging his mass between the two trees. He stretched downward and broke out into the air of Foo.

A horrific blast shook the ground.

The Dearth wrapped part of himself around the oldest tree, pushing the trunk away from Geth's roots.

Leven could see the black ooze rising up from the soil. He watched it wrap tightly around the trunk of the tree. He stood up and ran toward the tree with the axe above his head.

The tree grabbed Leven around the waist with one of his longest branches. He then heaved Leven heavenward with all his power.

Leven ripped straight up through the air like a missile. His cheeks and face jiggled and blew back as the force of the throw worked him over. His body twitched like a jumping bean.

Clover materialized, holding onto his neck.

"Don't let go of that axe!" Clover hollered, his own small body shaking from the force of the wind.

Leven tightened his grip on the axe but continued to shoot upward. The wind tore at his clothes, ripping his shirt. His brain rattled and his body went limp as he passed out again.

Clover grabbed the axe just as it was slipping away. He held onto Leven's shirt collar with one hand and the axe with the other. Leven's body slowed until it momentarily stopped. Then gravity took over and Leven began to race back down toward the ground.

"Wake up!" Clover screamed. "You're going to die!"

Clover whacked Leven with the axe handle.

"You. Are. Going. To. Die!"

Leven's eyes popped open and then shut.

"Please," Clover begged.

Then, as if politeness were the key, Leven's eyes popped open and stayed open. His eyeballs rolled back into his head and then jiggled back into place. There was blood on his mouth and he looked like a person who would have preferred death to what he was now doing.

"You're falling!" Clover screamed, slapping the axe into Leven's hand.

Leven was falling with his back toward the ground. He kicked, and his body whipped around so that he was facing the fast-approaching tree.

He wanted desperately to scream, but the effort seemed far too great. Leven saw the ground bubbling with roots. He could see some darkness climbing up the trunk of the tree. And he could see the tallest branches racing toward him.

His left shoulder hit the highest branch, and then his left leg snagged the next one and snapped at the knee. Leven reached out with his left hand, grasping to stop the fall, but his left arm got caught and twisted in a way that no left arm should ever be twisted.

Leven screamed as his back slammed into the low branches and he was spit out and deposited on the ground. Both the oldest tree and the Dearth seemed genuinely surprised to see him there. A loud hissing filled the air as Leven stood up on his right leg. Clover swiped at the tree branches as they tried to stop Leven, but they were too slow. Leven twisted his entire body and spun like a top, driving the axe through the Dearth and deep into the tree. Sparks flew, and the rich, oily darkness of the Dearth ignited and blew like a billion bombs.

Leven could see light and feel pain. The agony was so deep he moaned for death as he and the tree both fell forward to the ground.

CHAPTER FORTY-SEVEN

THE PERFECTION OF POSSIBILITIES

The sun shone down on the fresh green tavel and spread across the landscape like a soft blanket. Tea birds swooped down like ribbons, crisscrossing the air in celebration. The rivers and streams sang as they cut across Sycophant Run.

A long wooden table had been set up on a grassy knoll overlooking the Veil Sea. The waves sliding back and forth on the beach added to the magical sound of laughter coming from every direction.

The table was too small for Geth and Phoebe, so they sat on a stump near it. Phoebe was talking about the weather as Geth played with the paper-clip ring on his left index finger. Leven was lying on a blanket under the sun with Winter by his side.

It had been many weeks since the tree had died and things had spun back into place. Clover had wisely planted the seed, and Leven had lain in bed unconscious for almost three weeks before he had awakened to find Winter near him and the glow of millions of dreams flowing into a new Foo.

"Attention!" Rast called. "If you will."

Everyone stood up and gathered around the old sycophant. He smiled and raised a glass. Even the wind hushed up.

"It is a gift to be standing here," Rast said, "surrounded by so many friends and looking out on the Veil Sea with awe and not horror. It is the sycophants' sacred duty to assist Foo. It is a responsibility we do not take lightly. And while there are so many to honor, I feel that I must mention one. Clover . . ."

Rast looked around.

"Clover," he called again.

Clover materialized near the table. He combed his hair, straightened out his robe, and wiped what looked like lipstick from his face. "I was . . . snorkeling."

Lilly appeared on the other side of the table near Winter.

Rast cleared his throat and continued. "I think it only fair to point out what an exceptional job Clover has done."

"Hear, hear," everyone cheered as Clover smiled.

"When it was discussed that you would go to bring Leven from Reality, we never could have imagined how well you would do your part. Leven."

Leven stepped forward and pulled out a little box. Lilly and Phoebe began to cry.

"I remember when I first saw you under my bed," Leven said. "You told me you were there to help. And I'm certain the oldest tree would still be standing if it weren't for you."

Leven opened the box and pulled out a small leather strap with a clover on it. Clover took it and jumped up on Leven's right shoulder. Leven turned to look at him, and Clover hugged the life out of his head.

A number of people were wiping their eyes.

"Should we eat?" Rast finally said.

Everyone cheered and Rast clapped. Two rows of sycophants emerged from the bushes. They were being led by Amelia, and all of them were carrying platters of food. There were roasted potatoes and smoked meat covered in gravy. There were also buttered greens, creamy purples, and dry-as-a-bone pinks. Then came the cakes and drinks, so many they couldn't fit on the long table. Clover was about to serve himself, but then he remembered Lilly, and she went first.

Leven stood on the edge of the gathering with Winter. Foo was so different. The colors were brighter, the darks were deeper, and the dreams coming in weren't so singular—they seemed to mesh to make one frosty glow over the whole place.

"So you did it," Winter said.

"I didn't do anything."

"You know, it's okay if you're a little selfish," Winter smiled. "I mean, just for today."

The Want leaned in and kissed Winter as Clover helped himself to a third piece of cake.

CHAPTER FORTY-EIGHT

THE END

I have to be honest. I have not wanted to write this. I don't like ends; I prefer middles. I've stayed up many nights pacing the attic worried about how to close it up. But the fact of the matter is, things are no more closed than before. They're marvelously open. Every day I get up, I look around and notice things that Leven helped change—landscapes that used to be a bit different, dreams that weren't quite so vivid, and people who were once committed only to themselves now thinking of others.

I have stronger reminders as well. I had dinner with Tim and his family the other night, and it turns out that Swig is still hanging around their place. I also recently discovered something that leads me to believe that Dennis might not have died when he fell out of the helicopter. Plus, while stumbling around a deserted courthouse, I found a copy of Leven's birth certificate and was surprised to see

354

his birth name listed as E. Leven Thumps. I assume the *E* stands for *Elton,* and I have no idea why they didn't spell it out, but it's interesting to think that it took exactly *eleven* whacks or thumps to down the oldest tree. I have also stood at Blue Hole Lake and wondered how it ever could have survived.

You know, I have traveled many places in my lifetime, and I'm happy that I have had the opportunity to see so many foreign lands and so many unusual and amazing peoples. I've spent time on all eight continents and have bought postcards to send to friends from more than a thousand varied and unique convenience stores around the world. I've taken a plane to see a famous cave, a train to view a famous mountain, a bike to touch a famous home, a taxi to witness a famous temple, a boat to traverse a famous river, and a Segway to roll out over a famous canyon. I've enjoyed almost everything I've ever seen or witnessed. I must admit, however, that the first time I saw Blue Hole I was more than a little disappointed. The tiny little body of water in the barren wasteland of New Mexico first struck me as dry and unspectacular. But the second day, when I woke up and watched the sunrise light up the water and heard the birds sing in the sparse trees and touched the liquid, so clear and clean, I felt completely different.

Google it.

Look it up in the dictionary.

Visit it.

You'll be a bit different because of it. Of all the many things that I have seen and been a part of in dealing with Foo, I am most happy that Blue Hole still sits there looking just like it did before so many fantastical things happened to it. It is a reminder to me that small, unassuming things can be a part of true change.

I met a man the other day who insisted that Foo wasn't real. He was obnoxious and loud and bothersome and wore an ugly shirt. Still, I didn't have the heart to tell him that when things were really tough, when avalands were everywhere and the earth was spinning off its axis, he had actually curled up in a ball and cried like a baby waiting for it to end.

That isn't the case for all of you. So many of you fought for Foo and don't even remember. So many of you stood up and hosed down avalands or combated the sarus. You saw the importance of restoring good.

There will be days when you remember.

I don't know why I was lucky enough to be able to tell the tale. Or why I was picked to know Leven and Winter and Geth and Clover. I can only hope that somewhere in the back of our minds, beneath our deepest dreams, we'll remember.

So, the next time you see a toothpick, or witness clover growing in the field, or notice someone wearing wrinkle-free pants, or you experience winter, just shut your eyes and remember—Foo.

WHO'S WHO IN FOO

LEVEN THUMPS

Leven is fourteen years old and is the grandson of Hector Thumps, the builder of the gateway. Lev originally knew nothing of Foo or of his heritage. He eventually discovered his true identity: He is an offing who can see and manipulate the future. Lev's brown eyes burn gold whenever his gift kicks in.

WINTER FRORE

Winter is thirteen, with white-blonde hair and deep evergreen eyes. Her pale skin and willowy clothes give her the appearance of a shy spirit. Like Sabine, she is a nit and has the ability to freeze whatever she wishes. She was born in Foo, but her thoughts and memories of her previous life are gone. Winter struggles just to figure out what her purpose is.

GETH

Geth has existed for hundreds of years. In Foo he was one of the strongest and most respected beings, a powerful lithen. Geth is the head token of the Council of Wonder and the heir to the throne of Foo. Eternally optimistic, Geth is also the most outspoken against the wishes of Sabine. To silence Geth, Sabine trapped Geth's soul in the seed of a fantrum tree and left him for the birds. Fate rescued Geth, and in the dying hands of his loyal friend Antsel he was taken through the gateway, out of Foo, and planted in Reality. He was brought back to Foo by Leven and Winter.

SABINE (SUH-BINE)

Sabine is the darkest and most selfish being in Foo. Snatched from Reality at the age of nine, he is now a nit with the ability to freeze whatever he wishes. Sabine thirsts to rebuild the gateway because he believes if he can move freely between Foo and Reality he can rule them both. So evil and selfish are his desires that the very shadows he casts seek to flee him, giving him the ability to send his dark castoffs down through the dreams of men so he can view and mess with Reality.

ANTSEL

Antsel was a member of the Council of Wonder. He was aged and fiercely devoted to the philosophy of Foo and to preserving the dreams of men. He was Geth's greatest supporter and a nit. Snatched from Reality many years ago, he was deeply loyal to the council and had the ability to see perfectly underground. He was a true Foo-fighter who perished for the cause.

CLOVER ERNEST

Clover is a sycophant from Foo assigned to look after Leven. He is about twelve inches tall and furry all over except for his face, knees, and elbows. He wears a shimmering robe that renders him completely invisible if the hood is up. He is incredibly curious and mischievous to a fault. His previous burn was Antsel.

TIM TUTTLE

Tim is a garbage man and a kindly neighbor of Winter. In Reality, Tim and his wife, Wendy, looked after Winter after being instructed to do so by Amelia. When Winter goes missing, Tim sets out to find her.

DENNIS O WOOD

Dennis is a janitor whom fate has picked to carry out a great task. He leads a lonely life and has never dreamed.

JANET FRORE

Janet is a woman who believes she is Winter's mother but has no concern that Winter is missing. She has spent her life caring only for herself.

TERRY AND ADDY GRAPH

Terry and Addy were Leven's horrible-care givers in Reality.

OSCK

Osck is the unofficial leader of a small band of echoes. He is deeply committed to the meshing of Foo with Reality. He has also taken a very strong liking to Janet Frore.

AZURE

Azure is a lithen and a contemporary of Geth. He sat on the Council of Wonder and was a great friend of Geth's brother Zale. He turned to evil when he decided to stand still too long and let the influence of the Dearth overtake his mind and heart. A small bit of good still infects him, and it manifests itself by swelling and bleeding from his right ear. He is no longer his own man.

THE ORDER OF THINGS

BAADYN

The Baadyn are fickle creatures who live on the islands or shores of Foo. They seek mischief to a point, but when they begin to feel guilty or dirty, they can unhinge themselves at the waist and let their souls slide out and into the ocean to swim until clean. The clean souls of the Baadyn have been known to do numerous good deeds.

BLACK SKELETONS

These great warriors rose from the Cinder Depression many years ago. They occupy the land nearest Fté, and are known for their ability to tame and ride avalands.

COGS

Cogs are the ungifted offspring of nits. They possess no great single talent, yet they can manipulate and enhance dreams.

THE DEARTH

It is said that there is none more evil than the Dearth. His only desire is for the soil to have the last say as all mankind is annihilated. He has long been trapped beneath the soil of Foo, but has used his influence to poison Sabine and Azure and any who would stand still long enough to be fooled. In his present state, the Dearth works with the dark souls who have been buried to move the gloam and gain greater power on his quest to mesh Foo with Reality.

ECHOES

Echoes are gloriously bright beings that are born as the suns reflect light through the mist in the Fissure Gorge. They love to stand and reflect the feelings and thoughts of others. They are useful in war because they can often reflect what the opponent is really thinking.

EGGMEN

The Eggmen live beneath the Devil's Spiral and are master candy makers. They are egg-shaped and fragile, but dedicated believers in Foo.

FISSURE GORGE

Fissure Gorge is a terrific gorge that runs from the top of Foo to the Veil Sea. At its base is a burning, iridescent glow that creates a great mist when it meets with the sea. The heat also shifts and changes the hard, mazelike air that fills the gorge.

GIFTS

There are twelve gifts in Foo. Every nit can take on a single gift to help him or her enhance dreams. The gifts are:

See through soil	See through stone
Run like the wind	Shrink
Freeze things	Throw lightning
Breathe fire	Fade in and out
Levitate objects	Push and bind dreams
Burrow	Fly

GLOAM

The gloam is the long arm of dirt stretching from below the Sentinel Fields out into the Veil Sea. It is said that the Dearth uses the black souls of selfish beings buried in Foo to push the gloam closer to the Thirteen Stones in an effort to gain control of the gifts.

GUNT

The gunt are sticky creatures that seal up and guard any hole too deep, thus preserving the landscape of Foo and preventing disaffected beings from digging their way out. Once gunt hardens in the holes, it can be harvested to eat.

LITH

Lith is the largest island of the Thirteen Stones. It has long been the home of the Want and a breeding ground for high concentrations of incoming dreams. Lith was originally attached to the main body of Foo but shifted to the Veil Sea along with the other stones many years ago.

LITHENS

Lithens were the original dwellers of Foo. Placed in the realm by fate, they have always been there. They are committed to the sacred task of preserving the true Foo. Lithens live and travel by fate, and they fear almost nothing. They are honest and are believed to be incorruptible. Geth is a lithen.

LONGINGS

A near-extinct and beautiful breed, longings were placed in Foo to give the inhabitants a longing for good and a desire to fulfill dreams. They have the ability to make a person forget everything but them.

LORE COIL

Lore Coils are created when something of great passion or energy happens in Foo. The energy drifts out in a growing circle across Foo, giving information or showing staticlike images to those it passes over. When the Lore Coil reaches the borders of Foo, it bounces back to where it came from. It can bounce back and forth for many years. Most do not hear it after the first pass.

NITS

Niteons—or nits, as they are referred to—are humans who were once on earth and were brought to Foo by fate. Nits are the working class of Foo. They are the most stable and the best dream enhancers. Each is given a powerful gift soon after he or she arrives in Foo. A number of nits can control fire or water or ice. Some can see in the pitch dark or walk through walls and rock. Some can levitate and change shape. Nits are usually loyal and honest. Both Winter Frore and Sabine are nits.

OFFINGS

Offings are rare and powerful. Unlike others who might be given only one gift, offings can see and manipulate the future as well as learn other gifts. Offings are the most trusted confidants of the Want. Leven Thumps is an offing.

OMITTED

The Omitted are very insecure and untrusting beings. They can see everything in Foo except for themselves and their reflections. They are dependent on others to tell them how they look. They reside in caves and trees in the mountains outside the Invisible Village.

ONICKS

Raised near the Lime Sea, these winged beasts travel mostly by foot. An onick is loyal only to the rider on its back, and only as long as that rider is aboard.

RANTS

Rants are nit offspring that are born with too little character to successfully manipulate dreams. They are constantly in a state of instability and chaos. As dreams catch them, half of their bodies become the image of what someone in Reality is dreaming at the moment. Rants are usually dressed in long robes to hide their odd, unstable forms. Jamoon is a rant.

ROVENS

Rovens are large, colorful, winged creatures that are raised in large farms in the dark caves beneath Morfit. They are used for transportation and sought after because of their unbreakable talons. Unlike most in Foo, rovens can be killed. They are fierce diggers and can create rips in the very soil of Foo. When they shed their hair, it can live for a short while. They often shed their hair and let it do their dirty work.

SARUS

The sarus are thick, fuzzy bugs who can fly. They swarm their victims and carry them off by biting down and lifting as a group. They can communicate only through the vibration of water. They are in control of the gaze and in charge of creating gigantic trees.

SHATTERBALL

Shatterball is a popular sport played in a suspended giant orb of glass created by special engineers in Foo. The players are nits who have the gift of flight. It is a violent and exciting game that ends either when the orb is shattered or when only a single player remains inside. It is played with a small black ball called a pit.

SOCHEMISTS

The Sochemists of Morfit are a group of twenty-four aged beings who listen for Lore Coils and explain what they hear. They are constantly fighting over what they believe they have heard. They communicate what they know to the rest of Foo by using locusts.

SYCOPHANTS (SICK-O-FUNTS)

Sycophants are assigned to serve those who are snatched into Foo. Their job is to help those new residents of Foo understand and adjust to a whole different existence. They spend their entire lives serving the people to whom they are assigned, called their "burns."

THIRTEEN STONES

The Thirteen Stones were once the homes of the members of the Council of Wonder, with the thirteenth and largest, Lith, occupied by the Want. Each of the smaller stones represented a different one of the twelve gifts. With Foo in disarray, many of the stones are empty or are being used by others for selfish reasons.

THORNS

Thorns are possessive and whimsical beings. They are as small as bees, but they have great strength. They often live and hover around things they have grown attracted to, spending their days protecting and taking care of what they admire.

TURRETS

The turrets of Foo are a large circle of stone turrets that surround a mile-high pillar of restoring flame. The turrets sit on a large area of Niteon and are surrounded by a high fence. The main way to the flame is through the gatehouse that sits miles away.

THE WANT

The Want is the virtually unseen but constantly felt sage of Foo. He has a variety of gifts and can see every dream that comes in.

WAVES OF THE LIME SEA

The Waves of the Lime Sea are a mysterious and misunderstood group of beings who guard the island of Alder. Their loyalty is to the oldest tree that grows on the island.

WHISPS

Whisps are the sad images of beings who were only partially snatched from Reality into Foo. They have no physical bodies, but they can think and reason. They are sought after for their ideas, but miserable because they can't feel and touch anything.

There is nothing like a surprise.
Well, imagine mine when I reached
into my pocket and found this.

Everything's ready.
You'll find all you need
on the edge of the
Cinder Depression.
Our thoughts are
with you, Geth.
May fate be kind.

A NEW SERIES COMING SOON

GETH AND THE
RETURN OF THE LITHENS

◆

BY OBERT SKYE